THE THIEF OF DREAMS

Where had she gone?

He walked slowly through the rooms, tasting her presence with every step. Her absence awoke an ache inside him—a familiar hunger . . . If she was still in the city, if she was sleeping somewhere within its environs, he could find her. Asleep, dreaming, she was unique. Awake, the pattern of her psyche, while differing from those who did not dream true, was still too similar. But if she slept. . . .

He closed his eyes and let his mind range into the streets, sifting the dreams that spilled from the minds of the more common dreamers, searching. . . .

Ace Fantasy books by Charles de Lint

THE RIDDLE OF THE WREN
MOONHEART
MULENGRO: A ROMANY TALE
YARROW: AN AUTUMN TALE

Charles de Lint
YARROW

An Autumn Tale

ACE FANTASY BOOKS
NEW YORK

This book is an Ace
Fantasy original edition, and
has never been previously
published.

YARROW:
AN AUTUMN TALE

An Ace Fantasy Book/published by arrangement with
the author

PRINTING HISTORY
Ace Fantasy edition/October 1986

ISBN: 0-441-94000-5

Ace Fantasy Books are published by The Berkley Publishing Group,
200 Madison Avenue, New York, New York 10016.
PRINTED IN THE UNITED STATES OF AMERICA

for
Rodger, Pat & Jon
of The House of SF
in Ottawa

John, Terri
Tanya, Naomi & Jack
of Bakka Books
in Toronto

and not to forget
Sean Costello
—thanks for the loan of Zeus

ℋ

CONTENTS

❍

❍

Ж

Shadowings

Ж

Do not seek to follow in the footsteps of the men of old;
Seek what they sought.

—*Matsuo Basho*,
The Rustic Gate

1
❧

time was

OLD GHOSTS LIVED behind Cat Midhir's eyes, memories that had no home until they came to haunt her.

They came visiting in dreams, a gangly pack of Rackham gnomes, with long skinny arms and legs and eyes like saucers, dry-voiced like cattails rattling in the wind. Their tunics and trousers were a motley brown, their green and yellow caps pushed down unruly thatches of wild hair. Sometimes she sensed them outside of sleep, their wizened faces peering sharp-edged from sudden corners or, shy as fawns, soft-stepping behind her through parks and vacant lots—shadow companions who capered in her peripheral vision and were gone when she turned her head, dry voices piping strange music that became only the wind when she listened closely.

Rarer, they stepped her dreams in the shapes of tall and stately beings, like the children of fabled Dana or Tolkien's golden elves. When they came as such—the women in long embroidered gowns and the men in jerkins of soft leather, with their pale green eyes and silvery hair all braided—they told her ancient histories of the Otherworld and its people in voices liquid as water—tales that she transcribed in the light of day and wove into the fabric of her novels and short stories.

Rarer still, antlered Mynfel came, her eyes like honey, great branching horns lifting from her brow. Mynfel, whose very name was a charm against the riddling unknown, who sharpened Cat's intuition and filled the hollow places inside her with a quiet gladness, who made of simple living an art and made art a soaring swan with moon-tipped glittering wings. On those nights the stars held their breath and every sound, from the whirring buzz of a June bug to the scrape of a cricket's legs, hallowed her presence. Mynfel never spoke, but on such nights there was no need for tales or speaking.

Then the night visits stopped and her dreams, if they came at all, were empty. . . .

2

sunday night

It was August 29th, the last day of the 1982 SuperEx—Ottawa's annual exhibition of the tasteless and the tawdry, when the nation's bureaucratic capital removed its gray-flannel sobriety for ten days to reveal a garish underbelly. Lansdowne Park, the traditional site for this extravaganza, was choked with a gaudy array of concession stands and hucksters' booths, games and prizes, bargains and swindles, horse shows and music concerts, exhibitions that ranged from livestock to crafts to kitchen and household items, rides like The Bomb and the double Ferris wheel, and as many people as the organizers could induce to pack into the park's 25.6 acres.

The overspill of attendees and their various vehicles strangled the streets for blocks in every direction. This was a great irritation to most of the local businessmen and residents, but the enterprising souls who'd been renting out their front lawns as parking spaces for five to ten dollars a car and the owners of the Mac's Milk, Fat Alberts, smoke shops, and corner stores were happy as they counted their daily takes.

The sky above the park was lit up as though the Mother Ship from Spielberg's *Close Encounters of the Third Kind* had docked in it; the air smelled cotton-candy sweet as far away as Billings Bridge Plaza a mile south. The sound of the Ex was a cacophonous roar in the park itself, and washed in waves over the surrounding residential areas.

A half mile southeast of Lansdowne and a block northwest of the Rideau River, Albert Cousins crossed his sparsely furnished room and turned off his black and white television set, interrupting Johnny Carson in the middle of an interview with someone who looked like Tyrone Power but wasn't. His window was open in a futile attempt to alleviate the August heat; through it, replacing Johnny's voice, came the murmur of the Ex.

Albert smiled at that sound, a weary, old man's smile, full of remembrance. When Jean was still alive . . . He could still remember the last time they took the boys to the Ex. Tommy was . . . what? Sixteen then? And Billy a year younger. Of course, the Ex wasn't the same in those days. Not so big. Not so . . . what was the word? Commercial. Everybody talked a lot about whether or not things were commercial these days. Didn't much matter to him.

He and Jean had still gone a couple of times after that last outing with the boys. But that was the year Billy got hit by a car—in late September; the funeral was the first week of October. And Tommy didn't much care to have the old man and old lady tagging along with him and his friends the following year. Old man and old lady. They hadn't been old then. The way he lived now—*this* was what it meant to be old.

Being old meant being lonely. He'd outlived Jean and Tommy, and all of his friends. That was all it meant. It meant watching a black and white TV set in a rooming house for other old people just like him, living off his government pension, which barely allowed him to pay his rent and eat, much less go to the Ex. They called it the SuperEx now. But that didn't matter to him. It wasn't like he'd be going to it.

He'd sit up by the window a little while longer, maybe watch the late show, maybe not. It didn't matter. Time had a way of blending all the days and nights together, and the TV didn't help. All those little black and white actors looked and talked the same. The women all wore too little and the men looked like they'd stepped from the pages of a Sears catalogue. Not like in the old days. But at least it kept him from remembering too much.

Peter Baird's apartment was on Fourth Avenue, four blocks north of Lansdowne and just above the bookstore that he half owned and managed—the House of Speculative Fiction. After ten days of the SuperEx he kept the constant noise factor at bay by consciously ceasing to be aware of it. It was that or just go plain nuts. Sometimes you couldn't ignore it, but tonight he'd managed to—at least for a couple of hours.

It was going on to eleven-forty when he finished reading the last page of *The Borderlord* by Caitlin Midhir. This was the second time he'd read Cat's new book, but not the first time he'd stopped to wonder at the magic those printed words on paper could evoke in him. It wasn't so much the fantastical elements like elves and wizards—or in this case, the antlered Borderlord Aldon—nor the twists and turns of the plot. That he could find in myriad other books. No, there was a certain depth to her characters and underlying themes that reached out and grabbed him every time. The writing was lyrical, too, without ever descending into mush.

He glanced at the photo on the dust jacket and sighed. He could see why Ben was so enamored with her—could see it more than Ben, perhaps, because he'd known Cat for a couple of years now. She dropped into the bookstore every few weeks or so and they'd shoot the breeze over a cup of coffee. She didn't talk about her writing at first, so it had taken him a couple of months to put the shy woman he knew only as Cat together with the novelist Caitlin Midhir, whose four novels and one short story collection he carried in the store. He'd found out when he'd tried to sell her one of her own novels— the then-just-released *Cloak and Hood*. He'd known she liked that particular style of writing because she'd been picking up LeGuin's fantasies, McKillip and the like, and had even recommended Nancy Springer's *The White Hart* to him when it was still called *The Book of Suns* and marketed as a historical. So while she sat beside him quietly sipping her coffee, he'd handed her a copy of *Cloak and Hook* and started in on his sales spiel.

She'd looked at him strangely, and for a moment he thought he'd killed the book by raving it up too much. Then she said, in a very small voice, "I'm glad you liked it," and he flashed on what he'd been trying to do. It was the first time he'd ever raised a genuine laugh out of her.

Peter smiled, thinking back. Placing *The Borderlord* on his night table, he killed the light. He listened to the crowd noise coming from Lansdowne, pulled his pillow up over his ear, and tried to sleep.

Ben Summerfield pulled his cab up in front of the R&R Restaurant at the corner of Bank and Holmwood and leaned on the horn. He glanced at the much-worn copy of Christopher Stasheff's *The Warlock In Spite of Himself* that was sitting on his dash. Peter had told him the other day that a first edition of it was worth about fifty dollars American to a serious paperback collector. Seemed like a lot of money to pay for a yellowing book that had cost only seventy-five cents when it first came out back in '69. Not that it wasn't a good book, but you'd think for that kind of money you'd get something solid. Signed, maybe. A cloth edition for sure.

He leaned on the horn again and an attractive blonde wearing a tight T-shirt and tighter jeans came out the restaurant's door, followed by a tall, dark-haired man who looked like he thought he was Mr. Casual—designer jeans, shirt unbuttoned halfway down his chest, his hair swept back for that wind-tossed beer-ad look. They approached the cab, Mr. Casual making a show of opening the door for his companion.

"Gallantry is not yet dead," the man said with a grin that made Ben want to pull away before the grease in the grin got all over the cab's seats. "Five-thirteen Coronation, chief," he added to Ben as he got in beside the woman.

"Sure thing," Ben said, adding "asshole" under his breath. What was with this chief shit? What did women see in guys like this anyway?

He took his foot off the brake pedal, pushed down on the gas, and pulled away from the curb, cutting into the traffic. Behind him an irate driver sounded his horn.

"What a zoo that was," Debbie Mitchell said. She fluffed her hair, caught the cabbie's eye in the mirror and winked, smiling to herself when he blushed. "Every year I tell myself —that's it. I'm not going to the Ex again—not even if they get the Beatles to reunite for the Grandstand Show."

"It was pretty awful," Andy Barnes agreed.

He moved his leg closer to hers, laid his hand on her thigh.

Debbie nodded, replying to his comment rather than his unsubtle body language. What she really wanted was a hot bath. Going to the Ex made her feel unclean all over. And while normally she didn't mind Andy's attention—he could be a lot of fun if she was in the right mood—tonight his puppy-dog eagerness was wearing a little on her. She wondered if it was worth the bother to try and put him off tonight. His hand inched up her thigh. She glanced at the mirror again, but the cabbie kept his gaze studiously on the road.

Turning to Andy, she offered him her lips and dropped her hand down between his legs. His "brave little soldier," as he liked to call it, sprang to attention. Well, if he didn't manage to keep it up for any more than his usual fifteen minutes, she'd be able to have that bath she was looking forward to all that much sooner.

Mick Jennings' apartment was on Third Avenue, a little more than half a mile northwest of Lansdowne Park. The noise of the Ex didn't bother him at all. He and his girlfriend, Becki Bones, late of Toronto's punk scene, were listening to the Clash at full volume. Bass, drums, and guitars roared as Joe Strummer shouted out the lyrics to "Clampdown" from the band's two-LP set, *London Calling*.

Mick was an old hippie who'd gone punk. He kept his hair short except for the two-and-a-half-inch Mohawk band that ran from the top of his brow to the nape of his neck. The tattered jeans he wore were the same as those he'd worn in the old days, but he'd traded in his MAKE LOVE, NOT WAR and SUN POWER T-shirts for ones like the Clash's COMBAT ROCK, or the one he was wearing now: a skull with a crossed fork and knife under it, white on black, the legend EAT THE RICH in bold print above the skull. The earring he now wore in his left earlobe was a silver Anarchy symbol—a capitol A enclosed in a circle—replacing the peace symbol that had been there for so many years.

He was a mechanic at the BP station on the corner of Riverdale and Bank where Ben Summerfield took his cab when it needed repairs. Ben knew him as a good-natured, somewhat aggressive proponent of the whole British punk/ new wave scene—the music and ideologies of groups like the Damned and the Clash, Vice Squad and the Anti-Nowhere League. "I finally figured out that you can't solve everything with flowers," Mick had explained to Ben once. "Sometimes you've got to kick a little ass."

"Any beer left?" Becki asked during the silence between cuts.

She was about eighteen or nineteen—Mick didn't know which, and had never bothered to ask—with spiked black hair and strong Slavic features. The T-shirt she was wearing looked like someone had spilled battery acid all over it. There were rents and tears in all the strategic places, and you could only vaguely make out that it had once said SID LIVES.

"I'll check," Mick said. He left the room, returning with a couple of Buds.

"What're you smiling about?" Becki asked when he handed her one of the cans.

"I was thinking of Ben—working his ass off with the Ex. He'll have fares running him from one end of the city to the other tonight."

"I don't know why you hang around with him. He's so fucking straight."

"Hey, Ben's a good shit, you know what I mean? I don't hear him bad-mouthing you."

Becki shrugged. "Oh, I like him all right. I just think he's a little weird, that's all. All he does is drive that cab of his and read his space-and-elves books."

"Well, we can't all change the world," Mick replied.

He tilted his beer back, Adam's apple bobbing as he chugged. Paul Simonon, the Clash's bass player, was singing "The Guns of Brixton" now, something about having your hands on your head or on the trigger of a gun. When they came knocking on his door, Mick thought, he knew how he'd be stepping out.

Farley O'Dennehy was panhandling in front of the Ex at closing time that night. He had his battered suitcase hoisted in one hand, and kept an eye out for the cops while he scanned the crowd for easy marks. He was feeling bold tonight— fueled by a couple of bottles of Brights wine. So far he'd pulled in six bucks and change. If he could work the crowd for another half hour or so without getting busted, he'd be getting so piss-drunk tomorrow that he wouldn't even miss the Ex and its easy pickings.

"Hey, pal," he asked a man in white trousers and a light

blue shirt. "Can you spare me a quarter?"

"Fuck off, creep."

"Yeah? Well, you can—" Farley broke off when he spotted six-feet-three and two hundred twenty pounds of Ottawa's finest looking in their direction. "—have a nice day," he finished lamely, and shuffled off.

"You didn't have to be so mean," Stella Sidney told her boyfriend.

"Aw, the guy bugged me," Rick replied. "Why the hell should he get a free ride? At least I *work* for my money."

Rick Kirkby had just opened his own store—Captain Computer—and was filled with the righteousness of a small businessman standing up for the North American work ethic. Stella decided that it wasn't the time to remind him that if it hadn't been for *her* money, Rick would never have got the business off the ground in the first place. Bad enough he'd dragged her to the Ex tonight, without finishing the evening with a fight.

"Let's go find the car," she said.

"Yeah. Sure."

Stella followed his distracted gaze to see that it was centered on two high school girls in tie-tops and cutoff jeans that were so short you could see the cheeks of their rumps hanging out.

"Come *on*," she said.

"Okay, okay. I was just looking."

3

monday morning

BY THREE A.M., the streets were quiet. Humming the Human League's "Don't You Want Me" under his breath, a tall slender man stepped from the two-storied house he was renting on Willard Street in Ottawa South and ambled down the block to Cameron. He had short pale-blond hair and wore a lightweight suit with padded shoulders that hung stylishly from his lean frame. His eyes, when he stepped under the pooling glow of a streetlight, gleamed like blue crystals.

The name on the passport he was currently using identified him as Lucius Marn, residing in Canada on an extended visit from the United Kingdom. It was the same name that he'd used to sign his lease. The name he had been given at birth, however, in a time long before the use of passports or other identifying papers, was Lysistratus.

He paused at the corner of the block, moving into the shadow of the big red-brick house that, unlike his own, was divided into two half-doubles. Using honed senses he reached inside to touch the sleeping minds of its occupants—three on one side, two on the other. The texture of their dreams was coarse, diffused; sufficient to appease his hunger, but like a man given a choice between a gourmet dinner and simple nourishment, satisfying that hunger was not enough. Not when there was a choice.

Across the street, meeting the point of the V Willard and Bellwood made as they met Cameron, Cat Midhir unknowingly waited for him.

Her house was sheltered from the street by a tall hedge of gangly cedars and stood farther back from the street than its neighbors on either side. A giant birch on the right of the front lawn and a Dutch elm—one of the few in the city not yet stricken by disease—framed the front of the building. In the backyard a tall pine lifted from behind its roof like a second chimney.

The house was red brick, with a wooden veranda painted cream-yellow that ran the length of the front. An antique horse-drawn buggy stood forgotten on the left side of the long porch. The other half had been enclosed with screening. Decorous wooden eaves and gables, and the shutters on the dormer windows, matched the color of the veranda.

Yet for all the house's charm, there was a certain forsaken quality about it, as though it was a poor country cousin come visiting its more urban relatives. Not so much a sense of disrepair as being worn about the edges. In point of fact the house had once been in a rural setting. Originally part of the Billings Estate, a farm that had sprawled on either side of the Rideau River, the city had grown up around both the house and the estate, swallowing the farmland. The estate still stood on top of the hill across the river, spotlighted every night like a fairy-tale palace.

Lysistratus could not see the Billings Estate from where he stood. What light he did see spilled down from the upper right dormer of Cat's house, and it gave him pause. He didn't need the lit window to know that his prey was still wake. There was a distinct difference between waking and sleeping thoughts. The one he could feed on, the other... The other meant no more to him than the garish packaging of food in a supermarket. Waking thoughts carried dreams, but they were too difficult to pry sustenance from.

For a long time Lysistratus regarded the house. He began to hum again, "Anitra's Dance" from Grieg's *Peer Gynt Suites*, while he considered the woman inside. The quality of her dreams was such that they fed more than the gnawing hunger inside him; they fed the soul as well.

Mankind needed its dreams to keep its sanity. He needed mankind's dreams as sustenance. He took his bulk nourishment from those who didn't dream so true. The dreams of creative beings were more of a delicacy, while her dreams . . . they coursed through his system like a narcotic. They were rare gems, and he treated them accordingly, being careful not to be too greedy when he fed, lest he irreparably damage the source of his pleasure.

Before her, the best nourishment was to be found in primitive societies, strong-dreaming aboriginies unsullied by the vacuous glitter of the Western world. But such societies were closed to him. His skin was too pale to pass as one of them, and their shaman, knowing that such parasites existed, had developed harsh and successful methods of dealing with his kind.

The danger was less in a city like this—its inhabitants would not accept that he existed, except as a titillating fiction, and it was comfortable. He enjoyed its luxuries—theatres, opera, clubs. He took the same pleasure from Wagner as he did from David Bowie, from Bergman as from Lucas. He was safe, so long as he didn't overstay himself.

He had made a tour of the great cities of Europe and now planned a similar circuit of North America. A year here, a year there. He'd started small—Ottawa with its international flavor yet smalltown atmosphere—but planned to visit all the major cities: New York, Vancouver, L.A., Montreal, Chicago, Toronto, Washington.

He meant to enjoy himself, even with the one major drawback that the present age had delivered to one such as he:

Modern men and women moved too quickly. Their lifestyle was filled with too much stimuli, leaving them jaded, too easily satisfied, unable to use their imaginations. He found himself snatching half-formed images from those who dozed on public transportation or in parks and theatres. Where he once took lightly from one, perhaps two, throughout the dark hours, he was forced to feed on five or six now, occasionally killing his victims to harvest enough sustenance from their thin dreams.

"But you are safe," he murmured, gazing up to Cat's lighted window. "From death at least."

He remembered something that the poet Ibycus had said once: "There is no medicine to be found for a life which is fled." Dead, Cat could no longer feed him her true dreams. Dead, her dreams were lost to him forever.

He ran a hand through his hair, then gave Cat's window a brief salute before turning to go. The leather soles of his shoes made no sound on the pavement as he walked toward Windsor Park.

Albert Cousins never heard the door to his room open, never saw the slender man with the glittering blue eyes lean over his bed, never felt the stranger lay a hand on either side of his wrinkled face. Albert was dreaming of his wife, of Jean and him driving their old Chevy up the Gatineau, with the boys in the backseat—the one seven, the other six—and a picnic hamper in the trunk.

A final dream.

Lysistratus took the old man in the rooming house, took a lifetime of dreams and left behind a body with its motor-workings intact, but no soul to drive it. Standing over his drained victim, Lysistratus watched the body, bereft of its soul, slowly expire. His own body converted the old man's psychic essence into nourishment that would sustain his needs.

The basic hunger was satiated. But he thought of true dreams and the woman who dreamed them, and knew it was not enough. The simple satisfying of base needs could never be enough.

In the big house on Cameron where Willard and Bellwood join to form their V, Cat Midhir slept a dreamless sleep. In the morning she would wake with a headache, for on his return from the rooming house, Lysistratus had touched her sleeping mind with his and swallowed the night's dreams. Tomorrow she would sit at her typewriter, as she had every day for the past nine years, but tomorrow morning she would not keep anything that she wrote—if she wrote at all.

Three months ago she had stopped dreaming. Three months ago the words that had come so easily for so many years simply dried up.

Tomorrow would be no different.

Thief of Dreams

Sorcerers are not the same as other men. Part of their magic is to appear like us.

—*Islamic saying*

4

monday afternoon

MICK JENNINGS LAY on his back on a dolly, doing a brake job on a Honda Civic. His coveralls were more black than the gray they'd been when he'd first bought them, his hands and forearms were grimy, and he had a greasy streak on his forehead beneath the spikes of his mohawk. He was listening to CHEZ-FM because that was the station Jim had tuned in.

They were playing Zeppelin's "Stairway to Heaven"—as they seemed to every three or four hours. Remember progressive rock? Hard to forget it, mate, the way the radio stations still flogged it. Christ, he wished they'd let that song give up the ghost and die the death it probably yearned for. It wasn't as though he hadn't listened to it himself when it first came out—he probably still had a scratched copy of the album hiding somewhere in a milk carton with all his other oldies-but-moldy-goldies. But the song came out in '71. It was eleven years old. What was it going to take to convince the station's programmer that this was the eighties and they should be playing music relevant to *now,* instead of tired old licks and—

The *ping-ping-ping* of someone driving over the signal

cord by the pumps set his mind along a new track. Any bets
Jim's too busy to get that? he asked himself. He paused in his
work and counted to ten. Before he reached six, he heard his
boss call out from the office, "Hey, Mick. Can you get that?
I'm busy with a customer."

He rolled out from under the Civic. "Yeah. Sure."

He scratched his nose, leaving a new smudge behind, and
looked ruefully at his hands. Wiping them on his coveralls, he
headed out to the pumps.

"I'll be honest with you," Melissa Robinson said. "The
reason I flew up today is because I'm starting to get seriously
worried."

They made an odd couple. In contrast to the sleek, fashion-
able image that Melissa projected, Cat dressed haphazardly
and was slender almost to the point of being skinny, with a
heart-shaped face and intense gray-green eyes. Her dark curly
hair fell in a tangle across her forehead; she brushed it aside
with a quick nervous motion and sighed.

She'd felt as though she were on trial ever since she and
her agent had arrived at Noddy's Place for lunch. But no matter how much Melissa threatened or cajoled, Cat still couldn't
produce the new novel for her. It wasn't written yet. The way
things were going, it might never get written.

"The people at McClelland and Stewart are making nervous noises," Melissa continued. "Dana phoned me twice last
week as it is." She leaned across the table. "Can you at least
give me an outline to take back to them?"

"I don't use outlines—you know that. I get a theme and
then just go ahead—"

"Intuitively. I do know. What's the theme, then? Have you
settled on a title yet? Have you got *anything* I can give them?"

Cat had been putting off this discussion for two months—
exactly one month after she'd stopped writing and realized she
was blocked. She knew she should simply level with Melissa
—Lord knew, Melissa deserved that much courtesy. It was just
that if she *did* level with her . . .

There were a couple of questions Cat hated being asked.
The first was how to pronounce her name—"Kate-lynn
Meere," she'd explained wearily ever since grade school. The
second was, "Where do you get your ideas?"

It was easy enough to brush the latter off with a pat answer, except she always felt a little dishonest doing so. She didn't like being untruthful, but she didn't want to talk about her night-visiting either, didn't want to get labeled as a weirdo and see her name blaring from the front cover of *The Enquirer* in every supermarket: AUTHOR CLAIMS NOVELS ARE GHOST-WRITTEN BY REAL GHOSTS!

She felt guilty enough using those ideas as the basis for her writing as it was. The only way she'd managed to come to terms with it was by convincing herself that since the ghosts came to her in dreams, they must be dredged up from her own subconscious. Ipso facto, the stories *were* her creations.

Oh, really? Then why did she feel like she'd been deserted by her best friend?

Because she had been.

Her writing troubles were almost secondary to the loss of her dreams and the subsequent disappearance of the Otherworld and its inhabitants. They'd come night-visiting for as long as she could remember. As gnomes, they frustrated her with their wild antics. As elves, they had awed her with their unearthly beauty. And antlered Mynfel, with her night-deep eyes and resonant silences . . .

They had convinced her she was losing her mind, had in fact lost it long ago, then helped her rationalize away that same madness. They were her conspirators and her conscience, her freedom and her confinement. But mostly, through a lifetime of never feeling close, really close, to anyone, they had been her friends.

And now they were gone.

She could understand Mynfel's absence. The horned lady came seldom as it was. But the others . . . Lovely Mabwen with her silvery hair and doe-soft eyes. The poet-bard Kothlen who spoke of Myrddin and ancient kings from firsthand experience. What had become of them? And the gnomes? It had seemed that they were always around, in dreams or not, playing tricks about the house, tangling her already curly hair into elf knots, singing and joking. Especially Tiddy Mun, with his puckish grin and gentle nature.

"Cat? Have you heard a word I've said?"

Melissa was regarding her quizzically. Cat felt trapped, and wished she'd taken her own advice—never accept money for anything that wasn't written yet. Except she'd needed the money then, what with a mortgage payment coming up and the bank account balanced at zero.

She had a third of a novel sitting beside her typewriter. It had a title—*The Moon in a Silver Cup*,—characters, theme, the first few meanderings of a typical Midhir plot, but nothing else. Kothlen had started the story four months ago when she was still dreaming. Kothlen had started it, but never come back to continue it. She knew she could write something to finish it off, only it wouldn't ring true, and if it didn't ring true, she didn't want it published.

She took a deep breath and gathered her nerve. Melissa was a friend—one of the few she had outside of the Other-world—but that didn't make what Cat had to say any easier. It was more than admitting failure; it was as though she'd suddenly developed a weakness in her character, was a failure as a person as well as a writer.

"I'm blocked," she said at last. "I haven't written a word worth keeping in three months."

Melissa said nothing for a long while. The silence intimidated Cat, and she moved restlessly in her chair.

"It's not like I haven't been trying," she said into that silence. "It's just not working."

"Why didn't you say something sooner? We're supposed to deliver the manuscript in November. That gives us only three months and—"

"I *know* how long I've got to the deadline. It seems like that's all I can think of—that deadline looming up, getting closer and closer. I have visions of them sending men in pin-striped suits to get back their advance."

"Now don't be—"

"I've got a royalty payment from *Yarthkin* coming at the end of this month. I was planning to live on that money over the winter, but I suppose I could give them that and get a job or something."

Melissa shook her head. "We'll get an extension on the deadline. That won't be a problem. What's more important is getting you back on track."

"It won't work, Melissa."

"It just feels like it won't work. Everybody runs into these kinds of things."

"You don't understand," Cat tried to explain. "They're gone."

"They . . . ?"

"Ah . . ." Now was not the time to start blathering about

ghosts and night visits. But she had to say something. "I . . . I get my inspiration from dreams, and I've stopped dreaming."

Worry lines creased Melissa's brow. "You're a craftsperson, Cat," she said. "Writing's a craft, just like any other creative activity. You have to stay in practice. We both know there's more hard work involved in writing than any mystique."

"But I have to have something to write in the first place."

"Have you started anything?"

"I've started a million things, and they're all shit."

She wasn't going to mention the manuscript sitting beside her typewriter. Melissa would expect her to finish it, and she couldn't. Not without Kothlen, because it was Kothlen's story. Only he was gone. All the ghosts were gone.

"What you need is a change of environment," Melissa said. "You have to get away for a while. When was the last time you took a vacation?"

"I'm not sure. I was down in Vermont for a weekend last spring."

"You need more time away than that. Ottawa's a very pretty city, but there's something about it that leaves a gray film on your mind, don't you think? Too many civil servants all in one place."

"That's a typical Torontonian attitude."

Melissa smiled. "I still think you have to get away from this city for a while and scrape the fog from your mind. Do you have someplace you can go? Friends that live out of town, or even out of the country?"

"Correspondents in the States. A couple in Europe. But I can't just drop in on them."

"Why not?"

Cat shrugged.

"I'd invite you to stay with me, but knowing you, I don't think you'd find Toronto all that conducive either."

"I'll think about it," Cat said. "About going away. I'm just not all that sure it's the right answer. The problem's in here." She tapped her head. "This is where it's empty. Going someplace else isn't going to change that."

"Don't be so sure. Something you writers tend to forget is that you need outside stimuli to get those creative juices flowing."

A small smile tugged at Cat's lips. "The voice of experience?" she asked.

Melissa shook her head. "Those that can't, teach," she replied.

As the waitress in Noddy's was bringing Cat and Melissa their lunch, Peter Baird was just finishing up a stock check on the Del Rey backlist and wondering if he'd ever be able to keep Piers Anthony's Xanth series in stock. The damned books sold so fast, and what with *Ogre, Ogre* due in October and a sixth in the series to be released in January, he might have to call the store the House of Del Rey if the sales kept up.

Twenty-two blocks north on Bank Street, between Gloucester and Lisgar, Rick Kirby was in his own store, trying to sell a computer to Henri Cuiscard, who owned the shoe store down the block, and wishing he had a pert little salesgirl working for him so that he could just sit back and watch her work while he collected the loot. Not that Captain Computer was actually out of the red yet, as Stella liked to remind him whenever he brought the idea up. Didn't matter to her that it'd boost sales.

"Twenty-five sixty-five?" Henri asked him.

"Well, I could sell you something cheaper," Rick told him, "but if you're looking for efficiency. . ."

Just buy the sucker, he thought as he went through his spiel for the third time that day to the same customer. Henri Cuiscard nodded sagely, looking from the baffling—as far as he was concerned—array of hardware to his brochure and back again. He clutched the brochure as though it would impart comprehension simply by his holding it.

"These . . . ah . . . floppy disks," he began again. "How do they work?"

"It's very simple," Rick replied, trying to keep the irritation out of his voice. "They're like a phonograph record, except instead of one long spiral groove, they have a number of magnetic rings to store the data. This one can hold up to 576,000 characters. You insert it here and . . ."

Stella, he thought desperately. I *need* a salesclerk.

Two miles west and slightly north of Captain Computer, Stella Sidney was studying a statistical report in her office at

Tunney's Pasture and wondering, not for the first time in recent weeks, why she and Rick were still together. She sighed, trying to keep her mind on her work, but last night's argument after returning from the Ex stayed in the forefront of her mind and refused to be dislodged. It was as though they'd fallen into a downward spiral in their relationship, and the more they worked—or at least she did—at making it any better, the deeper and faster they fell.

Surprisingly, Cat felt better after lunch. Melissa had been very supportive, and Cat realized that it was her own fear of inadequacy that had kept her from confessing her block before this. The depression that had been glooming her steps for the past few weeks was somewhat lifted, burning away like mist before the sun. If she looked hard, she could actually see the odd ragged patch of blue sky. She didn't expect to go home and pound out a hundred pages of wonderful material. But Melissa *had* assured her that they'd get an extension on the deadline.

"I'll convince them to go for an autumn release," she said just before they left the restaurant. "*The Borderlord* should be doing well in paperback by then. Maybe we can get them to spring for a new double-headed promotion—the old paperback and the new cloth."

That would give Cat at least another five to six months to come up with something publishable. And it removed the pressure of the deadline that had been hanging over her head. Or at least the immediacy of it.

Standing on the sidewalk in front of Noddy's, she watched Melissa head off, then caught a glimpse of her own face on a poster in the window of Arkum Books, a couple of doors down from the restaurant. It was an ad for her latest book. "*The Borderlord,*" the blurb read. "By the author of *Yarthkin*, the winner of the World Fantasy Award."

The artist's conception of Aldon of the Borders wasn't exactly the way she'd pictured the character, but at least he hadn't been turned into a brawny barbarian hefting a sword, with some waxy-faced, impossibly-proportioned woman clutching at his leg. That had happened with the initial print run of *The Sleeping Warrior*. It was her first book, and when she got her author's copies and saw the cover illustration, she thought she'd die of embarrassment. For weeks she refused to go into bookstores, afraid that somehow the people browsing in them would connect her to that garish cover and judge her accordingly.

It was Melissa who'd written a cover-approval clause into all subsequent books—quite a coup for an unknown author, as Cat had been at the time. Melissa had also managed to convince McClelland and Stewart to pick up her latest book—another coup, considering that they weren't exactly renowned as publishers of fantasy. *The Borderlord* was her first book to appear from a mainstream publisher. It was also her first cloth edition—if you discounted the SF book club edition of *Yarthkin*.

If *The Borderlord* did well, it would be quite a boost to her career. The reviews that she'd seen so far were promising. If sales proved as good as Melissa thought they'd be . . .

Cat sighed. If and if. The problem with *The Borderlord*'s success, should it prove successful, was that it would put her next novel under that much closer scrutiny. And if Kothlen didn't come back soon to finish telling her the story . . . if he never came back . . . She didn't want to think about it. Besides, a successful career meant nothing compared to the loneliness she felt inside.

She tried to recapture the optimism that Melissa had left her with. Looking away from *The Borderlord* poster, she glanced at the rest of the window's display.

The man who owned Arkum Books believed in thematic displays. He had a soft sculpture dragon as a mascot whose name was Arkum as well, Arkie for short; every week it appeared in the window with a new costume that related to the current display. Today it was cookbooks, and Arkie had a tall chef's hat on his spiked head and was proudly brandishing a spatula. Last week it had been guidebooks, and Arkie had appeared in sunglasses, Hawaiian shirt and sandals, with a cheap Kodak camera slung jauntily over his shoulder.

Maybe, Cat thought as she turned from the window, she should write a story about a window-display dragon who got fed up with his job and went off on some mad quest. Tiddy Mun would like that. Maybe if she wrote it out for him, he at least would come back.

As Cat started for home, Farley O'Dennehy was still sleeping off last night's drunk, propped up against a tree on the heavily wooded slope between Parliament Hill and the Ottawa River. His suitcase lay on the ground beside him and he wore a tattered and stained pajama top over his clothes. He *always* wore pajamas when he was sleeping. Or at least as much of them as he could manage to put on before he passed out. Sometimes he even took off the clothes he was wearing first.

Five blocks south of Parliament Hill, on the fifth floor of the L'Esplanade Laurier complex, Debbie Mitchell was typing up Bill Worthington's correspondence. Worthington was the president of Worthington Tremblay Financial Services and Debbie's boss. Worthington was also responsible for the firm's financing one third of Captain Computer at a very reasonable rate of interest. Rick Kirkby and Bill went back a long way, but where Rick jumped from enterprise to enterprise, Bill had simply stuck it out with his partner Emile Tremblay, building up their business until it had become one of the most successful and respected financial services in the province.

Rick's name was on Bill's appointment calendar, and Debbie wondered if he needed another loan. If he did, he was going to be disappointed, because Bill had told her just the other day that he'd put all he was going to put into Captain Computer. The friendship notwithstanding, he wasn't going to throw good money after bad. Captain Computer had to make it or break it with the assets it now had on hand.

Well, that was between them. Debbie was looking forward to seeing Rick again. She knew he was attracted to her, and one of these days she'd take him up on his mock-serious advances. She just hoped that he'd prove to be a little less puppy dog than Andy. And a whole lot longer lasting, once he got it up.

Ben Summerfield could feel the man's eyes on him, and was trying to decide if he was about to make a pass or what. He couldn't figure out what else the guy could want. He would have laughed the whole thing off except for the intensity of the man's clear blue gaze, which he could feel settling on him every time he turned his back. There was something almost creepy about that lingering gaze, and it had nothing to do with Ben being definitely of a heterosexual persuasion when it came to sexual partners. When he had sexual partners. The man appeared to be in his early thirties, with stark blond hair and a pallor to his complexion that made the sudden blue of his eyes all the more disconcerting. He was slender, though obviously physically fit. His styled hair and trendy tan suit made Ben think of British rock stars like Duran Duran's Simon Le Bon or David Bowie, circa *Young Americans*. If he *is* gay, Ben thought, why isn't he hanging around the Market or on Elgin Street?

Ben turned away and stared at Tamson House, across the park from where he sat, determined to ignore the man he'd already dubbed as the Dude, as in Mott the Hoople's "All the Young . . ." He had the beginnings of a headache, and the pressure of that gaze on the back of his head just seemed to make it worse. He forced himself to stare at the gables and eaves of Tamson House and counted out a minute while following the lazy flight of a crow as it flew the length of the block-long building.

. . . a thousand - and - forty - two, a thousand - and - forty - three . . .

He could feel the pressure ease between his temples. The hairs at the nape of his neck laid down, one by one.

. . . a thousand-and-sixty.

He turned then, but the Dude was gone.

Vibed him out, Ben thought. He looked up and down the path that ran the length of the park, trying to pick out the man's lean figure, but couldn't find him. Fast walker. He rubbed at his temples. The headache was still there, threatening, but not quite so ready to make its appearance. Ben returned to the book he'd been reading before he'd dozed off.

Ben was a big, easy-going man—good-looking, despite the thinning hair up top and the extra weight he was putting on around the middle. The latter came from sitting around in his cab too much—he'd been driving one for five or six years now—and not getting enough exercise when he wasn't working. Like a cowboy and his horse, he never walked when he could drive his cab.

He had a basement apartment in a big old house that was the last building before the wedge of Central Park east of Bank Street cut across Clemow Avenue. Due to the incline on which the house was built, the back of his apartment overlooked the park as though it were on the ground floor. He had a private entrance on the side of the house and a back door that opened onto a small yard that merged with the common.

Because of that he considered the whole park his backyard, and only grudgingly allowed that the other people using it had as much right to be there as he did. He liked it best on weekdays, when the most you got were mothers pushing their newborns around in strollers, or late at night, when you rarely met anyone.

The book he was reading was a first edition of *The Borderlord* by Caitlin Midhir—he always pronounced her name carefully, Kate-lynn Meere, because he'd read in an interview somewhere how tiresome she found it being referred to as Kathlin Mid-here and all the permutations thereof. He was about a third of the way through, and as enthralled with it as he'd been with her previous four. He had the paperback and one book club edition of all her books, as well as the initial appearances of all the stories that had been collected in *Grindylow and Other Stories*, including "How Tod-Lowery Met the Moon," which had appeared in an obscure small press magazine called *Space & Time* that was published out of New York.

He wasn't exactly sure what it was that drew him to her writing. He read a lot of fantasy—from the classics by William Morris and Lord Dunsany, straight through to newer writers like Patricia McKillip and Parke Godwin—but no one else seemed to have the same touch of *rightness* about their tales. It was as though she didn't so much write the stories as relate histories that, while they might not be relevant to this here and now, *were* true somewhere. Or somewhen.

He knew she lived in Ottawa and had a mixed desire/fear of meeting her. While he thought—fantasized—that they'd get along famously, in reality he knew it would probably be awkward at best. What did you say to someone like her, that she hadn't heard a zillion times before? That was the trouble with famous people. They had people coming on to them all the time, wanting this, taking that. Not to mention the weirdos. He wondered if the Dude read her books, and smiled.

No, the way he imagined it should go was, they would meet casually somewhere, get to know each other like ordinary people did and completely bypass the whole fan/admiration shtick. Once they knew each other a bit better, he could profess his admiration of her work, friend to friend.

Ben sighed. *The Borderlord* lay closed on his lap. Cat's

face looking up at him from the photo on the back of the dust jacket. She'd trapped him with her first book. He'd passed on it when it first came out because the cover made it look like one more thud and blunder imitation of Robert E. Howard's *Conan.* But then Peter had recommended it to him. Two pages into it and he'd been hooked enough to go out and buy her second book, *Cloak and Hood,* which had just come out. A few months following that he'd run across one of the rare interviews with her in the then-current issue of *Fantasy Newsletter,* and that had been the start of his infatuation.

He'd been delighted with the personality that came through in the interview, even more delighted with the photo that had accompanied the text. Her features had haunted his dreams— a curious combination of frailty and strength that made him yearn to protect and be protected.

The whole thing was adolescent in its intensity, and he knew it, but couldn't stop himself. Peter teased him endlessly, never failing to remark when she'd been in to buy a few books, until Ben was nervous about going into the store on the off chance that she'd be there. He'd seen her on the streets from time to time—mostly in the Glebe where Peter's store was, or in Ottawa South, where he knew she lived—but that wasn't quite the same as being in the same room as her.

He knew she was shy. That came out in both the interviews and from what Peter had told him. But he'd bet she wasn't as shy as he was.

Ben looked away from the photo and watched the birds above Tamson House once again. Another pair of crows had joined the first one. He was mildly envious of Peter's casual relationship with Cat. Peter had her sign a copy of *Yarthkin* for him, and had offered to get her to sign *The Borderlord,* but Ben couldn't wait to read the latter. Peter had also said more than once that he'd introduce Ben to her, but it just wasn't the way Ben wanted it to happen. If it ever did.

He returned to the book, but his headache was starting to intrude too much for him to concentrate properly. He thought about the Dude and wondered again if the guy'd been thinking of coming on to him. It was funny. He'd been having a pleasant dream before the weight of that intent gaze had woken him, but he couldn't remember any of it now. All he had inside was a drained feeling. Probably too much sun.

It was hot and humid—the last couple of days of August.

He wore a pair of cutoff jeans and a loose cotton shirt that he'd bought at the Lung Mei sale last year—an annual three-day flogging of Indian styled tie-pants, wraparound skirts, shirts and the like—but even that was wearing too much.

Stripping off the shirt, he gathered it up with his book and started off across the common for home. He'd lie down for a while, sleep the headache away. Maybe he could plug back into the dream that the Dude had interrupted with his creepy stare.

As Ben went in through the back door of his apartment and Cat was just arriving home, May Featherston, the landlady of the senior citizens' rooming house where Albert Cousins lived, was telephoning the police. She was a widow of fifty-three, a bustling, rounded woman who loved to fuss over her tenants. She owned the house outright, and the rents she charged, while ridiculously low compared to the present level of rental rates, still brought in enough to keep the building financially solvent.

She dabbed at her eye with a Kleenex and tried not to think of Albert's lifeless gaze staring up at the ceiling of his room. Her finger trembled as she dialed the number—written on a piece of cardboard tacked to the wall above the phone, right under the one for an ambulance service and above the one for the fire department.

She loved old people and knew if she was going to continue to run a rooming house for them, she was going to have to get used to the fact that they weren't necessarily going to be long-term residents. But the day that she didn't mourn the passing of such a sweet old man as Albert was the day she'd hand in her right to be a human being.

The ringing stopped at the other end and a voice came on the line. "Police. Can I help you?"

May cleared her throat, then calmly and slowly, began to speak into the receiver.

5

that night

PETER LOOKED UP from the copy of Jack Vance's *The Dying Earth* he was rereading. A vague premonition stirred in him, charging the hairs at the nape of his neck. He set the book on his lap, Liane's flight from Chun the Unavoidable forgotten. His gaze went around his living room, then riveted on the floor-to-ceiling bookshelf across from him. For a moment he thought he'd seen something . . . a movement. . . .

A book leapt from the shelf and hit the floor with a loud slap.

Peter sat transfixed, staring at it. After a long moment he got up from his chair, moving slowly, as though in a somnambulant trance, and knelt by the book. It was Cat Midhir's *The Sleeping Warrior*. A shiver passed through him as he picked the book up, gaze locked on its garish cover. He weighed the book in his hand, then looked around the room as though something in it held an explanation for the strange phenomenon he had just seen.

Anyone working in a bookstore was used to a book falling from its shelf for no good reason. But this one hadn't been faced cover out, as those usually were. It had been sitting with only the spine visible, and had seemed to jump right off the bookshelf. Weird. He replaced the volume, half expecting it to come alive in his hands. The book fit snugly back into place.

It just fell, Peter told himself. It must have been hanging over the edge of the shelf or something and just fallen off. Funny how it had happened though. From where he'd been sitting, it looked like it had just lunged off the shelf of its own accord.

He returned to his chair and picked up *The Dying Earth* once more. From time to time he glanced at the bookshelf, but the books, row on row of multicolored spines, never moved.

After wasting the better part of the evening sitting through an endless string of boring sitcoms, Cat forced herself to go up to her study and read through the whole rough draft of *The Moon in a Silver Cup* manuscript. As she read, she kept Melissa's comments in mind and saw that there was more than a little truth to them. The story *was* as much hers as Kothlen's. The bare bones of the novel belonged to her absent Otherworld ghost, but she was the one who'd fleshed them out.

She took her time going over it, scrutinizing the pages word by word, looking for which parts were hers and which his. When it came right down to it, she'd taken more than a few liberties. The overall story was the same as the one Kothlen had told her, but here, where Haren met the Gypsies before he reached the keep—that was hers. And there—the whole segment with Kinneally in the tower. In fact the theme of the trickster as it touched the book, while a basic folk motif and nothing new, was entirely hers.

Kothlen had given her the what-would-happens, but nothing of the characters' motivations; the basic plot, but not the play-by-play action. The mood was hers. The pacing and thrust.

Okay. So Melissa was right in that regard. She was capable of dealing with the actual craft herself. So, while she couldn't finish *The Moon in a Silver Cup*, at least not yet, there was nothing stopping her from beginning a new novel. Nothing except a lack of something to write about in the first place. The novel had to have a reason to exist. Just following a story from A to B wasn't enough. At least not for her.

Where do you get your ideas?

Well, you see . . .

* * *

Cat was eleven when she decided she wanted to be a writer. It was one of those nebulous decisions that children are prone to, and came hard on the heels of her umpteenth reread-ing of *The Wind in the Willows*. Her head was aswirl with the adventures of Ratty and Mole and the incorrigible Mr. Toad, when the realization came to her all in a flash. *This* was what she wanted to do.

Her first attempts continued the adventures of Grahame's famous characters, but she soon enjoyed writing more about the new characters that she'd added to the Wild Wood's popu-lation than the ones that were rightly Kenneth Grahame's pri-vate domain. She filled a number of school notebooks with her own tales of Mouse and Sparrow, and still had a file folder full of those embarrassing efforts hidden away in a drawer somewhere.

It wasn't until a month or so later, in early winter, when she was walking with Kothlen in the Otherworld, that she shared her ambition with another person. She tried to explain it to him as they ambled through the hills that lay between the great oak and apple wood which was the domain of antlered Mynfel and the gray seas where the selchies and merrows could be seen sporting in the waves most nights.

Kothlen's father was Morer, the silver-haired harper of Gwyn ap Nudd's court, but his mother was a mortal, and it was from her that he got the blue in his blue-green eyes and the light-brown streaks in his own silvery hair. His features were not so sharp edged as the other elfin folk, and he always had time for the tangle-haired moppet who came night-visiting to his world. Next to Tiddy Mun, and for all the age differ-ence between them, Kothlen was her best friend.

Unlike his father, he was not a harper. But he *was* a bard all the same, and the stories that he knew . . .

He listened to Cat prattle on with a smile on his lips, well pleased that she should choose to follow his own profession.

"There are few joys to compare with the telling of a well-told tale," he remarked when Cat finally ran out of words.

Cat nodded. Though she was only eleven, she was already a voracious reader.

"I just *know* it's what I want to do," she said, "but . . ."

Her voice trailed off, and for a time they walked in silence. The tang of the sea was in the air. The Otherworld stars wheeled and spun in constellations unfamiliar to Cat's home-world, but well known to her.

"But what?" Kothlen prompted.

"I don't know what to write *about*."

"Sit with me a moment," he said.

He led her to an outcrop of stone that pushed its granite surface out of the heather nearby. Kothlen made himself comfortable while Cat perched like one of her namesakes beside him. Her parents called her Katie, but she was already thinking of herself as Cat. And *as* a cat, an outsider, an observer more than a participant, just like the cats she always had around her. It was a romantic notion that made up for the fact that she was the one who alienated herself from her peers. It would be another year before Kothlen gave her her own secret name.

"The tales I tell are old," he said. "When I relate them to you, I am merely retelling some ancient story or history in my own voice."

"You don't make them up?"

Kothlen laughed. "Oh, some of them. But mostly I just fill out the details. The tales themselves are what they always were. I think of them as the bones of some ancient beast that I must add flesh to so that it can live again. But while the tale itself, its truth, is of the utmost importance, it is the telling that allows it to be remembered or forgotten. The trueness of the telling is what makes up a storyteller's craft."

"So I could just work with the stories that you tell me, couldn't I? At least for starters."

"As long as you approach them with respect. The telling of tales is a most honorable profession, Cat. Remain true to the tale—never forget to give it its proper due, whatever you may add to it—and you will not go astray."

Her first short story—ignoring her *Wind in the Willows* pastiches—took her the better part of six months to write. She worked at it with a determination that surprised her, listened carefully to Kothlen's criticisms, and discovered that there was far more to writing than simply setting the words on paper. When she had finished that first story—at 30,000 words it was more a novella—and she could sit with her notebooks on her lap and flip through all those pages filled with her neat handwriting, knowing it was her own hard work that had gone into its making, she felt a sense of accomplishment

that would not be repeated until she made her first professional sale seven years later.

Throughout her teen years she remained busy transcribing
—at first Kothlen's stories, then Tiddy Mun's as well—scrib-
bling in her notebooks, rewriting, appraising, considering,
researching, trying to find her own "voice." She never considered sending the stories out in the beginning. In fact she never
shared them at all, because she had no close friends she dared
lend so much of her inner self.

She switched from handwriting to a typewriter when she
was seventeen, and after much heart-searching, submitted and
sold a story the following year. It was "The Three Daughters
of the Green Wizard," which appeared in the May '73 issue of
The Magazine of Fantasy and Science Fiction and was later
reprinted in her first collection, *Grindylow and Other Stories*.
The next year she sold three stories; in '75 she sold two.

On New Year's Day of the following year she began her
first novel, which took her a year and a half to complete. It
was rejected fifteen times before it finally found a home in the
back of her file drawer with the rest of her stories that hadn't
quite worked out. By then she'd finished the final draft of *The
Sleeping Warrior*, realized all the mistakes she'd made with
the first novel and why it would never sell, sent out *Warrior*
and received a contract for it in the mail three months later.

During those years she finished high school and moved
into her own apartment—a one-bedroom in Centretown at
$150 a month. Working as a waitress, a CR-2 government
clerk, a librarian, and in a bookstore, she wrote in the eve-
nings initially until she'd saved up enough money and nerve to
try her hand at writing full time.

And all that while, she went night-visiting in the Otherworld, grew closer to Kothlen and Tiddy Mun and more withdrawn from the world she lived in during the day.

Where do you get your ideas?

Cat sighed. Gathering up *The Moon in a Silver Cup* manuscript, she put it in an oversize manila envelope and stowed it
away in the bottom drawer of her desk under "things to get
back to." Where did she get her ideas? Where did other
writers get *theirs*?

She was beginning to feel depressed again. There was
nothing inside her that needed saying, nothing she wanted to

share. She needed someone like Kothlen to bounce ideas off of. She needed Tiddy Mun to tell her one of his presposterous stories, like the one that had become "How Tod-Lowery Met the Moon."

The light on her desk seemed too bright. She switched it off and sat in the darkness for a long time, not ready to face another night's dreamless sleep, but not quite prepared to stay up all night either. She wished she had someone to talk to, but found it hard to deal with people. At least on a personal level. Which was strange, for people seemed drawn to her; she was the one who drew back, who kept relationships at a certain distance. Like this afternoon. The only reason she'd managed to admit her block to Melissa was because it affected Melissa as well. If Melissa hadn't been her agent, Cat might never have told her.

She thought of calling Melissa—not now, but tomorrow morning. Melissa would listen. She'd understand. She'd proved that this afternoon. They'd spent three hours over lunch, and it wasn't just because Melissa saw her commission floundering under the weight of Cat's writing block. It was because she cared.

Cat stared around her shadowed study. She felt very small in the darkness. The silence of the house weighed on her. It was too big a place for one person and two cats. Except she needed the room for her books and records—both of which seemed to grow like weeds, they accumulated so quickly— and it fit her adolescent dreams of the sort of place she wanted to live in when she grew up.

She'd seen herself living in a place like this, but not with anyone else. She didn't need anyone else, not when she had her ghosts and her night-visiting. But now here she was, grown-up but lonely because her ghosts were gone and the house was empty. Just like her dreams. Even the cats, Ginger and Pad, were out for the night.

Other people admitted to invisible or imagined childhood companions, only they all seemed to outgrow them. Was that what had happened to her now? Had she mysteriously become too mature for her shadow friends? But if that was true, why did she feel so damned empty inside? Was she supposed to replace the ghosts with real people? That must be what others did. Only where would she find a man like Kothlen outside of the Otherworld? Another Tiddy Mun? A Mynfel?

* * *

Rick Kirby stood with his back to Stella, looking out her
living room window while he tried to contain his anger. Nit,
nit, nit. Christ, that was all she did these days. They'd been
arguing for three hours straight now. Around and around. The
same old push and nit and pry. About the only thing that
would stop her was to sew her fucking mouth shut.

Stella's apartment was on the seventh of ten floors in Le
Marquis, on the corner of Main and Lees, facing west. It had
an underground garage, with a laundry room and storage area
in the basement. The ground floor was taken up by Betty Brite
Cleaners, She of Piccadilly Hairdressers, Le Marquis Confec-
tionery and Groceries—where you could pick up every lottery
ticket from the Provincial straight through to Cash-for-Life.
The remainder of the ground floor consisted of offices and the
superintendent's apartment. Across the street was the École de
Mazenod, founded in 1933, and the Canadian Martyrs
Church. Beyond them was Algonquin College and the Rideau
Canal. Rick stared at them, unseeing. At this moment his own
reflection interested him more than the view.

Thirty-seven years old, but he didn't look a day over thirty.
He was a good-looking dude, no doubt about it, and if Stella
had any smarts she'd realize that there were one hell of a lot of
women who'd be grateful to have just a third of the time he
spent with her. Not that she wasn't a class act herself. But she
was just too caught up in this whole outdated melodrama of
one man/one woman, live within your means, don't take
chances. Fuck it. You had to live, didn't you? You had to get a
little high, get a little on the side, have yourself some fun. If it
wasn't for the fact that she was holding papers on two thirds
of Captain Computer, he'd have told her off a long time ago.

She talked a lot about love and trust, but where did she
come off having a lawyer draw up a contract between them
before she lent him the fucking money in the first place? She
just wanted a hold on him, that was all. Couldn't drag him to
the altar, so she got herself another piece of legal bullshit to tie
him down. Well, he was seeing Bill on Wednesday, and if he
could swing himself a little deal with good old Bill, he'd be
able to hand Stella back her money and say, Here's where you
get off baby. Either you live with me the way I am or you can
fuck off.'

The only hitch was, Bill just might not spring for the
bucks. He'd have to wine and dine Bill, maybe take along

Bill's sweet little secretary, who Rick knew had the hots for him, and see how things worked out. Until then it was sunshine and light time, that was all.

"Look," he said, turning from the window.

Stella sat on the couch, an unreadable expression in her eyes. Rick crossed the room and sat down beside her.

"I'm sorry," he said, using just enough of his salesman's sincerity to make his repentance appear credible. "I get a little, you know, out of hand sometimes. I know it. Must be in my genes or something. But you come first. Any time you catch me acting like an asshole, you just tell me, because the one thing I don't want to blow is what we've got going between us."

"Do you mean that, Rick? Do you *really* mean that?"

He put his arm around her shoulders and drew her close. "Straight A's, babe, and no turning back."

Stella leaned her head against his shoulder. If she could just believe him. But she was so confused with the way their relationship was going that she didn't even know what she wanted to believe anymore.

Rick murmured in her ear. As he felt the tension ease from her, a clear moment of genuine affection for her came over him that had nothing to do with what she could do for him or how she looked on his arm when they went stepping out. It was like when they'd first met at Jim Blair's party. Real. Honest. A reaching out of compatibilities. Then he started thinking about how, once he got the new loan, there might be some way he could turn her fucking lawyer's contract back on itself and just keep it all—her money *and* Bill's.

Cat got up from her desk and crossed the study to her thinking chair by the window. She curled up in it and stared up Willard Street. The people out there were real. She passed them every day, nodded hello to some, paused to exchange meaningless pleasantries with a few others. They'd all managed to become real, so why couldn't she? Why couldn't she shrug off the last vestiges of childhood, her shadow companions, and be like them?

Something moved out on the street and she leaned forward, trying to make out what it was. A figure. Another lost soul out looking for old ghosts? Should she run out and tell whomever it was that she'd lost them too? Maybe they could go looking for them together.

The figure on the street kept to the shadows, as though not wanting to be seen. Maybe it wasn't a neighbor out for a late evening stroll, Cat realized. There'd been a few break-ins in the area recently. Mrs. Beatty up on Bellwood had stopped her the day before yesterday and earnestly warned her to make sure every door and window was locked when she went out because "you just can't know anymore." The Thompsons on Belmont had been broken into last month, and Mrs. Beatty herself had lost a comforter that she'd left out on the line to dry overnight.

"I know the insurance will cover it," she'd confided to Cat, "but that doesn't stop you from feeling . . . violated."

With that in mind Cat felt a mild thrill of fear run up her spine when the figure stepped into the shadows of the red-brick house on the corner and simply stood there. Doing what? Her pulse quickened. He was watching her house. He was watching her!

She pushed herself back into her chair, keeping as far back from the window as she could while still being able to look out of it. Had he seen her? It had to be a he. A woman wouldn't go around staring at people's houses in the middle of the night, would she? Sexism, perhaps, but Cat was sure it was a man down there, watching her. Why? Would he stop at that? Or was he waiting to see if the place was empty or she was asleep?

She didn't know what to do. If it was a thief, the best plan would be to just walk around and turn on a few lights. But what if he wasn't a thief? What if he was something worse? What if he wanted *her*? Would turning on the lights draw him like a moth to flame? Did he have a scalpel hidden in a pocket? A butcher's knife?

She knew she was getting carried away, but couldn't stop herself. She thought of going downstairs to phone the police, but that would take him out of her sight and she couldn't face not knowing exactly where he was. Right now he simply stood there, watching. What if, when she went downstairs, he started across the street and broke into the house while she was still on the phone, or only just dialing? The police would never get there in time to stop him. She didn't even want to think about what they'd be stopping him from.

Throat dry, she seemed to sense another presence in the house already. She could still see the man, a slender dark shape in the shadows. Waiting. There wasn't anybody in her house, she knew. It was just the awful weight of his watching. You could always sense eyes upon you, the pressure of concentrated attention that could turn your head on a busy street. That was what she felt now. And, she realized, she'd felt this same presence before. Had the watcher taken up his post on other nights? Was he just trying to get up his nerve to—

She broke off that chain of thought. She had to decide. Turn on the lights? Call the police? Sit here in the dark and do nothing at all?

At that moment the pressure eased, the sense of impending doom rushing from her like air escaping a balloon. She saw the watcher slip along the side of the house and vanish into the alleyway behind it. Letting out a breath she hadn't been aware of holding, she sat weakly in the chair. Her legs were so watery that she couldn't have stood if she'd wanted to.

Now that the moment was over, she questioned her reaction to it. How much had been real and how much the workings of her own overactive imagination? God knows she was under a certain amount of stress as it was. For all she knew, what she'd taken for a prowler or worse—don't think about *that!*—could have been the fellow who lived in the house itself. Or someone who'd needed to relieve his bladder. How long had the whole incident taken anyway?

No. She shook her head. Whomever it had been, he *had* been watching her house, watching *her*. She was sure of it. Wasn't she?

Cat realized that about the only thing she was sure of was that she needed a friend. The pressure was beginning to tell on her. Her ghosts had left her alone for too long. She had to accept that she'd been deserted—by her friends in the Otherworld, or by her own imagination, or both—and if she didn't want to end up becoming some lunatic spinster locked away in a strange old house, she'd better do something about it. Now. Before it was too late.

Coming this early had been a mistake. He should have satisfied his hunger first. But Lysistratus was driven to this place, to the skimming of the woman's dreams and the heady euphoria they produced in him. It was more than the simple pleasure he took from her.

His gaze sought the window across the street and the

woman behind it. She went to her sleep later each night, and
tonight she had seen him. He wondered if it made a difference
as he retreated from his vantage point and faded into the
shadows.

He went across the river to Hull, where the clubs stayed
open until three, two hours later than those in Ottawa. He
moved from club to club, letting the pulse of Europop rhythms
and dancing crowds wash through him. A dark-haired woman
took him home. She had the face of one of Botticelli's angels
and the body of a harlot sheathed in a silk blouse and red
spandex trousers. As he brought her to orgasm, he swallowed
the quick spurt of pure psychic energy that exploded through
her, then put her to sleep. Skimming her dreams, he trailed his
fingers lightly across her flushed cheek, then left quietly.

On the way home he hunted in downtown Ottawa, seeking
the sleeping places of the tramps that haunted the same area
by day with their hands stretched out for spare change, their
eyes rimmed red from the consumption of too much alcohol,
their bodies reeking of too many bathless weeks.

He came upon three sleeping in the tiered parking lot on
Cooper near Kent. Feeding on their alcohol-sodden dreams,
he took enough to sustain himself without utterly draining
their souls. Come morning their psyches might have difficulty
coping with the bizarre visions that their own addictions
would inflict upon them in their weakened state, but he
doubted that they would notice any difference.

And while he made love to the woman, and while he fed
on the tramps, he thought of Cat, how he would stop by her
house once more on his return. And if she slept, if she
dreamed . . .

Her dreams were always a fitting nightcap, allowing him to
sleep easier himself. He knew that his need for her particular
essence was intensifying. One night he would drain her—take
it all. He never doubted it for a moment.

But not yet. He would choose the moment in a rational
manner, not have it forced upon him by a need that was no
more couth than that of a junkie scrabbling for a fix.

A hangover riding like a white fire though his head tore
Farley O'Dennehy from a fitful sleep. Flickering waves of
disturbing images raced ahead of the pain . . .

. . . a shadow with eyes of ice sitting on his chest, stabbing
at his face with talons of cold steel, its saurian tail wrapped

around his throat . . . claws reaching inside his chest, ripping out his lungs . . . his heart . . . the pain white and hot . . . like lava sliding over his skin . . . hissing as it turned his sweat to steam . . . searing his flesh from his body in long burning strips—

"Jesus fuck . . ."

He sat up, shook his head to clear it. Bad mistake. Something like raw sewage churned in his stomach. Pain hammered at his temples. And the images . . . fucking DT nightmares . . . He lurched to his feet, stumbled over to the parking lot's low stone balustrade and looked down. Vertigo flooded him. His body shook with dry heaves, and he sank weakly to his knees.

It didn't make any sense. He'd split a twenty-sixer with Poke and Ron Wilson, then the bottom of a bottle of Alcool mixed with some wine. Nothing they hadn't chugged down before. But his head. The hangover wouldn't quit. He held out his hand. He had the shakes so bad it was vibrating. There was an emptiness inside him, and he had the jeebies like he couldn't believe.

He looked to where Ron and Poke were lying, sleeping the sleep of the innocent or the damned—if you were innocent, you just didn't know any better, and if you were damned, you just didn't care. His vision blurred, doubled. He squeezed his eyes shut. The pain was lessening, but he kept getting flashes of ice-blue eyes and fire. Crawling to where his suitcase lay, he worked open the two worn clasps, dragging out his pajama top. He had one arm in a sleeve when he passed out again, falling across his suitcase.

6

tuesday

THE WEATHERMAN ON the CBC Late News forecasted rain for
Tuesday. It came as promised, disguised as a thin drizzle, and
threatened to remain throughout the day. In the tiered parking
lot on Cooper Street Farley still had his hangover when he
woke up, but it was nothing special. Nothing a hair of the dog
wouldn't cure. He only vaguely remembered the previous
night's hallucinations. Sitting up, he rubbed the two days'
worth of stubble on his chin and poked Ron with his foot.

"How's the moola holding out, Ron?"

Ron was a thin, red-haired man with prominent blue bra-
chial veins on his forearms and red-rimmed eyes. He dug into
the pocket of his corduroys—so aged that the ribs were worn
flat—and came up with a dollar bill and a handful of change.

"Got me two . . . ah . . . two forty-three."

"I've got a dollar. Poke?"

Jimmy Pokupra was tall and big-boned, with a deep tan
and no weight on his rangy frame. He unwrapped a sandwich
that he'd just pulled out of the side pocket of his patched and
torn Sears-special sports jacket which had come his way cour-

tesy of the Sally Ann. He'd gotten the jacket in their store on Somerset. It had had a price tag of $5.25 on it, but didn't cost him more than the time it took him to put it on and walk out.

"I'm skint," he said. "Anybody want a bite?"

Farley and Ron shook their heads.

"We've got to be moving," Ron said. He looked out at the wet haze without any pleasure. "Bill-Boy doesn't mind us sleeping here, but if his boss catches us . . ." He drew a finger across his throat.

Farley tugged his pajama top off of the one arm it was on and stuffed it back into his suitcase.

"I tell you," he said, "I had the weirdest nightmare I ever did have last night. I thought I woke up and had these snakes crawling all over me—or maybe it was something that was like a snake, but a man at the same time. . . ."

"Whoo-ee, who's got the DTs?" Poke grinned, showing a mouthful of half-chewed sandwich and the gap between his teeth.

"You need something hot and black," Ron advised Farley.

"Hell with that. I need something with a punch to put my head back together." He stood up, hefting his suitcase. "You guys coming?"

Ben didn't sleep well Monday night. By Tuesday morning he'd managed to shake yesterday's headache—at the cost of three Anacin—but he'd picked up a queasiness in his stomach that stayed with him overnight and into the morning. He'd tried reading some of *The Borderlord* last night, but the print kept swimming before his eyes. In the end he'd watched the late movie on Channel 12 out of Montreal—*Captain Blood*, the 1935 version which was Errol Flynn's first swashbuckler —and dozed off sometime after two.

In the morning he was able to keep down his toast and coffee and read yesterday's newspaper and two chapters of *The Borderlord*. By eleven he felt well enough to take out his cab and pick up a few fares. His rent was due and he was about fifty dollars short. That came from stopping in at Peter's store too often and buying all those pricey hardcovers. He glanced at Cat's book lying beside him on the seat, and shrugged. There were some things you just couldn't pass up.

He picked up his first fare in the Glebe—a real Mr. Jetsetter, bound for the airport in an outfit right out of *Esquire*

—and listened to a blow-by-blow description of where, and with who, and how Mr. Jetsetter was planning to spend his next three weeks. The cab's wipers kept time to the man's droning voice.

"Nothing Disneylandesque, you understand. There's nothing that's more of a pain than a beach full of senior citizens basking in the golden sun with their golden years hanging out of their swimsuits—except maybe packs of noisy brats kicking sand in your cocktail. . . ."

Ben changed the man's misnomer from Jetsetter to Joe Ritzy and promptly shut him off before they'd gone a mile, nodding once in a while or sticking in an odd "You don't say?" when it seemed appropriate.

"You just wouldn't *believe* what they're charging for an apartment in Paris this year," Joe Ritzy told him earnestly.

I probably would, Ben thought. But who cares?

That morning Cat woke from another dreamless sleep. By daylight, last night's fears seemed foolish. She tried to imagine what she would have said to the police if she *had* called them, and became embarrassed just thinking about it. Thank God she hadn't. They had more important things to worry about than illusory prowlers, while she . . . she had a novel to write.

Trying to ignore her usual morning headache, she made her way downstairs to put the kettle on for coffee. She could remember a time when she used to wake up inspired, but that was before—*when* she still dreamed. It seemed a very long time ago now. She stared out the kitchen window, watching the thin drizzle come down in her backyard, and waited for the water to boil. Briefly she wondered where Ginger and Pad were on a wet day like this, then decided they'd come in when they were ready and not before. It might be a wet day for her pets, but inspired or not, it was a perfect day for staying inside and getting something done. No more excuses.

After she'd washed and dressed and the first morning's caffeine was kicking through her system, she was ready to sit down and give it a try. She cleared off her desk, dug up a travel guide to Northern Ireland and Lady Gregory's *Gods and Fighting Men,* and tacked up a few pictures on the wall behind her typewriter. One was of an old Ulsterman, taken from an issue of *National Geographic,* two were photos of round

towers that an Irish correspondent of hers had sent. The fourth
was a drawing by another correspondent, who lived in Pough-
keepsie, New York. It was of a raggedy elfin maid, curled up
asleep in amongst the roots of an old oak tree. Tiddy Mun
would like her, Cat decided as she pinned it up.

The pictures gave her something to settle her gaze on when
she looked up from the typewriter, something that wouldn't
distract her from the tale at hand. Even though her writing
consisted of retelling Kothlen's stories, she still used the pictures and reference books, for Kothlen chose only certain details to enlarge upon, and while she wrote intuitively, she
trusted neither intuition nor her memory to see that she got
everything just right. The difference this time was that the
pictures and books would have to serve as inspiration, without
her dreams to point the way.

A poem by Yeats had come to her earlier while she was
trying to convince the thicket that passed for her hair to be
more reasonable. Looking up the poem now, she studied the
lines that had brought it to mind:

> . . . in a dream
> Of sun and moon that a good hour
> Bellowed and danced in the round tower. . . .

She typed the words out and studied them some more,
imagining what Kothlen might do with them, where they
would take *his* fancy, and slowly the beginnings of a story
took shape in her mind. The old man and the elfin woman.
Was she once a daughter of Dana, one of the Tuatha de Dan-
ann, or had she always been of the *daoine sidhe*? Had the old
man been young when they first met? Had the years drawn the
youth from his flesh while they passed her by? Did they first
meet by the tower, or were they parting there?

She titled the story after the poem, "Under the Round
Tower," and though she knew that it wasn't going to become
the novel that McClelland and Stewart were waiting for, at
least it would be something. Choosing a cassette from the
stack on her desk, she stuck it in her Aiwa, pushed the play
button on the deck, and returned to her typewriter. As the soft
sounds of Vaughn Williams's "The Lark Ascending" drifted
from the speakers, she began to work up the opening scene of
her story.

* * *

Debbie Mitchell was planning to spend her lunch hour picking out a new outfit for herself in the shopping concourse below her office. Bill had just asked her if she was free tomorrow night, and if so, did she want to go out for dinner with Rick Kirkby and himself. Debbie agreed readily enough. Having spent last night with Chris Stone—who was as wearisomely me-Tarzan-you-Jane as Andy was fawning—she was in the mood for someone like Rick.

She could tell at a glance that Rick was the kind of guy who thought mostly about himself, but that didn't worry her. He was also the kind of guy who, in making sure he was having a good time himself, livened things up for whomever he was with. She was as tired of being followed around by puppies as she was of this whole bed-as-jungle scene. Rick would be straightforward, and that suited her fine. About the only pressure she could foresee with him was if they were going to bed, and when.

Something black to set off her hair would do, she decided, tight at the hips and breast, with a slit along the side—midlength; sexy, but not overtly so. She was going to let Rick make the opening moves.

Ben pulled up at the pumps at the BP station, shut off his engine and watched Mick approach from the garage, wiping his hands on his coveralls.

"Hey, Ben. How's it going?"

Ben grinned as he stepped from the cab. He leaned against its door while Mick worked the pumps. "I just took the longest, most boring drive out to the airport that I've ever taken. I mean, this guy would make Joe Clark sound exciting."

Mick laughed. "Ah, the joys of working with the public. Warms my heart through and through. You working tonight?"

"Not if I can make the rest of my rent today. Why?"

"Some friends of mine are doing an opening set at Barrymore's tonight—thought you might want to check it out. The sound's by yours truly."

"Loud?"

"Well, the guitars are all plugged in. . . ."

"How punk *are* they?"

Mick ran a hand across his Mohawk. "Well, I'm the punkest guy in the band, and I'm only on the soundboard. These guys play ska, Ben. You know—like fast reggae. Like the Beat and the Specials."

"I'll give you a call around suppertime, okay? I didn't sleep so well last night so I might crash early. How much do I owe you?"

"Sixteen even. Anyone ever tell you that you sleep too much?"

"Anyone ever tell you that punk died when the Pistols packed it in?"

Mick shook his head. "Died? Fuck, it's just starting to kick in, Ben."

By late afternoon, all Cat had to show for her efforts was a wastepaper basket heaped with crumpled twenty-pound bond stock. The Selectric in front of her was silent, the paper in it as virginally white as when she'd rolled it into the machine. She felt like pitching the typewriter through the window. Everything she wrote had all the awkward charm of those *Wind in the Willows* pastiches that she'd written when she was eleven. ("Mouse felt Very Important at that moment, because Badger had asked *him* to help with the decorations. . . .")

She was supposed to be a professional, a writer who'd been described by one critic as producing work that ". . . flowed effortlessly across the page." Oh, really? These days her writing was more like a wooden crate bouncing down a long flight of stairs.

She tried to tell herself that it wouldn't all come back in one day. These things took time. She had to work at it little by little. But though all that made sense in its own way, it ended up sounding like just so many well-intentioned platitudes, empty of comfort. Surely to God she could produce one or two pages of readable manuscript after a day at the typewriter? She had never had any patience with writers who complained of being blocked. You just sat down and did it. Only now . . . now. . .

She could remember a time, not so very long ago. The Otherword stars shone down on the henge atop Redcap Hill. Inside the hill the gnomefolk were partying and up to their tricks, but outside, where the fairy thorn stood midway between the base and crest of the hill—and midway between the faint sounds of revelry that came from underfoot and the silence of the night skies above—Cat and Tiddy Mun sat, knee to knee, listening to Kothlen spin the beginning of a new tale.

"The daughter of the King of Burndale Yellow had a silver cup," Kothlen said, "and in that cup she meant to catch the moon."

His voice was resonant and clear, his eyes turned dreamy-gold in the starlight. At Cat's side Tiddy Mun squirmed, delighted that the elflord was beginning a new story. His eyes were wide as saucers and he bit at his lower lip in anticipation, holding Cat's hand tightly in his own.

"Do we like her?" he asked. "The princess?"

"Shhh," Cat said, but Kothlen smiled.

"That you will see," he said.

"But what was her name?" Tiddy Mun wanted to know.

Cat and Kothlen exchanged knowing looks. The little gnome was always like this at the beginning of a tale—unable to contain either his curiosity or excitement. The proper unfolding of a tale, each event following the previous like the measures of a dance, didn't hold the same meaning for him as it did for them. He wanted to know it all. And to know it all at once.

"Her name was Alyenora," Kothlen told the little man, "and she was as fair as a rowan in bloom. Well loved she was by all the folk of Burndale Yellow, well loved by all save Hovenden the witchman who lived in the Old Wood with a one-eyed raven and a wingless dragon."

Tiddy Mun shivered and gripped Cat's hand more tightly.

The next morning when she woke, Cat had begun *The Moon in a Silver Cup*. The words had come flowing effortlessly through her—not Kothlen's tale, exactly, but without his tale, the story she was writing would never have come. As it took shape on the paper, it became not so much Kothlen's telling, nor her own writing, but some magical combination of the two. And as the tale was a dance, so her fingers danced on the keyboard of her IBM, pausing only long enough to take out a page and insert a fresh one, five to six hours a day, seven days a week, until the manuscript stacked beside her typewriter was a half-inch thick, and then . . . then she stopped dreaming and the dance stumbled to a halt, the magic fled, and—

Ripping the blank page out of the Selectric, Cat crumpled it into a small ball, flung it at the already filled wastepaper basket, and stomped out of the room. What she was going to

do was go for a walk. She might never try to write another
word. She might never go into that room again. She might
never come back home again.

Lysistratus hungered once more, the pleasures of the previous night already forgotten. But the thought of faring out
into the streets by day, snatching what dreams he could, as
much a scavenger as the winos he'd fed from last night, was
distasteful. If only the dreams he stole could give him more
than sustenance and longevity, if only they could render him
immune to death—to a bullet, a knife, or a simple accident.
Then he would not have to exercise such caution as he did. He
could stride amongst mankind like the superior being he was.

Instead he had to remain a scavenger—like the jackal that
the African rootmen named him when they drummed their
magicks and drove him from their veldts and jungles; like the
ghost death that the Australian bushmen named him when they
drove him away with their ritual shouts; like the lone wolf that
the Inuit shaman named him when they used their chants and
drum magic to drive him south from their frozen wastes; like
the buzzard that the Hopi shaman named him when they raised
their ghost winds and drove him north from their deserts.

The strong dreamers cast him forth because he was no
match for them—he didn't have their physical brawn, nor the
mystic power to withstand their devil-castings. But the strong
dreamers no longer ruled this land—not as they had when
he'd first visited it in previous centuries. He had returned because the men of the cities ruled now. They were weak
dreamers; that very weakness was what kept them from dis-
covering what he was and casting him forth as their aboriginal
cousins had. But it left him with a constant hunger.

If only they could all be like Cat Midhir. Powerful
dreamers, blind to his existence. He wondered if perhaps she
could be bred. . . .

He turned his gaze to a small painting of the Kikladhes that
hung on the wall of his living room. The islands were washed
by the same Aegean waters that hid Poseidon's palace from
the eyes of man. Andros. Myconos. Southern Thera. Though
he'd not been born there, he still thought of them as home.
Ancient strongholds of dream.

Coarse-dreaming Turks had driven him out once. He had
needed to wait four hundred years for the rebellion that al-

lowed his return, only to be driven out again when the Nazis
pounded their hard-heeled boots into their soil. Those arrogant
Nordic dreamers had been gone forty years now, but he no
longer thought of returning. That time might come, but not
until he was stronger. Not until he was no longer a scavenger.
Not until he need never be forced into exile again.

Lysistratus smiled to himself as he slipped on a lightweight
tan raincoat and went out into the drizzle, his moment of
moody introspection forgotten. Only the small-minded would
complain in his situation. Eternity was his, wasn't it? And all
of mankind's dreams.

On a day like this the library would be a good place to
visit. The museum. A shopping mall. Anywhere that a weary
soul might close his eyes for a dozing moment.

Cat had walked off her anger by the time she reached the
Glebe. There was still a dull ache inside her, where something
that needed expressing could find no vehicle of expression,
but there was nothing she could do about it. Standing in front
of The Merry Dancers Old Book and Antique Emporium, she
looked up and down Bank Street, wondering what she was
doing here. It was going on six and everything that wasn't
already closed would be closing soon.

She didn't really want to have dinner alone in one of the
restaurants that had sprung up in the area over the past few
years. On the other hand, she didn't want to go home just now
either. She decided to go over to the House of SF. If they were
still open, maybe she could pick up a book. That would give
her something to do tonight. She wasn't going to spend another evening sitting in front of the tube, and she wasn't going
to stare stupidly at her typewriter all night either.

The "Come in, We're OPEN" sign was still in the window
when she arrived, and she hurried up the stairs before Peter
could change his mind and close. She wouldn't keep him
long. Just a book and she'd be off.

The House of Speculative Fiction—on the blue-and-white
sign outside, the sounds "eff & ess eff" were added to the
name—took up the ground floor of a half-double on Fourth
Avenue. The store itself was in what had once been the living
and dining rooms of a ground-floor apartment, while the
kitchen, complete with stove, fridge, and sink, doubled as a
makeshift storeroom. Beside the sink was a narrow stairway

that led to the apartment upstairs where Peter lived. There was also a broader stairway at the front of the store, giving access to the second floor, but Peter rarely used it.

He could be found behind the low counter everyday except for Thursday nights and Saturdays, when the other owner, burly Rodger Turner—who worked for the federal government five days a week—took over. Yet even at those times Peter was generally about. He looked up now as Cat burst in, and grinned when he saw who it was.

"How do, Cat. Long time no see. Where've you been keeping yourself?"

Now that she was here, she wished she hadn't come. She liked Peter Baird. He was a fairly handsome man with short light-brown hair, not tall but taller than she, with hazel eyes that were quick and warm. He was one of the few people Cat felt comfortable with, but right now, after his effusive welcome, she realized that she wasn't up to any sort of extended conversation. She didn't want to seem rude, but—

"Are you okay?" Peter asked.

Oh, God, she thought. How long have I been standing here like a dope, not saying anything? She quelled the sudden urge to bolt out the door—because how would she explain *that* later?—and tried to find a smile. By the look on his face, she wasn't being very successful.

"I'm fine," she said. "Really. I've just been having one of those days."

"I know what you mean. But at least you're doing something productive with your time instead of being cooped up in a place like this all day, twiddling your thumbs while the drizzle does its damnedest to keep customers away. Say, how's that new book coming?"

Cat's lower lip began to tremble, and all the past few months' losses and pressures swelled up inside her. I'm not going to cry, she told herself. A real cat wouldn't cry.

But she burst into tears.

Peter had long enough to think, Oh, shit—what'd I say? Then he was up and around the counter, steadying her by one arm as he led her back to his chair. He left her there for the time it took to turn the "OPEN" sign to "Sorry, We're CLOSED," lock the front door, and return to hunch down beside her.

For a moment he stared helplessly at her, but when her sobs grew louder, he drew her head down to his shoulder. He

didn't say anything about everything being okay, or Hey,
come on now, realizing that neither had much meaning. If
everything were okay, she wouldn't be crying. Instead he just
held her until the sobs dwindled into sniffling. He fetched her
a Kleenex that she accepted gratefully, though she wouldn't
meet his gaze.

"God. I feel so . . . stupid," she said after she'd blown her
nose.

Peter shook his head. He switched off the store lights to
take away the glare, knowing she'd feel more comfortable if
she didn't think he could see her too well. The room was lit by
the light in the storeroom/kitchen, throwing her face into
shadow.

"Don't feel stupid," he said, drawing up the chair he kept
for visitors.

She kept her head down so that her hair spilled across her
face. "I can't help it. I can just imagine what you're thinking."

"I'm not thinking anything bad. I'm wondering what's
upset you, and hoping it wasn't me, but Jesus, Cat. People cry
all the time. If you want to talk about it, I'll listen. If you
don't want to talk about it, that's okay too. But don't feel
embarrassed just because you let go for a minute."

"Yes, but . . ."

She looked up finally and Peter shook a finger back and
forth in front of her.

"But nothing. I don't know what's upset you, but if you
need a shoulder to cry on, it's okay. What do you think I'm
going to do? Write it up as a news flash for *Locus* or something?"

Cat sniffled, but the beginnings of a smile started on her
lips. "I can just see it," she said. " 'Writer Has Breakdown in
Sci-Fi Store.' "

"Ouch."

"Okay. Ess-eff store."

"Better. Not perfect, but better." He regarded her for a
moment, wondering not for the first time just who the person
behind the writer and occasional visitor was. "Say," he said.
"You got anything planned for the next couple of hours?"

"No." Sniff. "Why?"

"Well, I thought maybe we could go out and get a bite to
eat."

Cat put her hands over her eyes. They were a bit swollen and would look all red. Everybody'd stare at her and know she'd been bawling.

"Oh, no," she said. "I couldn't."

"Well, how about having something here? I can offer you leftover chili."

"No. I really should be getting home. . . ."

Except she didn't want to go home. The cats were probably still off wherever it was that they went. She'd just sit there, knowing the typewriter was standing silent upstairs, feeling the big empty house all around her. It was funny—she never used to feel that way about it.

"Okay," Peter said. "I just know that when I'm feeling lousy, nine times out of ten I feel better just being with someone. But if you've got to go . . . Well, at least let me walk you home."

Cat barely heard what he was saying. She kept thinking of the big lonely house. And what if that man came by and stared at her again? She just *knew* it wasn't the first time he'd stood there. What if he did more than stare tonight?

"Earth calling Cat, earth calling Cat."

"What? Oh, I . . ."

If this was what it was like being real, Cat didn't know if she wanted to be real. Everything was wound up tight inside her again. She wasn't relaxed like she always felt in the Otherworld, but if she couldn't go night-visiting, she wanted to stay here. She *couldn't* go home. Not yet. But it was hard to get the words out. When she finally did speak, she surprised herself.

"Peter, I haven't written a word in three months."

As soon as it was said, she felt better. She realized immediately—just as she had with Melissa—that it wasn't such a hard thing to say after all. She stole a glance at Peter to gauge his reaction. Don't let him shrug it off, but don't let him make a big fuss about it either. God, she didn't know what she wanted him to do.

"Jeez," he said. "No wonder you're feeling so shitty. You must be climbing the walls. How'd it happen, do you know?"

"I . . ."

She wanted to tell him about Kothlen and the Otherworld, but everything closed up inside her.

"Hey," Peter said, sensing that she was beginning to withdraw again. "Why don't we talk about it later—if you're up to it. Meanwhile, let me show you how a rich bookseller lives."

The pressure inside her eased as soon as the subject was changed.

"I'd like that," she said.

7

tuesday night

LISA HENDERSON HURRIED south along Bank Street, turned left on Sunnyside then right on Willard. She glanced at her watch: 9:45. Her mother was going to kill her. She'd promised to phone her before nine to make arrangements for her birthday dinner on the weekend. "Now are you *sure* that's what you want for dinner, dear? Roast chicken, broccoli, and scalloped potatoes? It seems rather plain. And I *do* think you should bring a friend—like that nice young man with the mustache. No? Well, call me on Tuesday, *before* nine, *just* to be sure. Now you won't forget?"

Except she had forgotten, because after work she'd gone for a coffee with Brad Windsor—who didn't have a mustache like Jon Fisher, whom she'd stopped seeing a month ago, though her mother didn't know that yet—and ended up having dinner with him and spending the better part of three hours just talking. Brad was nice. He listened to what she had to say, didn't peel away her clothes with his eyes, and . . . well, so far as she could see, he just didn't have any bad habits.

Lisa worked at Rhapsody Rag Market—a clothing store

close to the corner of Bank and Cooper that sold the kind of
clothes she wore, uptempo folksy in natural fibers. She was
twenty-three—twenty-four on Saturday—and a graduate of
Carleton University, where she'd acquired a B.A. in English
that didn't do much for her except make her mother happy.

As she reached the half-double that housed her second-
floor apartment and was digging about in her purse for her
keys, she glanced at the darkened windows of the adjoining
double, wondering, not for the first time, just exactly what the
fellow who lived in there was like. He was such a dreamboat.
If only he wasn't so standoffish. Everytime she'd tried to
strike up a conversation with him, it went absolutely nowhere.

She gave a mental shrug as she ran up the steps to her own
house. What she should be doing was getting an excuse ready
for her mother, not mooning over the man next door. Her
mother—Ottawa's expert in emotional blackmail, but still the
only mother she had. Now let's see. We had to do inventory
—no, she'd used that one last month. Then . . . She smiled
wickedly as she fit her key into the lock of her apartment door.

She should just tell her mother the truth. Something like:
you see, Mom, I've been seeing a lot of different guys, sleeping with some of them too, but I haven't met anyone I feel
really serious about yet. Her mother, she knew, would have a
cardiac arrest on the spot. And if she survived the heart attack,
Lisa would never hear the end of it. "Bad enough you live on
your own, unmarried as you are, but to throw yourself around
like some common prostitute . . ."

Lisa sighed. Some parents changed with the times while
others—like her own—never lifted their eyes from their own
narrow view of the world. The best thing to do was to say that
she ate out and forgot the time, then listen to her mother sigh
and moan and wonder aloud how she could have raised such a
thoughtless daughter, and leave it at that. Anything else and
she was just asking for trouble.

The phone started to ring as soon as she got her door open.
There was no need to guess who that would be.

Debbie had the evening to herself for a change and was
enjoying the quiet. After a light dinner of a spinach and feta-
cheese salad, washed down with a glass of white wine, she
took a long leisurely bath, then watched *Happy Days, Laverne*

and Shirley, and *Three's Company* while her hair was drying. She passed up *9 to 5* — she'd liked the movie better anyway —to try on her new dress.

It was low-cut, gathered tight at the waist, the skirt falling loosely to her knees—a little slinkier than she'd originally planned on, but she hadn't been able to resist the way it accentuated her figure when she'd tried it on in the store. She studied herself in the mirror, with her blonde hair pulled up in a loose bun and wearing a pair of spiky high heels—the kind Judy in the office called CFMPs, Come-Fuck-Me-Pumps. Smoothing the skirt, she bent as though to pick something up to see how much leg showed through the slit, and smiled as she straightened.

Rick Kirkby, she thought. You don't stand a chance.

Tomorrow night she'd see how much of him was innuendo and how much the real thing. She changed into a loose gown and curled up on her couch to read the last few chapters of Ludlum's new book, *The Parsifal Mosaic.*

"Hey, Ben," Becki said. "You wanna dance?"

They were sitting at a table in Barrymore's, facing stage center, the vaulted ceilings loftly above them. The building had been, in its time, a theatre, a movie house, a strip joint, and now a rock 'n' roll club, retaining the garish furnishings of all its previous incarnations.

It was situated on Bank Street, above another club that was a biker's hangout and a pinball and video-game arcade, and across the street from a chip stand and the Royal Oak—a quasi-British pub. The coloring of Barrymore's was all gilted, velvet red and black, with ornate chandeliers and brass railings separating the various tiers that had once been balconies in its theatre days. The rows of seats had been removed and replaced by tables and chairs which, though the arrangement appeared curious at an initial glance, proved to give every patron an excellent view of the stage.

Adding a final tackiness to the worn-edged glitter were the costumes of the waitresses—a last nod to the club's days as a strip joint. The women moved between the tables wearing black low-cut bathings suits, top hats and tails, black fishnet stockings and high heels. Ben shook his head as one of them approached their table to ask if they wanted a refill.

"You want *me* to dance?" he asked Becki.

She was decked out in her full gear tonight. Three earrings in one ear, none in the other; the thick raggedly-cut hair uncombed and spiked like a hedgehog's back; a red, white, and blue British flag T-shirt with the arms torn off; tight black jeans with the knees torn. Her deep-blue eyes sparkled mischievously as she grinned.

"Of course you. Mick's too busy playing Dread at the controls."

Ben glanced up to where Mick was working the soundboard. He looked like he knew exactly what he was doing as he fiddled with what appeared to be a hundred different sliding knobs, and by the sound that eventually issued from the speakers, he apparently did.

"Sure," Ben said. "I'll give it a try."

"Great."

By the time they reached the small dance floor to the right of the stage, the band had ended one number and were starting another. They were called Too Bad, after the band's lead singer, and consisted of four young men—two white and two black. The music was just as Mick had described it—fast reggae with a touch of R&B. The rhythms were infectious, the harmonies clean.

Ben started out feeling awkward, then got into the swing of it, much to Becki's approval. She grinned at him in the midst of a dance that was a combination of a very vigorous twist and a hopping motion called pogoing. Ben glanced up at the soundboard again and caught Mick's gaze. His Mohawk-topped head was bobbing in time to the music and he lifted his hand from the board to give Ben a thumbs-up. By the time the song ended—the chorus was a repetition of "Goin' down to de riddem, goin' down, goin' down" with one of the black men, his dreadlocks flying as he shook his head, doing a rap overtop of the harmonies—Ben was thoroughly enjoying himself.

"You want to stick it out for another?" Becki asked him.

"Try and stop me."

"All *right*."

Farley and Ron sat in the parking lot across from Barrymore's, huddled behind the chip wagon, finishing off a bottle of wine. Poke had drifted off sometime around noon.

"You still seeing snakes?" Ron asked.

Farley blinked. It took him a moment to digest the words, then he slowly shook his head. "Nope," he said very seriously, took a swig of the cheap wine and passed the bottle to Ron.

"That's good," Ron replied, equally serious. "I don't like snakes."

Ron had been bumming some spare change down in the Market late that afternoon, when a woman had pressed a twenty-dollar bill in his hand, saying, "You get yourself something to eat, you poor man."

"Yes, ma'am," he'd replied, grinning so hard he was likely to split his face. "I surely will, ma'am. Thank you very much. God bless you, ma'am. God bless you."

With the three dollars Farley had acquired, they'd bought themselves four bottles of wine and had enough left over for two breakfast specials in the morning and a healthy start on tomorrow's alcoholic intake.

"I *especially* don't like snake-headed men," Farley said as the bottle came back to him.

"The worst," Ron agreed. "They're the fucking worst."

Rick spent the evening at Stella's, bored out of his mind as they watched some made-for-TV movie that even the actors didn't seem to care about. About its only saving grace was the way that woman—what was her name? She was on *Dallas* or one of those shows—looked in a bikini. It made you want to get her out under some palm trees somewhere and hump the brains out of her.

He sighed as they sat through the news. *The National.* The Prime Minister was leading Joe Clark in the Gallup Polls. Big deal. *The Local.* Some church burned down. Who cared? Did people even go to church anymore?

Tonight was his big effort at "getting along"—especially important because he wasn't going to be around until late tomorrow night, and he sure didn't want Stella tagging along. Not with Bill's secretary coming. But until he had Bill's money in his hands . . . Yeah. Well, all that was going to save tonight was when they finally turned off the boob tube and hit the sack.

Stella might have her faults, but she sure had all the right

moves when it came down to the skin game. He might get a
little on the side—hell, he might get a lot, who was count
ing?—but what made those affairs so sweet was knowing he
could always have Stella as a sort of icing on the cake. Who
said you couldn't have your cake and eat it too?

By eleven Cat and Peter were sitting on a couch on Peter's
balcony. It had cooled down somewhat over the evening and
Cat was snuggled in an old sweater of Peter's, feeling drained
of words again, but in a pleasant way. She didn't think she'd
talked this much, especially about herself, to anyone before.
They'd been enjoying a companionable silence over the past
fifteen minutes, broken only by the traffic on Bank Street, a
few houses away.

"The dreams are the key," Peter said suddenly.

Cat started at the sound of his voice. She'd been just drifting along, not really thinking of anything.

"You believe me?" she asked.

That in itself was hard to believe. She'd found herself telling him everything, from how she felt about cats and people
when she was a teenager, to her night visits in the Otherworld;
how she felt she was living a lie, that her ghosts should share
as much of a byline as she did.

"What's to believe or disbelieve?" he asked. "I just think
you're luckier than most, that's all. I wish I could remember a
quarter of my dreams, much less have them be one connecting
narrative. You're certainly not the first artist to be inspired by
dreams and visions either. Just think of William Blake. What
we have to figure out is how to get you to remember them
again."

"But they don't just come to me in my dreams," Cat said.

Peter shook his head. "Uh-uh. I can't buy that. You said
yourself that it was only a feeling. You *thought* you felt pres-
ences. You never actually saw them. I can see where that
would happen. I mean, your dreams were like having a whole
other life. It stands to reason that you'd feel those people—
your 'ghosts'—around you in the day. They were so much a
part of you, how *could* they go away? Are you with me so
far?"

Cat was willing to go along with that for now, no matter
what she privately believed. "Okay."

"Well, from the little I know about dreams and dreaming,"

Peter continued, "we go through two different kinds of sleep in a night. REM sleep—that stands for Rapid Eye Movement —and non-REM sleep. It's during REM sleep that we're supposed to dream. When you wake up and remember what you dreamed, remember it clearly, that means you woke up during one of your REM cycles. I figure what's happened to you is, somehow you shifted into waking up during your non-REM cycles."

"It's that simple?"

"I'm not sure," he admitted. "I don't know a whole lot about it, and I've never heard of anyone who dreams the way you do."

Cat thought about it all for a moment. What he said sounded very rational and plausible, but something didn't sit right. She told him as much.

"I'm just not dreaming *period*," she added.

"You mean you're not remembering your dreams."

"It doesn't feel like that."

"But that's what it's got to be. Otherwise . . ."

"Otherwise what?"

"Otherwise I *really* don't know."

"So how can I wake up in the right cycle?" Cat asked. "How do I know when I'm in one or the other?"

"You don't. In sleep laboratories they've got all kinds of equipment that let the researchers know when you're in one and when you're in the other. They hook you up to an EEG to measure your brain activity. They've got gizmos to measure everything. I wouldn't be surprised if they haven't already figured out a way to actually record dreams by now."

"I don't want to go into a laboratory."

"I don't blame you," Peter said. "But you *do* want to remember your dreams, don't you?"

Cat nodded.

"What I'd do," Peter said, "is stay with a friend and have them wake you up every half hour or so. Trial by error, you know?"

"But I don't know anyone who—"

"Or you could use an alarm clock."

Loneliness, he realized, was as much the problem as her insecurities about her writing. And while he was willing to believe that she dreamed what she did, he couldn't accept that her dreams wrote her stories for her. Only how was he supposed to go about convincing her of that?

"Do you really think that would work?" Cat asked.

It took Peter a moment to realize that she was responding to what he'd said earlier, not to what he'd been thinking. "It can't hurt to try," he said.

"I suppose not."

They fell silent again. Cat knew she should be getting home, but she still couldn't face the empty house. Nor the possibility of the watcher returning.

She wished she could just stay where she was. But although Peter had been sweet, and she was grateful for his taking the time he had with her tonight, she didn't feel it was fair to ask him if she could stay. It would be imposing, for one thing. And he might take it the wrong way. Romance was all very fine, but she was more interested in just having a friend right now. What few romantic relationships she'd had in the past had never been exactly ideal. The last one had been a year or so ago. Tom Sinclair. Sensitive. A graphic artist. But he'd left her because she was "too flaky."

She felt good about Peter right now and realized that he could be a real honest-to-goodness friend. Not a big deal for most people, but for her, outside of the Otherworld . . . She didn't want to spoil it.

"Penny for your thoughts."

"Mmm?"

"I guess, what with inflation, it should really be a quarter, but somehow it doesn't have the same ring."

Cat smiled. "I was thinking of going home," she said, "but . . ."

"But?"

There was nothing underlying the word—no come on, just curiosity because she'd let the sentence trail off. Emboldened, Cat went on.

"But I don't want to be alone. I don't want to give you the wrong impression or anything. . . ."

There. She'd said it.

Peter regarded her for a moment, then understood her hesitation. "You can stay here if you like," he said. "No strings attached. The couch folds out into a bed—not this one, but the ratty one in the living room. Will that be okay?"

Cat nodded gratefully.

"Just one condition though," Peter added.

"What's that?"

"I absolutely refuse to wake you every half hour."

Cat started to giggle.

Cat was a real sweetheart, Peter thought as he lay in bed. Mixed up as hell, but a sweetheart. He heard the couch springs squeak as she changed positions. But it was weird the way she'd convinced herself that she had these ghostly collaborators. He supposed that so long as it worked out, so long as she was producing, it didn't really matter. But what about now? How could she be persuaded that she could write just as well without her dreams?

He knew a few writers—that came with the territory when you had a bookstore—and they were all touchy about one thing or another. Gary Felding could only write when he sat in a certain chair—didn't matter where the chair was. Eloise Peltier needed a Dixon HB pencil and yellow, unlined foolscap before she could produce a single coherent sentence. Pat Kozakiewicz wrote the endings to his stories first, while going home from work on the bus. He couldn't write the endings at home, and if he didn't have an ending, he couldn't write a story.

Cat needed her night visitors.

He supposed they were all habits that for one reason or another had developed into iron-clad rules. They certainly added to the mystique of a writer's idiosyncrasies. But then you had someone like Harlan Ellison, who could write anything, anywhere. Of course, he needed his trusty Olympia—so there you were. Still, none of that helped solve Cat's problem.

What she really needed was to get out more and meet some people. She obviously had a lot of smarts—that came out both in her writing and talking to her on a one-to-one basis—so it was hard to figure out how she could live so cut off from the rest of the world.

Because she had an Otherworld. And Otherworldly friends.

Right.

His thoughts turned to Ben, and he wondered what Ben would say when he found out that Cat had spent the night

over. On second thought, scratch that. He'd better not tel
him. Ben was more than a little jealous of the fact that Pete
spent time talking to her in the store as it was.

He wondered what kept Ben vacillating between wanting to
know Cat "like a friend, you know, Peter?" and being afraid to
exchange two words with her. Maybe he was afraid that when
he met her, she wouldn't match up to the fantasy image he had
of her. Maybe he really *was* too shy. Just like Cat seemed to
be.

Peter smiled in the dark. And just maybe he could do
something about both of their problems.

Lysistratus took in an opera at the National Arts Centre that
night. After the performance he managed to include himself in
a reception that was being given for the performers. The so-
prano intrigued him—her waking thoughts gave off the promise of rich dreams—but there was too great a crowd around
her. Instead he let one of the company's young men take him
up to his hotel room. He was easy to bring to climax, but his
dreaming was shallow, leaving Lysistratus in a discontented
mood as he walked home by way of the canal.

He paused twice to skim dreams from sleeping victims
whose houses and bedrooms he entered like a ghost. But there
was nothing magical about his manner of gaining entry. After
years of necessity, especially in the present age when locks
were so prevalent, there were certain skills that he'd had no
choice but to acquire. There were few commonly used locks
that he could not bypass in a few moments.

He was in a better mood as he continued on his way, humming an aria from the evening's performance, but his good
humor drained away as he stood in front of Cat's empty
house. In the three months that she had fed him with her
dreams, she had not spent one night away from the house.
Why now? Because she had spied him last night?

He dismissed the thought as unlikely and drifted across the
street from his usual vantage point to step through the gap in
the hedge that the walkway made. There he stood, merging
with the shadows. He saw an orange cat sleeping on one windowsill. Another brown-and-gray tabby dozed on the worn
leather seat of the buggy. But the house was empty.

He moved closer, onto the porch, up to the door. The cats,
startled by his sudden and silent appearance, fled. For a long

while Lysistratus stared at the door, then slowly he bent over the lock. He inserted two slender metal rods, working them until the lock made a soft snicking sound. Then he was inside.

He walked slowly through the rooms, tasting her presence with every step he took. Her absence woke an indefinable ache inside him—that familiar hunger for her essence, combined with something else that he could put no name to.

There was no sign of packing, nor of a hurried departure. He unfolded one or two balled-up scraps of paper by her wastepaper basket, then let them fall to the floor after he'd read their awkward phrases. Where had she gone? He sat down in the corduroy easy chair that fronted the window of her study and viewed the street.

This was where she had been sitting when she spotted him last night. He wondered what it would feel like to be inside her, how much different, how much stronger the essence he would gain from her orgasm would be compared to what he stole from her sleeping dreams.

If she was still in the city, if she was sleeping somewhere within its environs, he could find her. Asleep, dreaming, she was unique. Awake, the pattern of her psyche, while differing from those who didn't dream so true, was not quite so singular. But if she slept . . .

He closed his eyes and let his mind range into the streets, sifting the dreams that spilled from the minds of more common dreamers, searching.

This was the first time that Cat hadn't slept in her own bed for a very long time. It was a strange feeling. It was nice to know that there was someone else just a call away, to know there could be no crazed prowler—imagined or not—standing across the street, planning who knew what terrors to inflict upon her. But the very things that made her feel safe, made it hard to get to sleep. The couch squeaked every time she moved, so that she ended up lying very still so as not to wake Peter. And then there were the shadows in the room. They were all so different from the familiar ones in her own bedroom.

She thought about Peter's explanation of REM and non-REM cycles and wondered if he was right. It all made sense in its own reasonable way. The trouble was that she called her night visits dreams simply for want of a better description.

They weren't really dreams per se. Not by any standard definition. Nor visions either. It was like being awake—only in a different place. She went somewhere else when she slept. Or at least she used to.

Lying there in Peter's living room, with the sense of him all around her, she began to have second thoughts about having confided so much to him this evening. What must he think? Bad enough that she'd ended up telling him about her writer's block without laying her whole life story on him as well. Had he been understanding, or subtly condescending? He'd seemed to understand more than she'd thought anybody could—only how much of that had been his humoring her?

She was being unfair and she knew it. She was putting a taint on the whole evening, but she couldn't help it. Her forehead was damp and an emptiness had settled in her stomach. What if she *had* been deluding herself for all these years— talking to shadows, making phantoms real. They had places for people who couldn't relate to the real world, who couldn't see beyond their own delusions. Mostly it was the dangerous ones that they put away—the ones who might hurt themselves or others. But who was to say that she wouldn't become dangerous herself? Lord knows she was walking on the edge these days.

That uncertainty was always present—more so now than usually, because the dreams themselves were gone. The dichotomy—sane, insane—was what got in the way whenever she tried to have a normal relationship with someone. Thank God she didn't blather away to her correspondents, though even her letter-writing had tapered off these past few months.

It was easier to put something into writing, to relate to a person who was made up of words on a page that showed up in her post office box, than it was meeting people face to face. But since she'd lost her dreams, since the ghosts had gone, she'd felt too empty to write even a postcard. There was a tottering pile of unanswered letters sitting on her desk at the moment.

She turned over and the couch springs squeaked. There was too much going around in her brain, and it never changed. She was so tired of it all. She closed her eyes, fiercely willing herself to sleep. As wound up as she was, she was sure it would elude her, but surprisingly, sleep came quickly. And with it a dream.

She knew immediate relief. Peter had been wrong with his

REM/non-REM nonsense. *This* was her dreaming. And when she got up from his couch in the morning, she knew she'd recall it as clearly as though she was remembering the previous day's events. If it meant she was crazy, fine. Better this than the empty ache inside, the emptiness that nothing in her waking state could fill, except for her writing.

A breeze lifted her hair. She could taste the salt tang in it, and drew a deep breath. She was standing on Redcap Hill, with its three dancing longstones for company and the twisty-branched fairy thorn on its lower slope; the hill that housed Tiddy Mun's gnomish kin. Kothlen's moors unfolded before her into the northern horizon. The gray seas were to the west; behind her, Mynfel's oak and apple wood.

The moon was bright above, washing the hill with its cool light. For a moment Cat was so happy she couldn't breathe. She was home. She could walk Kothlen's moor, or sit here on the hill amongst the standing stones. She could travel to the wattle and daub huts of the marsh folk, or make her way to the craggy foothills of the mountains where Mynfel's wolves ranged. But then she became aware of a difference in the Otherworld, an emptiness that stole the heart from the land, and her happiness dissolved.

A vague dread stole over her—shapeless because she couldn't put her finger on its source. There was a wrongness in the air, a feeling of being watched—from a great distance, but being watched all the same. It was as though the night itself was searching for her.

Where were her friends? Why was the hill under her feet silent, where the gnomes usually held their nightly revels in its hollowed chambers? She was in the Otherworld, but it didn't seem to be the Otherworld that she knew. She was alone in its mysterious reaches—alone except for whatever it was that was searching for her.

She shivered. The night wasn't cold, but fear had its own way of sapping strength. Goose bumps started up and down her arms.

I don't want to be here, she thought. I don't want to be found by whatever it is that's looking for me.

But she didn't seem to have a choice. The dream shifted into a nightmare as she turned in a slow circle, trying to watch all directions at once, seeing the familiar landscape of the Otherworld alter as she perceived it through fear rather than wonder. Everything familiar seemed strange. Haunted. The night held menace in every inch of its darkness.

Something stirred, down by the fairy thorn, and she spun
to face that direction, her breath catching in her throat. She
saw a shape rise up from amongst the tree's roots, the moon-
light reflecting catlike in large eyes. She wanted to bolt, but
fear rooted her legs to the ground. Then the apparition spoke,
called her by her secret name, and she sank to her knees with
relief.

"Tiddy?" she called in a husky voice. "Is that you?"

Gaze flitting nervously left and right, the gnome approached her. His entire body was taut with tension and he
looked ready to bolt at the slightest provocation.

"It's me, it's me," the little man said mournfully. He came
up close, saucer eyes searching her face. "Why did you leave
us?" he asked.

Ben had gone to bed more than a little tipsy. The clock
beside his bed showed two-thirteen when he crawled under the
covers. An hour later he woke in a cold sweat with the after-
images of a bad dream floating before his eyes and a buzzing
in his ears.

There had been a man stalking him in his dreams—a man
with skin like white frost and glittering blue eyes. His finger-
nails were curved like talons. When he smiled, his lips pulled
back to reveal row upon row of incisors like a barracuda's. He
had Ben backed up against the wall of an alleyway, the bricks
pressing against Ben's shoulder blades, the man's eyes flat and
cold, his grin widening. And then suddenly the mouth of alley
was filled with cats—a wave of them that crested and swept
over the man, clawing and biting. . . .

That was when Ben woke.

Too weird, he thought. He sat up against the headboard,
still shaken by the intensity of the images. He didn't normally
have dreams—or at least he didn't normally remember them.
But even the ones he remembered had never been like this.
And there'd been something about the man who was stalking
him—something familiar that eluded him the more he tried to
place it.

After a while he lay down again, calmer, but still puzzled.
He turned his thoughts to the evening just past, Becki's pleasure that he'd danced with her—"Guess you're not such an old
fart after all," she'd teased him—and hanging out afterward

with her and Mick and a couple of guys from the band—
Johnny Too Bad and Ras . . . Ras Danny Dread.

He fell asleep again, the nightmare all but forgotten.

"I didn't leave you," Cat said. "I just . . . I don't know what
happened. I just couldn't get here anymore. Something was
stopping me. Oh, Tiddy, I've missed you. Why didn't you
come to me?"

"I couldn't find the way," he replied in a small voice.

"But where have you been?"

"Hiding."

"Hiding from what? From me?" Just the possibility of that
made the knot in her stomach tighten.

"Not from you," Tiddy Mun told her. "Never from you.
From . . . from the evil one. . . ."

"Evil. . . . ?" That was what filled the night, she realized.
What was seeking her. Not the night itself, but something
inhuman all the same. Something evil. "Where are the
others?" she asked. "Mabwen and Kothlen . . . and all your
kin?"

"Gone, gone. Kothlen is dead. Mabwen is fled." Tiddy
Mun began to shiver uncontrollably. "All the . . . others are too
scared to do anything but run and hide."

Cat stared at him in shock. "Kothlen . . . is dead?"

"The evil killed him. It comes like a great shadow to steal
your soul. We thought . . . I thought he'd killed you too."

Cat drew the little man close and held him. Tears spilled
from her eyes, ran down her cheek unheeded. Kothlen dead.
That tall bright lord—dead. She couldn't accept it, but the
truth plummeted through her like a rock plunging through
water, sending up ripples of sorrow that threatened to drown
her as they widened. She'd never be with him again. Never
see him smile. Never sit with Tiddy Mun at the tall elflord's
knee, listening to his stories or just sharing a companionable
silence. He was dead. Dead.

"How can he be gone?" she cried.

Her despair rang across the hills, and Tiddy Mun grew
very still in her arms. They both sensed the gathering of whatever it was that hunted in the night. Its searching narrowed,
focused on them. A pressure beat at them from beyond the
protection of the standing stones. It came from the darkness,

sapping their wills, drawing them out from between the stones.

They stumbled on trembling legs, collapsing just outside the safety of the dolmen. Unprotected, they huddled under the night skies and felt the darkness sweeping near.

Lysistratus could sense her now. She wasn't far—a mile, perhaps two. She slept alone, in another's house. She was too far to feed on, but close enough to draw her to him. She hid, but hiding would do her no good. If she didn't come to him, he would go to her, but feed he would tonight.

"Come home, sweet dreamer," he whispered into the night. "Come to the comfort of your own bed, your own secret place of solace. No one can harm you here. . . ."

Cat felt weak, as though she'd tried to get up too soon from a sickbed and had slumped helplessly to the floor. She wanted to be safe at home, in her own bed. Not in an Otherworld where Kothlen was dead and everything except for Tiddy Mun was strange. Nor to wake in a strange apartment, on a strange couch, to see the four enclosing walls of a living room that belonged to someone else surrounding her.

Tiddy Mun whimpered in her arms. The darkness above them took the impossible shape of a great dark-winged pterodactyl. They clutched each other tightly. Cat knew that they had to move, to get back inside the protection of the longstones, but they were both too frightened to move. Then that black saurion shape in the darkness above them swept down with an icy rush of fetid air, talons outstretched and raking the sky.

Cat heard a wailing scream pierce the night and was only dimly aware that it had been torn from her own throat.

Peter sat bolt upright in his bed, the scream that had woken him still ringing in his ears. It took him a moment to get his bearings, then he thought: Cat!

"Oh, Jesus."

He lunged from the bed and skidded across the floor to the living room, hitting the light switch as he went in. In the sudden glare of light, he saw Cat crouched in a corner of the open daybed, holding what looked to be some sort of doll in her arms. Except it was too large to be a doll, Peter realized, and who'd make a doll as wild and tattered as this one was? Raggedy clothes, bone-thin limbs, wild hair, eyes too big for the pinched features of its face. Then the doll moved and Peter took a step back, stumbled over an end table, and sprawled on the floor.

When he got to his feet and half-fearfully looked back, there was only Cat, huddled on the couch, eyes wide with fright, hair plastered wetly against her forehead. She moaned, hands opening and closing on the blanket that she'd drawn up to her chin.

"Easy," Peter said, wondering just what the hell he thought he'd seen. He moved toward her. "It's okay, Cat. It was just a bad dream."

She looked blankly at him, then slowly her eyes focused. He sat on the edge of the daybed and drew her to him, rubbing her back with the palm of his hand in long soothing strokes. The shirt she'd borrowed from him was damp with perspiration.

"That was a bad one," he said when she finally drew back.

She nodded, swallowed with difficulty. "He's dead," she said numbly.

"Who's dead?"

"Kothlen. And—" She looked wildly about the room. "Tiddy Mun!"

"What—" Peter began. Then he heard a scuffling on the stairs that led down to the store.

The image returned to him—the image of what he'd thought she was holding when he first flicked on the lights, before he'd stumbled and fallen. It had to have been a trick of the light. He'd seen the blanket bunched up in her arms and given it features. Or the pillow that was now lying on the floor. Except . . . He turned toward the stairwell. The sound hadn't been repeated, but that didn't mean—

"You saw him too, didn't you?" Cat asked. "Tiddy Mun. A little man. A moment ago. I know he came back with me. . . ."

He hadn't seen anything, Peter told himself. Especially not some lingering figment of her dreams. He just didn't need something like that to be real. But his whole body was tense and he found himself straining to hear another sound from downstairs. Was that the front door? Again the sound wasn't repeated. There was only silence.

As though she were following his thoughts, Cat asked,

"You're going to pretend that you didn't see anything, aren't you?"

"Look, Cat. I'm not sure what I did or didn't see. All I know is I heard you scream and got out here so fast that I wasn't even awake yet."

That wild face with its huge eyes returned to him. It was like something out of a Rackham print or one of Charles Vess's illustrations.

"He *was* here," Cat said. "We were in the Otherworld, but everything was changed. There was something . . . hunting us. And then just when it was about to get us I . . ." Her voice trailed off. She'd been about to say, I woke up.

"It's okay," Peter said. "It's over now."

As soon as he spoke the words, he realized that he was being too quick to offer comfort, too pat. She wanted to talk it out, while he just wanted to forget it. Now she was withdrawing again. Bottling it all up inside because he was being too pigheaded to admit that maybe he *had* seen something.

"I can't stay here," Cat said abruptly. "I'm going home."

Peter glanced at the clock on the mantle. "For God's sake, Cat. It's just going on four. Why don't you just go back to—"

"I can't stay here. I have to go home. At home I'll be safe."

"You're safe here. I don't bite."

She didn't crack a smile. "I'm going," she said, and stood up.

Picking up her clothes, she headed for the bathroom and shut the door firmly behind her. Peter started to follow, then realized he'd better get dressed himself. All he was wearing was a pair of boxer shorts. She was ready to leave as he came out of the bedroom, and looked at him strangely.

"Why are you dressed?"

"I'm going with you."

"I want to be alone, Peter."

"That's okay. I'm just going as far as your front door. Humor me, won't you?"

They went downstairs in silence. Peter looked carefully around, but nothing seemed disturbed. He glanced at Cat. What if he *had* seen something?

"Who was he?" he asked as they stepped out onto the street.

Cat stood silently, studying the sky. She shivered as she

remembered that great winged shape dropping down out of the Otherworld darkness. Where was Tiddy Mun now?

"Cat—" Peter began.

"Don't patronize me, Peter."

"I'm not." He shrugged. "Okay, so maybe I was. But just take a look at it from my point of view."

"You saw him," she said. "You just won't believe that you did. Or you won't admit it."

Her temper was rising. She was about to tell him to just leave her alone, but then she thought of last night's watcher and tonight's feeling in the Otherworld.

"Tiddy Mun is a gnome," she said softly. "One of my . . . my ghosts, I suppose you could say."

Peter realized how much that had taken out of her. Yesterday evening had been different. That had been a cleansing of sorts. This morning she was all closed up again. Somehow he had to get past that block, as he had last night. But he couldn't do it by playing along with her fantasies—no matter what he might or might not think he'd seen in her arms earlier.

"I thought you said they only visited you in your dreams."

"The gnomes used to always follow me around, here as well as in the Otherworld, though mostly it was Tiddy Mun. I'd feel him watching me from around a corner, but when I turned he'd be gone. It was sort of a game that we played. But then I stopped dreaming. . . ."

"You said someone had died."

"Kothlen. He . . ."

She couldn't go on. All the sorrow she'd been suppressing came surging up inside her. For the third time in less than twelve hours, Peter held her close, desperately trying to bring her back to the plain reality of the here and now. They stood near the corner of Bank Street and Fifth. He could see their reflection in the front window of Britton's Smoke Shop—the small form pressed against him, hair as wild as her gnome's. . . .

The thought trailed off. Damn it. He *had* seen something. All he had to do was close his eyes and he could call up those alien features in his mind. The triangular-shaped face, pinched and brown as bark. And the eyes, like two small moons, glinting gold . . .

A cab drove by and Cat pulled away from him as though even that passing driver was too much of a crowd to witness her grief. Peter thought of flagging it down, but by then it was already far down Bank, taillights winking red. He turned back to Cat, reached for and captured her hand.

"I did see something" he said. "What it was, I don't know. I just find it really hard to accept that it was a little man from your dreams, Cat."

Hard to accept? Try impossible. But *she* believed. And her grief for the death of one of the dream companions—that was real for her as well. So what did that mean? That she had a good imagination? He could tell that from reading her books. But no matter how real it was for her, he knew he shouldn't play up to her fantasy. It was just going to support an illusion, and that wouldn't help in the long run. It would make it harder for her to accept that it was her subconscious mind peopling her sleep with the companions she was too shy to meet in real life.

An excellent theory, barring one small detail. He'd seen something too.

Cat watched his face through a film of tears, trying to understand what was going through his mind.

"C'mon," he said simply, squeezing her hand.

They walked along in silence, past the Civic Centre and Lansdowne Park. Halfway across the bridge they paused and looked down at the still waters of the canal, arms propped on the balustrade.

"Kothlen was like water," Cat said, searching for words to express what her friend had been like, trying to bridge the gap of disbelief that still lay between Peter and herself. "When he was still, he was as quiet as that water down there. You could just sink into his silences, and when you came out of them, you were refreshed. Filled again. He was like Mynfel in that way."

"The horned woman?" Peter asked, remembering her talking a bit about her yesterday evening.

Cat nodded. "She's like a goddess. Being with her is like being in the presence of something . . . I don't know. Solemn. Holy. Kothlen could be like that, but he could also be fun. Did you ever go up into the Gatineaus in the spring and hear one of those small brooks come tumbling down a hill? That's what his laugh was like. And that's why I think of him being like water. He was as hard to understand as the sea, but as immediate as . . . as rain on your face."

The depth of her feelings reached Peter. He found himself wishing he could have known this man, wishing Kothlen hadn't been just a fabrication, but someone real. Someone Cat could have introduced him to. Someone he could have talked to himself, to sit around and shoot the breeze with. . . . Again he returned to the question: Did Kothlen's unreality make any difference to the validity of Cat's feelings? No matter what Kothlen had been—imagined or not—didn't the feelings stay real?

"You're going to miss him, aren't you?"

She nodded again, quietly, holding back a new rush of tears.

Lysistratus smiled in the darkness of Cat's study. He had felt her coming to him ever since he'd broken her dream. Now every footstep brought her closer. He thought again of breeding a woman like her. Was she in a fertile cycle tonight? What sort of child would spring from a union of such a true dreamer and a being like himself?

When Cat and Peter reached the corner of Belmont and Willard and were looking down the street to where Cat's house rose above the cedar hedge, Peter sensed a change come over her.

"What's the matter?"

Somehow she couldn't tell him about the watcher—not after everything else that had come up between yesterday afternoon and this morning. He'd go from thinking her quaintly eccentric to out-and-out paranoic.

"Cat?"

She didn't know why she'd insisted on going home. Looking down the street to her house, it appeared sinister. She felt the same disquiet she'd known in her dream—just before everything went wrong. She'd come to be safe in her refuge. Nearing it now, it seemed anything but safe.

"Are you okay?" Peter tried again.

"It's nothing," she said with false bravado. "I'm just not having a good night."

When Lysistratus saw the pair of them coming down the street, he rose from the chair he was sitting in and stepped back from the window. His seed would not fill her tonight, the

way her dreams filled him. Not unless he dealt with her companion, and he wasn't prepared to do that. He considered
waiting in her study to see if her companion was just dropping
her off, then shook his head. Downstairs would be better.

There was something odd about the night. He could almost
sense a second Cat Midhir abroad—had ever since he'd
pulled her from her dreaming. It existed as a disturbing presence that nipped just at the edge of his awareness. When he
reached for it, it flitted from his scrutiny, sliding away into the
seas of the night with all the quick grace of a manta ray. Here
one moment, gone the next. Hidden. But close.

He could put no name to it. It felt so much like Cat, like
the essence of her dreams . . . as though some part of her
dreaming had broken free and strayed to wander loose on its
own.

Soundlessly he left the room and slipped down the stairs.
He could hear their footsteps on the porch as he paused in the
hallway in front of the door. The taste of her, of her essence,
was strong in the air. Her anodynic dreams . . .

He wanted to take her right there on the floor in the hallway, even though it would mean he'd have to deal with her
companion and all the problems that could ensue. If he simply
put the man to sleep and took her, they would realize something was amiss when they awoke, sprawled in the hall, or
however naturally he might arrange their slumbering bodies in
her bed. If he killed the man, the police would be brought in.
Either way he stood the chance of losing his easy access to
her.

Undecided still, he drifted toward the rear of the house. If
only the hunger wasn't so strong tonight.

Cat dug in her pocket for her key.

"I was sure they'd be around," she said lightly, hoping to
make the end of their very strange evening more normal. She
had the quixotic notion that if they parted ordinarily, all the
weirdness could be forgotten.

"You thought who'd be around?"

"Ginger and Pad. My cats. I haven't seen them for a day or
so."

Peter smiled. "Cat's cats."

She had her key out now. "They can be a couple of monsters, let me tell you, but . . ." Her voice trailed off. The front

door swung open as she touched her key to the lock.

"Cat?"

The watcher reared in her mind with all the menace of the dark-winged searcher on top of Redcap Hill.

"I locked it before I left," she said. "I know I did."

Peter stepped past her into the house. Pinprickles marched up his spine. There was suddenly a very real sense of danger in the air that was neither imagination nor dream. As he started forward, Cat put a hand on his arm. Every horror movie that she'd ever seen came rushing into her head. Ghouls. Maniacs with meat cleavers or long wicked knives...

The back door slammed, and they both jumped.

"There's somebody in here!" Peter cried and ran ahead to the kitchen.

"Peter! Don't!"

They stopped in the kitchen to stare at the back door. It swung wide. Heart thumping, Peter moved forward to look out. On the lawn he could make out footprints in the dew— widely spaced, like a running man would make.

"Oh, God," Cat said as she saw them. "It's real."

Peter swallowed hard. "What's real?"

His own imagination had started to take quantum leaps. He was ready to believe almost anything when she started to tell him about her watcher. When she was done, he almost sighed with relief. A weirdo he could handle. That fit into his world-view, no matter how unpleasant that kind of a person could be. He just couldn't have faced the possibility of more dreams becoming real.

"You'd better call the police," he said.

"I . . . I can't."

"What do you mean, you can't?"

"They'll just laugh at me."

"For Christ's sake, Cat. It's their job to check out this kind of thing. Would you rather be dead?"

She sat mournfully at the kitchen table, feeling as though her world was tumbling into a freefall from which there was no escape. Reality, even her ghost-laden brand of it, had turned topsy-turvy. Order had fled and no one had been thoughtful enough to provide her with a new set of rules.

"Why'd he have to pick on me?"

"I don't know." Peter massaged his temples. "We don't

even know what he wanted."

But with all you read in the papers or saw on TV these days, you had to be prepared for the worst. Especially if you were any sort of a public figure—even as low-profiled as Cat. Hinckley came to mind—attempting to assassinate Reagan just to impress Jodie Foster. Lennon's murderer. Fans. Hero worship that went a giant twisted step too far.

He said as much to Cat. She looked shocked.

"I get letters from my fans all the time, Peter. They're not weirdos."

"You don't know that." Looking up, he saw the fear in her eyes. He tried to put on a reassuring smile. "Maybe you're right. Still, you'd better not stay here."

Cat shook her head. "I'm not going to let him chase me out of my own house."

"Okay. I can see that. But if you won't call the police, how about if I hang around for a bit—just until it gets light out."

Cat nodded, grateful for his offer. Her bravery only went so far, and after tonight . . .

Peter pushed himself up from his chair. "Maybe we'd better go over the house," he said. "Just to be sure. Do you want—"

"I'm coming with you."

There was no way she was going to sit in the kitchen by herself. Peter nodded, understanding how she felt.

At the front door he had to step aside as her cats edged their way in. They watched him warily as they sidled through the door, then bolted for the kitchen. Peter stared out at the hedge. He felt as if he were in a net that was just starting to draw tight, a net from which there was no escape.

He looked beyond the hedge to what he could see of the street. Was the prowler still out there, watching? Nothing had been taken, or even disturbed inside. And while this wasn't even his house, Peter still felt the same sense of outrage that Cat did. Outrage and fear. Hard to say which was stronger right now.

"Shit," he muttered under his breath. Slowly he closed the door.

Lysistratus saw the door close. Dawn was less than an hour away. Would she sleep before it grew too light for the shadows to hide him? He watched as, room by room, lights came on in the house to stab the shadows outside their windows with their bright illumination. They probably thought he was still inside.

He smiled. That much of a fool he wasn't. Nor would he linger here any longer. There would be other nights.

As he turned away, he searched the night one last time for that strange presence he'd sensed earlier—that stray bit of dream, cast loose on the world to fend for itself. An absurd notion, he realized, but it stayed with him. He reached out with his mind, casting the net wide, but it came up empty.

He frowned. Hunger gnawed inside him.

Lisa Henderson slept poorly that night. She'd had another argument with her mother—about her birthday, naturally enough, which certainly put a sense of gloom over the coming festivities. It was at times like this that Lisa wished she lived in another city, even another country, just to get away from the family obligations her mother insisted she maintain. Everything from Christmas to that most holy of holies, Mother's Day.

But her birthday was supposed to be *her* day, wasn't it? To do whatever it was that she wanted, even if it meant spending the whole day in bed, or going out and getting pleasantly sloshed with a bunch of friends. When she'd made some reference to that, the shit had really hit the fan.

Why can't you keep your mouth shut? she'd asked herself as she was forced to listen to another tirade of what a thankless daughter she was, and how did she think her father would feel, and how hurt *she* was herself that her own daughter would . . .

Lisa got off the phone with a headache that aspirin would not get rid of. It just lay there between her temples, centering mostly behind her left eye, where it felt like there was a little man with a long needle giving her brain a sharp jab every few moments. She got those headaches a lot.

Stress, her doctor had diagnosed when Lisa went to her with that problem a few months ago. "This is a case of prevention, rather than treatment," she'd added as she prescribed a relaxant. Diazepam, 5 mg. One tablet every six hours, when needed. Valium. Lisa never got the prescription filled. It seemed too . . . too Middle America somehow.

When she got off the phone tonight, she wished she'd taken about a half dozen of them before answering.

She laid down for a while. When the headache subsided into a bearable dullness, she tried reading the paper, but it was too depressing and the print seemed too pinched tonight. Trying to reread Dylan Thomas's *Quite Early One Morning*, she couldn't get into the mood to appreciate it properly either, and ended up settling for the TV. She watched the late movie on Channel 13, the late-late movie on CFCF 12 out of Montreal, and finally got into bed around four A.M., only to sit up a couple of hours later, dead tired yet wide awake.

She got out of bed and went to sit by the window in her living room, which overlooked the street. Movement caught her eye and then, before she could draw back from the screen, she was looking into the piercing blue eyes of her next-door neighbor where he stood on the walk below, his gaze fixed on her window.

She tried to look away, but her limbs went all weak and a buzzing started up in her head. She couldn't have turned her head if her life depended on it, which in some bizarre way seemed all too real at that moment. She felt as though a part of her was being drawn into him. A great darkness welled up before her eyes. There was something waiting for her in that darkness—something too frightening to have to face.

As though in a dream, she felt a hand touch her on the shoulder, lift her from her chair, and lead her to the bed. Her nightie left her body. She was caressed, teased, brought up to the brink of climax, only to fall again. When she finally came, her eyes opened wide and she saw her neighbor's face inches from her own. Then he was inside her, filling her with his need, but stealing something from her at the same time—a part of herself more precious than any moment's pleasure.

Lysistratus looked down at the woman's limp body, holding a pillow in his hand. She *knew*. In that moment that he'd taken a piece of her, she had opened her eyes wide, recognized him, and understood what he did. He toyed with the pillow, then tossed it aside. Now was not a good time. It was too close to home. He left the room as silently as he'd entered.

When Lisa woke the next morning at ten, she was already a half hour late for work. It wasn't until her lunch hour that she remembered last night's erotic dream. She smiled. The man next door had been in it. The smile faltered as the memory grew a little sharper. Tied up with the eroticism was something ugly that she couldn't quite place. But it left her with a vague unease and edgy nerves, and the disturbing sensation that it hadn't been a dream.

By her afternoon break she was feeling so high-strung that she dug out her prescription from the bottom of her purse and had it filled at the pharmacy across the street.

8

wednesday

PETER LEFT CAT'S house with a certain amount of misgiving. She was much calmer now and had promised to meet him at the store later in the morning. She'd promised as well to keep the doors locked while she was home, and that when she did leave, she'd make certain there was more than one person on the street. In the light of morning it all seemed a little foolish, but while the stranger aspects of last night still needed some suitable explanation as far as Peter was concerned, the very real threat of an intruder—of Cat's watcher—couldn't be denied.

Peter still felt they should have called the police. They were equipped to handle this sort of thing. Ordinary people might be able to deal with a psycho in a Brian De Palma film or in the pages of a Stephen King thriller, but this was the real world, and out here on the streets it just didn't work that way.

He meant to stay at her house tonight and if they saw anyone lurking about, if they saw *anything* out of the ordinary, he'd call the cops himself. But before that, before he even opened the store, he had another part of Cat's problems to deal with. He liked her a lot, but she needed more than just a friend right now. Maybe she and Ben would hit it off or maybe they wouldn't. But it sure as hell wouldn't hurt to give them the opportunity to have a go at it.

"Mick?"

He turned back to the bed. Becki sat up, the sheets falling back from her breasts. She grinned.

"Where ya going?"

"To work."

"Capitalist."

"Slug-a-bed."

She stretched, ruffling her spiked hair. "Do you have to go right this minute?"

"Well . . ."

Mick let his jeans fall to the floor and climbed back into bed. Becki pushed him down and sat on his stomach, running her hands down his chest.

"You know your friend Ben?" she murmured. Her mouth was right beside his ear, her voice breathy.

"Mmm?"

"He's not such an old fart after all—told him so myself."

Mick laughed and pulled her back as she started to sit up again. "I kinda thought you'd changed your mind about him," he said. "Now are we going to talk or—"

"We're going to 'or'," Becki told him seriously, and then they both laughed.

Mick only just made it in to work before Jim. They no sooner got the station open than an old Ford ran over the signal cord. *Ping-ping-ping.* Mick glanced at Jim.

"Hey," Jim said. "I've got the bank deposit to do."

It'd be nice, Mick thought as he headed out for the pumps, if they could have just one more full-timer working here.

Ben caught the phone on its third ring and muttered a sleepy hello into it. He sat down at the kitchen table, dressed only in shorts and a T-shirt, and stared blearily at Central Park through the window.

"Did I wake you up?" Peter asked on the other end of the line.

"I'm not sure that *awake* is the word I'd use to describe the way I'm feeling right now. What's up, Peter?"

"Just thought I'd let you know that the new Ellison showed up late yesterday afternoon. You still want a copy?"

"You called me at eight-thirty to ask me that?"

"Hot item, pal. They'll probably all be gone by noon."

"So save me one already."

"You're sounding grouchy, Ben. Have a late night?"

"I checked out Mick's new band last night at Barrymore's —a group called Too Bad that he's doing the sound for. How about you?"

"Well, the woman of your dreams stopped by and stayed for the evening."

"Who?"

"Cat Midhir. Weird thing. I walked her home and we found that some guy'd busted into her place."

"Are you serious?"

"Uh-huh. He left empty-handed and the place wasn't busted up or anything, but I got the feeling he was waiting for her. She spotted someone casing the place the night before. Being who she is, I hope it wasn't some crazed fan—you know what I mean?"

"Christ, Peter. If you think *I* had anything to do with—"

"Give me a break, Ben. I know you better than that. Infatuated, yes. But crazed? Not likely."

Ben looked across the kitchen at the poster of Cat that Peter had given him—it was the same as the one hanging in the window of Arkum Books advertising *The Borderlord*.

"I tell you, Peter," he said quietly into the phone. "Sometimes I worry about it—the way I go on about her, collect everything she writes, everything that's written about her. I've even got all the columns that she did for her community newspaper—*The OSCAR*. Remember those?"

"You don't have to explain, Ben. Besides, you're mad-keen on other writers too."

"Yeah, but it's not the same."

"So it's not the same. That doesn't mean you're going to start going weird on us."

"I suppose not." What Peter had said earlier about Cat coming over for the evening sunk in then. "Are you . . . starting to see her?" he asked with a twinge of jealousy.

"I was with her last night, Ben, but it's not like you might think. She came into the store just before closing last night and she was really depressed. I mean, bottoming out."

"What's she got to be depressed about?"

"Well . . ." Peter didn't want to compromise Cat's trust. But having inadvertently let part of it slip out, he realized that he had to say something. He wouldn't tell about the dreams. That was too private. But . . . "Just between us, she's having trouble with her writing lately."

"She's—jeez. What a bummer. Are you giving her a hand?"

Peter laughed. "Who are you kidding? I'm just giving her a sympathetic ear. She hasn't got a whole lot of friends, Ben."

"Yeah. You've told me." He glanced at the poster again. "Sometimes I wish—"

"All you've got to do is do it. She's shyer than you are."

"I think it's kind of late for that, Peter. Any sort of friendship'd be tainted by this whole hero-worship trip that I fell into."

Peter disagreed. "Writers love ego-boo, Ben. I've never seen such an insecure profession. I think it comes from the fact that they don't get any immediate feedback on their stuff. You know. Like when a musician plays a gig, people either like it or they don't, and she knows right away. But a writer just sits away in a garret somewhere, pecking the stuff out and having to wait for the reviews, which won't even necessarily be representative of what the general public thought of her book anyway."

"It still wouldn't work."

"Yeah. Well, if you're convinced, you're convinced. I think you're making a mistake, but what can I say? I've got to run, Ben. You'll be down this afternoon to pick up the Ellison?"

"Fifty-five Canadian, boxed and signed—you think it's worth it?"

"You bet. Course, I've got my rent to pay."

Ben laughed. "Right. Okay, Peter. See you this afternoon."

Lysistratus sat facing his painting of the Kikladhes, his thoughts turned inward. The sounds of Klaus Schulze's synthesizer washed from the speakers of his stereo at a low volume. Lysistratus imagined that sound as the blue-green waters of the Aegean Sea lapping Myconos's shore. He concentrated on it, hearing more than the waves on that strand. There was a gull's cry, the rattle of a fisherman's oars as he brought his boat to beach, the bleating of goats on the headland, a man's voice lifted in song as he trimmed his vines. . . .

He thought it curious how such a contemporary music could evoke such pastoral memories. But he supposed it was no more different than the dichotomy that he himself represented. He appreciated the glitter and flash of the contemporary world as much as he did the simple pleasures of the past. That was his principal complaint with modern society—they didn't seem capable of maintaining a happy marriage between the two. It was either all empty sparkle, or a dead serious return "back to the earth." Although there were exceptions.

He thought of Cat Midhir and her true dreaming. Tonight they would explore a deeper union than they had thus far. But first he would have to deal with the woman next door. She had recognized him for what he was, and though he doubted she could represent any danger on her own, he had not survived this long by being careless and letting such loose ends lie unravelled.

There was something very satisfying about a victim's final dream. As the life left their body, as their last psychic essences fled to fill him . . .

Much as Cat appreciated all Peter had done for her last night, she was glad to see him go. She needed time to be alone with her grief, time to try and understand what was happening to her. Accepting that Kothlen was dead was the most difficult. How could he be dead? He was one of her ghosts. Ghosts don't die.

The day was already threatening to become a scorcher. Taking her coffee with her, she went up to her study, flicked on a fan and sat in her thinking chair by the window. It was strange how everything was happening all at once. First she lost her dreams and with them her ability to put them on paper. Now the source of her inspiration was dead—just when she'd finally dreamed again. On top of that was Peter's theory that whoever'd been here last night, whoever'd been watching her, might be doing so because of the very writing she couldn't do anymore.

At least she didn't have her usual morning headache. Small comfort, all things considered. No comfort at all, really. Kothlen was dead. When she dreamed, she dreamed nightmares now. The other ghosts were all hiding, all except for Tiddy Mun, and where was he? Where was she without Kothlen?

Gone, gone, gone . . .

She forced back the tears that came welling up. She had to be braver than that. If she didn't feel so wide awake, she'd try to dream again. She'd find Tiddy Mun and— Except who knew what would be waiting for her when she dreamed again? The Otherworld had changed, and horror haunted it.

Her dreams and writing had always been her catharses, giving her something to turn to when the world seemed too big and frightening, filled with people who didn't care, a way of communicating that didn't require personal intimacies. Now when she needed an intimate, when she was trying to reach out, it seemed too late.

Melissa and Peter were the closest she had. She'd already tried Peter, but he simply hadn't understood. Not really. Not where it counted. And she wasn't prepared to try Melissa again. The fewer to know how close she was walking on the borders of being all-out crazed, the better it was.

Lines from a poem came to her.

> *That crazed girl improvising her music,*
> *Her poetry, dancing upon the shore,*
> *Her soul in division from itself*
> *Climbing, falling she knew not where. . . .*

Yeats again, but that was what she was. Divided inside herself. The Cat with a secret name who lived with ghosts, night after night, who dreamed. That was one. Not so shy, not so withdrawn. But there was the other one as well, the one who was sitting here now, trying to make sense of it all. This Cat who didn't dream, or dreamed horrors, who had no secret name—what was she to do?

Well, she could start by getting out of this house and up to the store, as she'd promised Peter she would. She didn't have anywhere better to go. Anywhere else to go at all, really.

Maybe she could lie down on his couch again and look for ghosts. Maybe she'd open a cupboard to find Tiddy Mun there, waiting for her. Maybe she could dream a place where Kothlen wasn't dead and shadows didn't drop from the sky with her secret name branded on their talons. Maybe she could sit behind the counter with Peter and watch the people come in and out of the store, and pick up a few tips on how to be real from them.

She looked out the window. Mrs. Beatty was fussing with her flower bed on Bellwood. On Willard, Nate Timmons was doing bodywork on his car. In the schoolyard that filled the pie-wedged shape between the two streets, the usual storm of shouting, running, jumping children were racing to and fro, filling the air with their shrill cries.

There was no one lurking, and there were no shadows to lurk in. It's perfectly safe, Peter, she thought. She changed into a pair of shorts and a loose cotton blouse, stuffed a book into her shoulder bag, and went downstairs. As she reached the front door, the phone began to ring.

"I'm on my way," she told it, and stepped out into the September sunshine.

Double-checking the door, she set off for Bank Street, the Glebe, and Peter's store, having already decided to walk rather than take the car.

Ben saw the Dude walking down Bank Street as he turned onto it from Clemow. It's funny, he thought. Once you spotted someone you thought was a little odd, you just kept seeing them. The city was full of characters. You could go your whole life without seeing one, but as soon as you did, you saw them everywhere. Like that old guy everyone called the Walker who lived somewhere in the Glebe. He'd lived there for years, apparently, but Ben had never noticed him until Peter pointed him out one day.

The Walker was tall and almost bald. He wore a shabby overcoat most of the year and walked everywhere. Ben saw him at least once a day now, anywhere from St. Laurent out in the east end of the city to as far west as Bayshore. But mostly you saw him in the Glebe. Everybody had a story about him, but no one really knew anything about him. Just a harmless old fellow with nothing to do but walk. Well, it sure beat some of the weirdos you could find downtown.

Not that the Dude was exactly in that class. Ben checked his rearview mirror and saw that he was heading into the park. Looked like he was going to be another Central Park regular. Just what the place needed. Some duded-up fugitive from a music video, out putting the make on the boys.

Farley was in the Glebe, hanging out in Central Park with Ron, working on what remained of their last bottle of Brights wine. The sun was high and the air was hot, they were both getting corked, and what the hell, he had no complaints. Farley took a long swig, handed the bottle to Ron, then laid back, his head pressed against the grass, the blue sky immense above. He leaned up on his elbow as the wine came back to him, tilted the bottle back, then froze.

His throat went dry as he saw the young man making his way across the lawn in the distance. For a moment his vision blurred and in place of the man's face he saw a snake's head, topped with a shag of dyed-blond hair. The bottle fell from his fingers.

"Jesus Christ, Farley!" Ron scooped the bottle up before much of its precious contents could spill out. "What the hell's the matter with you?"

"I . . ." He glanced at Ron, then back to the man. There was no snake's head. The man ignored them, acting as though they didn't exist. But for one moment he'd seen something in those glittering blue eyes. . . . He shook his head. "Too much sun," he said hoarsely. He grabbed the bottle, Adam's apple working overtime as he tried to kill the dryness in his throat. But the strange feeling that had come over him wouldn't pass. His hands were sweaty, his bowels tight.

"I don't know about you," Ron told him, taking the bottle back before Farley finished it off. "You getting the heebs or something?"

Farley looked down at his trembling hands. He didn't know what the fuck he had, but it was starting to scare him.

You too, Lysistratus thought as he glanced away from the two winos. I remember you, but you were not meant to remember me.

He continued across the park, leaving it in search of easier prey. The wino could wait.

It was shaping up to be a busy night.

It wasn't until midafternoon that Ben headed for the bookstore. Turning onto Fourth, he had to drive halfway down the block before he could find a place to leave his cab. That was the trouble with having the store so close to the post office. There was never any place to park. People just pulled up in the no-stopping zone in front of the squat brown-brick building and left their cars anywhere they pleased. The Green Hornets had a heyday writing out tickets on this stretch of street.

As he walked into the store, Ben thought about this whole

weird trip with Cat Midhir. Maybe he'd stake out her house tonight and see if he couldn't catch whomever it was that was bothering her himself. Be a hero. A nice idea, he thought with a laugh. Only what would he do with the guy if he *did* catch him? Magnum, P.I. he wasn't.

Peter was with a sales rep from the newly amalgamated Berkley/Jove/Ace/Playboy when Ben came in. They had a big binder on the counter between them and were going through the new releases for the next month. The binder was full of flat book covers and release sheets, each one protected by a plastic covering.

"Hey, Ben!"

"Hi, Peter."

"Look. We've just got a few more of these to go through. Why don't you get yourself a coffee?"

"Sure. You want one?"

Peter shook his head. He stepped aside so that Ben could get through to the back room. Ben glanced at the shelf just to the right of the door to see what special orders for other people had arrived. That was where Peter stored them, and you just never knew what you might see in there that you might want to order for yourself.

At that moment he realized there was someone else in the back room, sitting in the easy chair near the fridge. Looking over, he thought he'd die. You bastard, he thought to Peter. Curled up in the chair and glancing up from her book as he came in, tousle-haired and big as life, was Cat Midhir. Though she wasn't really all that big, Ben thought. She fit snugly into the chair, bare legs curled under her. Ben could feel his whole body turning beet red.

Peter had really set him up this time.

"Just a second, Tom," he heard Peter say to the sales rep. "I guess you guys don't know each other," he added cheerily as he filled the door beside Ben. "Cat, this is Ben Summerfield, my best friend. And let me tell you, if he stopped shopping here, we'd probably go broke. Ben, this is Cat. Look, I'll be with you in a moment, okay? I just want to finish up with this Berkley/Jove—jeez, Tom, couldn't you come up with a shorter name?"

"You should hear our receptionists try to get it all out in one breath."

"I can imagine." To Cat and Ben: "I'll be about five minutes, okay?"

"Uh, yeah. Sure," Ben said. I'm going to kill you, he thought.

He pulled up a chair before his legs gave way on him, and swallowed nervously. What was he going to say? He had to say something quick or she'd really think he was a jerk, but all that came to mind were inanities. I've always wanted to meet you. I love your new book. I've got everything you've ever written—at least what's in print, ha, ha! Pardon me while I shrink down into nothing and disappear through a crack in the floorboards. Nothing personal, you see. It's just that if I open my mouth I'll probably put both feet straight in it.

"Hi," was what he managed, the word coming out only slightly higher than his natural speaking voice. He cleared his throat. "What are you reading?"

Stupid, stupid. He could see from the dust jacket that it was the new Ellison. The title leapt out of the top right-hand corner of the cover, white lettering against a bright orange background: *Stalking the Nightmare*. There was a big hand coming from the spine, dropping a handful of odd beings. A red-faced man with ram's horns. A cat with cybernetic paws. A woman in a white jumpsuit. Even Mickey Mouse.

"Something that just came in yesterday," Cat said. "I've never really read any of Ellison's stuff before, but Peter insisted that I read the introduction if nothing else. 'Quiet Lies the Locust Tells.' I never knew Ellison could be so . . . poetic, I suppose. All I ever knew about him was his angry young man image."

For Cat that was a long speech. Especially delivered as it was to someone she had just met.

"A lot of people feel like that about him," Ben said, "until they actually sit down and read something by him. Now I'll be the first to admit that he's written some real clunkers, but when he's good, he's dynamite. And he's more often good than not. You should read something like 'Lonelyache,'" he added, warming up to his subject, "or 'Jefty is Five.'"

"Didn't that win an award?"

"Umhmm. Two of them—the Nebula and the Hugo in the same year."

Listening to them as he went through the last of the new

releases, Peter had to smile. He should have thought of this
ages ago. It was about time Ben actually met Cat. Maybe now
he'd take her down from that pedestal and start thinking of her
as a real person. And who knew where it might lead? Dear
Abby, eat your heart out. I might be taking over your column.

"How about the new Asprin?" Tom asked.

Peter nodded, ordering thirty-five of *Storm Season* and ten
of each of the previous Thieves' World collections.

"That it?" he asked as Tom started to put the binder away.

"Unless you want to go over the backlist . . . ?"

Peter shook his head. But he did want to keep busy out
here, at least for a while longer. "How are you and Brewster
getting along these days?" he asked.

"You don't want to know," Tom began, and launched into a
recital of the latest feud between himself and the cantankerous
owner of Brewster Books, which was located downtown at the
corner of Cooper and Bank.

This, Peter thought as he settled back to listen with satis-
faction, should be good for at least another twenty minutes.

Ben felt like he was walking on clouds when he left the
store a couple of hours later. He'd turned down an invitation
to dinner, citing work as an excuse, though the truth of the
matter was he was just too full of the wonder of it all to be
able to stay in Cat's company any longer. There'd been a few
awkward moments there at the beginning, but . . . He had to
admit that Peter had been right. All he'd had to do was meet
her. And now that he had . . .

Jesus, he felt good.

When he reached his Buick with its Blue Line Taxi on top,
he slid in behind the wheel and then just sat there, enjoying a
sense of well-being. What a great lady. What a damn-fine,
great lady! They'd even got to talking about her books. She'd
seemed genuinely flattered that he liked her work as much as
he did, and then surprised both herself and him by asking him
if he'd like to take a look at the new manuscript she was
working on.

Would he? Are bears Catholic? Does the Pope shit in the
woods?

Last night's break-in never did come up, but Ben vowed
that if there *was* someone watching her house, he wouldn't be
doing it for long. The idea of someone harassing her pissed

him off in a way that it couldn't have this morning, when she
was still a two-dimensional personality he knew only through
her books and the articles written about her.

We'll see, he thought as he pulled away from the curb.
Tonight we'll see. If Mr. Hide-in-the-Shadows was still hanging around, he'd have more than a woman living on her own
to deal with. The ferocity of his feelings startled him. But the
more he thought of it, the more he strengthened his resolve to
do something about it if he could.

"What a nice man," Cat said when Ben left.

"One of the best."

"He's like a big bear—all gruff and round."

"You should put him in one of your books—he'd probably
buy the whole print run."

Cat laughed. Right now she felt so good she almost
thought she could go home and write up a storm. Sitting behind the store's counter, meeting and talking to more people in
one day than she'd normally see in a week, and finding in Ben
a real kindred spirit, her earlier black mood seemed to belong
to another person. Nothing had really changed. All the problems were still there, the frustrations and the sorrow. But for
the moment she had a different vantage point to look at them
from.

"Would you like to eat out somewhere?" Peter asked.

Cat shook her head. "Let me make dinner for us tonight."

"I don't eat squash or beets," Peter warned.

"So who does?"

Stella pulled off Briarhill Drive into Rick's laneway and
wondered why on earth she'd agreed to wait for him at his
place tonight. He was going to be at another business dinner
—read "suck up to Worthington for another bad-risk loan"—
until at least ten-thirty tonight. That was if he didn't get too
sloshed to find his way home. Stella sighed. She turned off
the ignition and stepped from the car. He'd said he was going
to get his act together, and he certainly seemed to have been
trying this past day or so. The least she could do was give him
a chance to prove himself.

What they really should do was move in together, she
thought as she went into the house. The money they'd save on
rent alone would make the necessity of another loan redun-

dant. But as she always did when she came up against that idea, Stella wasn't so sure she was ready for that herself. It was too much give on her part. And she'd given a lot already. Too much. First she'd let him prove himself—really prove himself—then they could take it from there and see where it went.

She tossed her purse onto the sofa and wandered into the kitchen to see what she could scrounge up for her dinner.

At five past seven Mick was just finishing with his last customer of the day—a safety check on a '76 Pinto that just barely squeaked by the Provincial standards. Jim had already gone home—tonight was his bowling night. Mick shook his head as he did every Wednesday night. It was hard to believe that people still went in for that kind of shit. He turned off the lights above the pumps and inside the office, then sat down across from Ben.

"If you ever have a problem," Mick had told Ben once, "any kind of a problem, you come and see me. I mean, if someone's hassling you, we'll see if we can't fix it—you catch my drift?"

That had been a couple of years ago, and Ben could remember laughing off the whole mafioso inflection in Mick's voice. He'd replied with something to the effect that he doubted he'd ever need to get anything "fixed," if Mick caught *his* drift. But now he found himself sitting in the garage, eating his words as he told Mick his problem.

"Cat's the writer you're so big on, right? The one who drives the VW and always comes across so hesitant like I'm doing her a big favor by working on her car." Mick gave Ben a grin. "And now you've got the real-life hots for her?"

"It's not like that, Mick. I mean, she was always this unattainable person before—like someone in *People* magazine. I always thought that knowing her would spoil the image I had of her. But now that I've met her . . ."

"You've got the real-life hots for her," Mick repeated, laughing.

"Will you give me a hand?" Ben asked.

"Hey," Mick said, "would I let you down?" He pulled a switchblade from his pocket, depressed a small button with his thumb, and four inches of blade sprouted from its end with a sharp click.

"Jesus! We're not going to need that."

Mick shrugged, putting the knife away. "You never know," he said. "You know what I mean?"

9

tasting the waters of acheron

RICK ARRIVED AT the Caffè Italia Trattoria to find Bill and his secretary already there waiting for him. The restaurant was on Preston Street, down in Little Italy—a relatively small dining room with white stucco walls, dark wood beams, innumerable posters and framed photographs of Italy, country-styled ceiling lamps, and seventeen tables—each spread with a red-and-white checkered cloth. Rick grinned as he came in the front door and nodded familiarly to the hostess—a tall, sloe-eyed Italian woman. He shook hands with Bill, then turned to Debbie, giving her an openly admiring look. She was stunning tonight, her pale-blond hair falling loosely to her shoulders, her body sheathed in a slinky black dress, a single pearl on a silver chain hanging just above the low cut of its neckline.

"Been waiting long?" he asked.

"We just arrived ourselves," Bill told him. "Nice place."

Bill caught the immediate undercurrent that passed between Debbie and Rick and understood now why Stella wasn't part of their company. It made him wish he hadn't asked Debbie to accompany them. He liked Stella. God knew what she saw in Rick. She just fell for that same boyish charisma that everyone else did, he supposed. Like Debbie was doing now.

He often thought that if Rick could just settle down with someone like Stella—someone attractive and level-headed, a steadying influence—the success Rick needed would be attained a lot more quickly. Stella was mostly the reason that Bill had loaned Rick the remaining money he'd needed to start up Captain Computer. Maybe this time, he'd thought, but knew as he was handing over the check that it wouldn't work out any differently than any of the other endeavors Rick had plunged into with equal enthusiasm.

Knowing Rick as long as he did, it was easy for Bill to see the cold edge that undercut the charming front he wore. He realized now that hoping Stella would be the one to blunt it had been just another exercise in futility.

"You're going to love the food here," Rick said when they were seated and had ordered their cocktails. He was having trouble keeping his gaze from Debbie's cleavage. "Ever had prosciutto ham? It comes with the antipasta along with the usual salamis and Italian pickles."

"I thought I'd try the marinated artichoke hearts," Debbie said.

Rick shrugged. "Okay. But then you've got to go for the fettucine—homemade and served just like they make it at Alfredo's in Rome. *Al dente*."

He pronounced the Italian words with an atrocious accent, and grinned. Bill settled back in his chair, wishing he'd just had Rick come up to his office. Then he could have refused the request for a loan—which was bound to come up at just the "appropriate moment"—without having to sit through an evening of watching his erstwhile friend preen himself as he worked up to a new conquest.

Rick's college mentality of always having a good time still surprised Bill. It wasn't that Bill was a prude. He just felt there was more to life than this constant, almost desperate striving after women and booze. Looking at Rick right now, it wasn't hard to strip ten years or so from his face and hear him saying, as though it were only yesterday, "Met this chick like you wouldn't believe, Billy-boy. We got plastered—I mean *piss*-drunk—and made out in her old man's car, right there in the backseat while he was out mowing his lawn. The old bastard never saw a thing. I mean there's me, humping his 'princess,' while he's pushing the old mower back and forth. . . ."

Bill sighed, and signaled to the waitress for a refill on his scotch.

Lisa Henderson and Judy Hudson stepped out of Rhapsody Rag Market just after six.

"God, it's hot," Lisa complained as Judy locked up.

"It's not so much the heat as the humidity," Judy said, repeating the most often-used description of an Ottawa summer. She dropped her key ring into her purse and turned to Lisa.

"Want to go for a drink?"

Lisa shook her head. "Brad had the day off, but he said he might give me a call after dinner, so I'm going to go home to take a shower and plan to spend the next couple of hours or so picking out something to wear."

Both women laughed.

"Don't settle for a movie," Judy said. "Hold out for dancing."

"On a night like this?"

"You could always cool down with another shower afterward—if you even wanted to cool down."

"'Save money—shower with a friend,'" Lisa said.

Judy's eyebrows lifted. "I thought we were *both* too young to remember that."

Lisa said goodbye to her co-worker and turned toward her bus stop. She was halfway down the block when she felt the tap on her shoulder. She turned, caught in the middle of daydreaming about showering with Brad, a blush on her cheeks.

All she could focus on were the eyes. Lysistratus's presence went through her like a shock. Last night's erotic dream returned in a flood of memory—not a dream!—and she started to back away, her feet entangling with each other. Lysistratus steadied her with a firm grip on her arm. His icy eyes enfolded her gaze, drew her into him, forced his will upon her with the sheer intensity of their presence.

"Won't you walk with me?" he asked.

No, she thought, but the word never got past her throat. The Valium that she'd taken to get her through the afternoon wasn't helping now. Tense, strung like a tight wire, she found herself nodding in reply.

Lysistratus led her down Bank Street. They turned right at Somerset and continued for a block and a half before they came to Dundonald Park—a block of mown lawn, bushes, and trees across from the Brewer's Retail.

When they sat down on a bench, she realized for the first time that he didn't look the same. The eyes were unchanged —powerful, blue as crystals, sucking all the warmth out of her body so that she shivered despite the heat. But his hair was dark now, and he had a mustache. Instead of his usual trendy clothes, he wore an old pair of faded jeans, a T-shirt, and carried an Adidas gym bag. Passing him on the street she might never have recognized him, except . . .

His eyes. When she'd turned, all she could see was those eyes.

They sat on the bench for long moments. The inability to control her own body movements paralyzed Lisa as effectively as the hypnotic spell in which he held her. Her thoughts were in a turmoil. *What does he want with me? Why does he keep staring at me? Why can't I move?*

His face leaned close to hers. Inwardly she shrank from him, but her body betrayed her and never moved.

"Sleep," he said softly.

His eyes enforced the word until it was all she could do to keep her remaining sense about her to fight the command.

"Sleep."

The voice stayed soft, sibilant as a snake's kiss.

No, she wanted to cry, but she still couldn't speak. What was he doing to her? This couldn't be happening to her. They were in the middle of a park, and it wasn't even dark yet. Didn't anyone see what was going on?

That man, walking his dog. Mister! Please help me!

But the man kept right on strolling, pausing only long enough to let his pet lift its leg against a no-parking sign before going on.

Sleep.

The voice was inside her head now. A bleak emptiness welled up behind it. She fought it, panicked beyond reason.

"Remember me to Hades," Lysistratus said.

The bleakness washed over her like a black wave. Lysistratus leaned forward, pressing his lips against hers. She slept. He forced her sleep to give birth to dreams, then drew their essence from her, sucked them in, through her skin, through his own, until his body was filled with their sweet nectar.

When he drew back, her body was stripped of its motor-workings—alive, but not alive. She might expire here on the bench. She might last until she was brought to a hospital, living the last bit of her life as a vegetable, but nothing could revive her now. He had stolen her soul.

He placed his hand across her eyes and closed the lids. He leaned her weight against the back of the bench and stood, dipping his head to her in a brief salute, before he walked off through the park.

Blocks away he stepped into an alleyway. When he was certain that he was not being observed, he exchanged the T-shirt he was wearing for a long-sleeved casual dress shirt from his gym bag. He rolled up the sleeves. The wig of dark-brown hair disappeared into the bag and a red one was removed and set in place on his head. He took a small mirror from his pocket and regarded himself critically. Into his cheeks, between the cheek and gums, he inserted cotton wadding to change the shape of his face. The mustache joined the wig in the bag. A pair of sunglasses completed his new disguise.

When he emerged from the farther end of the alley, walking with a slouch and the slight hint of a limp, not even his own mentor—three hundred eighty-two years dead now—would have recognized him at a quick glance. And a quick glance was all that anyone he passed on the street would give him.

One down, he thought. Two to go.

After dinner Cat and Peter took their coffees out to Cat's screened-in porch and sat there quietly, enjoying the cool breeze that had finally come with the fall of night.

"Were you planning on doing some writing tonight?" Peter asked after a while.

"No. I don't want to think about it for the moment. I think part of my problem might have stemmed from the pressure I was putting on myself. You know—produce, produce!"

"For the introverted writer you were telling me about last night, you sure opened up today."

"I know. It was funny. I didn't feel any of my usual inhibitions at all. I can't explain it. I guess I just felt safe, sitting there behind your counter. And some of your customers were so nice. Like that fellow with the red hair and the wire-frame glasses."

"Lewis Reed."

"Umhmm. And your friend Ben. Does he write?"

"Not that he's told me. Why?"

"He seems to have such an immediate grasp as to what makes a story work and what doesn't. I think that's why I asked him if he'd take a look at my *Silver Cup* manuscript. Maybe he can help me work out my writing block, in case my dreams don't. . . ." She looked away, suddenly uncomfortable, but before Peter could say anything, she went quickly on. "You know Ben's the only person to have picked up on the fact that Tattershank—the wizard in *Cloak and Hood*—really *was* one of the Middle Folk. That's why he *had* to help Meg. Most of the reviewers complained that he was acting out of character, but . . ." She paused again, this time feeling a little embarrassed. "Listen to me. I'm just rambling on."

"That's okay. I like listening."

"Anyway," she continued, "that's why I'd like Ben to have a look at *The Moon in a Silver Cup*. Without Kothlen . . ." She faltered, swallowed hard, then plunged on. "I've never shown anyone my unfinished stuff before. Not even Melissa—that's my agent, Melissa Robinson."

"Ben cares," Peter said. "It's that simple. If he's your friend, then he's your friend for life."

"That's the feeling I got," Cat said. "You know, I wish I'd known people like you and Ben when I was growing up. Everyone always talks about the physical changes you go through—puberty and all that—but nobody talks much about the changes you go through in your head.

"The most frustrating thing I can remember was being treated like a child when I didn't feel I was thinking like one. I always felt that I was being patronized—by my parents, by my teachers. From about the time I was ten I felt old. So I found it hard to relate to kids my own age as well. I guess I just turned inward. If I hadn't had my ghosts—I know what you think of them, but to me they're real—if I hadn't had them, I think I would have gone completely bonkers.

"With them I could be myself. I could be a ten-year-old with an old woman's mind, and nobody would treat me condescendingly. If I had questions, someone like . . . like Kothlen was there to answer them. To *seriously* answer them. If I got scared—just about being alive, maybe—they would talk me down. And if I wanted to be a hooligan or just plain silly, there was always Tiddy Mun and his cohorts. Especially Tiddy Mun."

She looked out into the darkness, lost in memories for a long moment.

"Going to the Otherworld was always great," she said suddenly. "At least for while I was there. But the trouble was, I still had to go through all the hours when I was awake—when I was in *this* world. I don't know this world all that well. Not the things that seem to count. All that having to cope with this world's done is to drive me further inward."

"I think everyone goes through something like that," Peter said. "To some degree or other. It's just growing pains. How you deal with them shapes what sort of person you become. I suppose there are some people who, no matter how old they get, never learn to deal with them."

"Like me?"

Peter shook his head. "No. Like the people who lose all their ability to stretch their minds. Our minds are very malleable when we're young. Most people lose that as they grow older."

"I wouldn't want to lose that. Not ever. And I still wish I'd known people like you and Ben when I *was* young."

"We were probably as confused as you were then, so we wouldn't have been much help. But we're here now. And there's not just Ben and me. There must be lots of people out in the world that you could relate to. All you've got to do is reach out—like you did yesterday with me. And today in the store. You might get burned sometimes, but that's the chance you've got to take."

Cat sighed. "I guess you're right. But it seems too hard. And what about the Otherworld? Do I have to hand in my passport to it, just to get along out here?"

"I don't know, Cat. I don't know what it is you feel when you're dreaming—where it is you go. If you even go anywhere. That inner world might *seem* real, but—"

"What about last night? I know you saw Tiddy Mun."

"I . . . I saw something, Cat. I just don't know what it was that I saw."

"Do you think I'm crazy, Peter?"

"No."

"Do you think I'm weird?"

"A little. But I like you that way."

She looked away again, wishing that things could always be just as normal as they felt right now. The night was so peaceful. The wind had just a breath of a Sibelius string concerto caught in its breathing. If there could be no prowlers . . .

"Do you ever get scared, Peter?"

"Sure. Everybody does. I think about our future: the way the economy's going and what it means for the store and my livelihood. I think of Reagan sitting south of the border, all primed to set off World War Three, and there's not a damn thing we can do about it. I'm scared of going to the dentist. Scared of dying . . ."

"That's the one thing that doesn't scare me," Cat said. "I figure that when I die I'll become a ghost for some other lonely kid."

"I'd like to meet one of your ghosts."

Cat looked wistful. "I wish there was a way that I could arrange that. I've been thinking of Tiddy Mun off and on all day. I wonder where he went?" She looked through the screen to the hedge, and goose bumps lifted on her arms. "I think there's something about my house that scares him now."

"Nobody's going to get into the house tonight, Cat. That's why I'm here."

"But what if someone *does* come? What if he's got a gun or something?"

"Then we call the police."

Cat thought about last night's visit to the Otherword, of what Tiddy Mun had told her about the evil thing that was hunting them—her and him and all the ghosts.

"What if it's something worse still?" she asked. "Like . . . like some kind of monster?"

God, that sounded stupid, she thought. But she couldn't shake the creeping feeling from her. Last night, when that malevolent presence came swooping down at her in the Otherworld . . .

"It's a monster all right," Peter said. "But a very human one. Someone who likes to harass women who live alone in big houses."

"I want to go inside," Cat said.

The night no longer seemed friendly. It gathered beyond

the spill of the living room's lights, which were all that lit the porch, throwing shadows that were dark and impenetrable. Cat picked up their mugs. Before Peter could protest, she had already slipped inside.

Farley was cold sober and on the edge. Ever since that moment in Central Park this afternoon . . . Reality seemed to have taken a long step to one side, leaving him behind. He had a constant buzz between his ears, a feeling that hovered between a hangover and a headache. But the worst thing was this inescapable sensation of living on borrowed time. A feeling of impending doom.

"You're nuts," Ron said when Farley had tried to explain it to him. "What you need is a bellyful of hard juice, my man. Nothing else will do. The whole world loves a drunk. Or at least it loves a drink. I forget which."

Farley left Ron somewhere down on Rideau Street and went off to look for someplace safe. He was hunched down in the alley that ran through the four-story apartment building at the corner of Laurier and Bank. It was an old building, and it was dark in the alley. He didn't know if it was a safe place or not because he didn't know what he was hiding from. From himself, he might have said had anyone been there to ask.

He clutched his suitcase tightly to his chest. There was no one in the alley to ask him questions or keep him company. He was all alone, and how did you hide from yourself anyway?

Christ, he could use a drink.

"You don't understand," Rick said.

Bill took a sip from his second cappuccino. The coffee was rich and foamy, and it almost made up for the turn the conversation had taken. In one corner of the restaurant a man who looked like he'd stepped right off the set of some Italian extravaganza, complete with striped shirt and thick mustache, was playing sentimental music on an accordian.

"No, *you* don't understand," Bill said.

The argument had started after they'd finished their main course. While the waitress was serving their zabaglione—a custard and egg yolk mix, laced with marsala wine—Rick had begun his pitch.

"It's just another three, four thousand," Rick was saying now. "With the Christmas season coming up . . ."

Bill shook his head. He glanced at Debbie who, whatever

other plans she might have for Rick tonight, was sensibly keeping out of this discussion.

"I know you, Rick," he said. "The only reason I went along with the first loan—against Emile's better judgement, I might add—was because I knew that if you did screw up like I expected you to, I could always write the whole thing off on my tax return. Why the hell do you think I had our contract drawn up the way I did? You might own Captain Computer in name, but on paper and *until* you make good your debt to me, I've got a piece of your business. I'm not liable to any other debts you might accrue, but when you go under you can bet your ass *I* won't be screwed. In fact, as things stand now, your going bankrupt right now would stand me in far better stead than if we let things go on as they were."

"Bill. We're old friends. . . ."

"We *were* friends, Rick. But I haven't any more patience for your get-rich schemes. Not when you won't work at them yourself. I'll tell you this: if I thought you'd clean up your act and give it an honest go, I'd help you out. But the way things are going—"

"The way things are going? You sanctimonious bastard. What the hell do *you* know about how things are going?"

His voice was loud, and people at the neighboring tables were starting to turn their way. Bill stood up.

"You can think what you want, Rick. I've never tried to hurt you. The only person that's standing in your way is yourself."

With that he nodded brusquely to Debbie, who gave him a wry grin, and left the restaurant.

"The cheap fucker," Rick muttered. "He even stiffed me for the tab."

"Hey," Debbie said, laying a hand on his arm. "Take it easy."

"Take it . . ." For a moment there was a coldness in his eyes that made Debbie wish she'd left with Bill, then Rick shrugged and smiled. "What the fuck," he said. "Easy come, easy go. It's the story of my life."

"Why don't we go down to the Market?" Debbie said. "There's some nice bars down there. We could talk, have a few drinks, and then . . . see where the evening takes us."

Rick regarded her wolfishly. "Hey, hey," he said. "All of a sudden the night's bright and things're looking good."

He knew Stella was waiting for him at his place, but there

was no way he wanted to see her right now—not go home and
have to listen to her go on about something or other on top of
the shit Worthington had just laid on him. And besides, he
thought as he studied Debbie's cleavage, he had a point or two
he wanted to work out with his present company. Stella could
wait. Hell, she liked waiting, and it'd give her something else
to moan about when he saw her.

Something moved at the end of the alley, and Farley looked
up. The night had gotten cooler and he was in the middle of
taking a jacket out of his suitcase when he sensed the motion.
He saw a shadow blocking the mouth of the alleyway. A tall
figure. Squinting, he tried to make out who it was.

"Hey, Ron," he said in a voice barely above a whisper.
"That you?"

The figure moved toward him, blue eyes glittering like a
cat's in the dim light. Evil flowed from those eyes like blood
from a fresh wound.

"Oh, Jesus fuck," Farley moaned. "Don't hurt me, mister."

The suitcase fell from his lap and clunked on the ground.
He put a hand out to the wall, seeking purchase, but he was
shaking too much to stand. The eyes closed in on his own,
demanding, overpowering him.

Please . . . leave me alone . . . don't hurt . . .

Farley tried to say the words, but they froze in his throat.
He couldn't move. He couldn't even shake anymore.

The stranger bent down low, face inches from Farley's un-
shaven features. Suddenly Farley remembered the snake-
headed man and the man in the park. His bladder gave way
and urine soaked his pants. He saw a glint of bright metal in
the man's hand. The blue eyes swallowed him. He felt the
snakes from his nightmare crawling down his throat, in
through his ears and nose, right up his asshole.

Darkness came up and swallowed him.

Lysistratus leaned forward. He laid a hand against Farley's
cheek, felt the coarse stubble under his palm. The reek of
sweat, alcohol, and urine filled the air, but he ignored it. He
touched his forehead to that of his victim's, willed him to
dream, then drew the dreams out of him, wine-sodden but still
nourishing. And then, just as they weakened, just before their
last essence spilled into him, he plunged his knife into the

wino's throat and gave a small cry of pleasure as the life spark leapt from the dying mind into his own.

He moved back before the blood could fountain over him. Stepping over the growing puddle, he paused long enough to wipe his knife blade clean on the dead man's shirt, then slipped on through the alleyway, took its right turn, and found himself in a parking lot. The knife vanished into his gym bag.

The dreams he'd stolen tonight set the blood to pounding through his veins. He lifted his head to the sky and almost wailed like the wolf the Inuit shaman named him. He bared his teeth in a grin instead and started for home.

And then there was one, he thought.

"This is weird, you know that?" Mick said.

He and Ben were sitting in Ben's cab. It was parked where Cameron met Riverdale—about five houses down the block from Cat's place. They slouched low in their seats, rearview and side mirrors adjusted so that they could see the street behind them without having to show themselves.

"He might not even show up again," Ben said. "He almost got caught last night."

Mick shook his head. "Nah. Those kinds of guys always come back. The more risk there is, the better they like it. What I'm wondering is whether maybe one of us should be watching the back."

"Peter said Cat saw him standing in the shadow of that house on the corner. If he does show up tonight, I think it'll be to look around, not to break in."

"Maybe." Mick hooked his hands around his knees and leaned his head back. "I tell you," he added, "if we catch this sucker tonight, he's going to be sorry he ever messed around with this kind of shit. It's gonna be one, two, three." He smacked his hands lightly against his knees. "And that'll be all she wrote. You got the time, Ben?"

"Quarter past two."

"If he's coming, he'll be coming soon."

By the time Houlihan's was closing and Rick and Debbie hit the street, neither one of them was exactly sober. They made their way down York Street to where they'd left Rick's car, managing to get into their respective seats without undue mishap. Rick stared blankly at the keys in his hand.

"Where do these go?" he asked.

Debbie giggled. "Don't you *know*?"

"Ish a joke—get it?"

Debbie didn't, but it didn't really seem to matter. Rick fiddled around with the keys until he finally fit the proper one into its slot and turned the motor over. It caught with a roar as he gave it too much gas.

"My . . . place or yours?" Debbie asked.

Her head felt too dizzy to keep upright, so she leaned it against Rick's shoulder. He dropped his hand down to her thigh and she closed her legs, trapping it.

"We'll go to . . . mine," Rick announced. "I want you to meet Shtella. You'll like her. She humps like a bunny."

Debbie regarded him with drunken worry. "But I don't do it with women."

"Thash okay. Neither does she."

He pulled away from the curb in a series of stops and starts, steered the car around the block until they wove their way out onto Sussex Drive. They cruised down Colonel By Drive, deaked up through the parking lot at Defense Head-quarters and headed south on Nicholas Street. Rick began to whistle through his teeth while Debbie dozed contentedly on his shoulder.

Cat and Peter sat in the darkened study. Though a bed had been made up on the couch for Peter downstairs, neither of them was ready to try to sleep. Once they'd come inside, Cat's nervousness had stolen into Peter, so that by the time midnight arrived, they were both starting at every sound.

They didn't speak much. Cat sat in her thinking chair by the window, Peter in the rocker they'd brought in from her bedroom. When Cat started to doze around two o'clock, Peter chose a cassette at random from the twenty or so stacked up beside Cat's Aiwa. The one he picked was a homemade col-lection labeled "Misc. Classical." Returning to the rocker, he half dozed along with Cat as the solemn organ and strings of Albinoni's "Adagio" whispered through the room.

Ten-thirty rolled by without Rick showing up, and Stella wondered why she was surprised. She looked around his liv-ing room, mad enough to trash something. Like the picture window. His Sony Trinatron would go nicely through it. Or maybe his stereo, one component at a time.

She didn't know why she had ever expected him to change, didn't know why she should even care. They were so obviously mismatched that only she and a blind man could have missed it. All that kept her from leaving right now was that she wanted to confront him when he came in, to find out just what he had wanted out of this relationship. The money she'd invested in Captain Computer? Well, he could kiss that goodbye. She'd see her lawyer about it first thing in the morning and have that money out of the company so fast it'd make his head spin.

She got up to pace the living room and caught her reflection in the big picture window. Was it her body? She wasn't exactly Bo Derek, but she wasn't ugly either. Before she started seeing Rick, she'd never had any trouble getting dates. The trouble she did have was trying to find a meaningful relationship in a world that had turned its back on commitments.

So how did she go about meeting someone nice? Someone that cared. Who was willing to give as much of himself as she had to give him. How the hell did she make sure she didn't end up with someone like Rick again? She was tired of being ragged. When it came to men, she always seemed to pick the wrong ones. If they didn't need mothering, they were like Rick and didn't really give a shit about anyone but themselves. What they wanted were whores—there when they needed a fuck, gone when they didn't want to see them.

She glanced at her watch. They were running *The Playboy and the Bobby-Soxer* on Channel 11 in ten minutes—Shirley Temple as a teenager, but sounding just the same as she did in *The Good Ship Lollipop*—with Cary Grant, handsome as ever. She'd seen it before, but maybe it'd be just the thing to calm her down.

Where were the guys like Cary Grant in her life? Why did she have to get stuck with the Ricks? If he'd been with another woman tonight, she was going to kill him. She was going to kill him anyway, but if he'd been out playing Hot-cock Kirkby, she was going to *really* kill him. It wouldn't do anything to help their own relationship—because that was finished as of tonight—but if it made him think twice about the next woman he dragged into his life . . .

Stella sighed. Who was she kidding?

Lysistratus ignored his usual vantage point tonight. There was something in the air that made him nervous, so when he left his home after dropping off his gym bag, he took a more circuitous route to Cat's home. He still kept to the shadows, but tonight he hid in the deeper ones along Bellwood. The house wasn't so easy to watch from here. He could see the lights were out. But the street seemed too awake.

He sensed that she had someone with her again. The two of them were drifting in that twilight place between waking and sleep. He reached out for Cat with his mind, snatching at her half-formed dreams. As the first taste of their opiate sweetness entered him, he knew he needed physical contact with her. Last night he had withdrawn because of her companion, but tonight . . . the man would have to take his chances. Tonight Lysistratus was in the mood for killing whatever got in his way.

Peter awoke with a start, wondering what had woken him and how long he'd been asleep. The tape was still playing, so it couldn't have been that long. He looked from the cassette machine to Cat, and his eyes went wide with shock.

There was something perched on the arm of her chair, shaking her arm as though trying to wake her. Last night's hobgoblin, all eyes and gangly limbs. It seemed almost insubstantial, as though he could put his hand right through it, but it was there—something *was* there!—all the same.

For a long moment he and the curious apparition regarded each other. The creature was poised as if for flight now, like a startled hare just before it bounded off, or a squirrel suddenly aware that a cat was stalking it. Slowly Peter reached a hand toward it. He had to feel if it was real. He had to know if it was really there. Then Cat made a sharp, moaning sound.

The hobgoblin vanished. One moment it was there, saucer eyes watching him, and the next it was gone, replaced by a small glowing ball of gold light. Then that too, like the Cheshire cat's grin, winked out.

The room grew cold. Peter swept it with his gaze, but Cat drew his attention. Her Tiddy Mun—if that was what it had been—would have to wait. Cat was twisting in the chair, her features tight with pain. Peter took her by the shoulders and gently shook her.

"Wake up, Cat. Wake up!"

That's what the strange being had been trying to do as well. Why was it so important that she woke up? What was happening to her? If she was in trouble in . . . in her Otherworld . . .

The chill in the room grew more pronounced. Cat no longer fought her dream. She lay slack in his grip, head lolling to one side.

"Cat!"

At that moment Peter knew the first inklings of terror. The hobgoblin, strange as it had been, hadn't frightened him. But what came now . . . creeping up his spine . . . spreading through his nervous system . . .

His gaze was drawn to the window and beyond it, to the street, to the shadows of a house and the gaze there that searched for his own. Cat slipped out of his numbed fingers, falling back against the chair as paralysis gripped him. Something was in his head, shredding his feeble attempts to push it out, and he knew if it stayed there he would never return from the blackness that came washing up to swallow him.

A curious memory came to him: He was sitting in his own living room, reading, when one of Cat's books leapt from the bookshelf to hit the floor. He saw it again, falling in slow motion, and wondered if it had been a premonition of some sort, some warning that he had neither realized nor accepted for what it was.

Then the darkness was all.

Lysistratus drank in the heavy nectar of Cat's dreaming psyche. As the first fires coursed through him, he knew that he had to go to her. He had to feel her skin under his hands, feel her heart tremble against his. He had to fill her with the hardening penis that swelled between his trousers and leg.

The net of his power reached out to draw Peter into its web. Lysistratus saw the face at the window and locked his gazed into the other man's. Peter dropped unprotestingly, dropped like a stone into the dark sleep that Lysistratus woke inside him, and soon his psyche was feeding the parasite as well.

With their combined essences rippling through him, Lysistratus stepped from his hiding place and crossed the street. He was still only skimming the surfaces of their souls. He needed physical contact now to complete the bridge—flesh to flesh. He would drain the man until he was empty. Then he would fill the woman with his seed, fill her and take her pleasure back into him again, multiplied a hundredfold.

He imagined the bubbly voice of Clare Grogan, lead singer for Altered Images, and smiled at the song she sang in his mind—"See Those Eyes." His own eyes glittered like blue fire.

Cary Grant was in the middle of an obstacle race at a country fair when Stella heard Rick's car pull into the driveway. She turned off the TV with the remote and went into the hall, standing under the framed Magritte print that hung to the left of the light switch. She had a half-dozen scathing comments ready on the tip of her tongue, but nothing had prepared her for what came through the door.

Rick stood framed in the doorway with a stunning blonde on his arm, both of them pissed to the gills. Stella stared at them, her mouth half open, and didn't know what to say.

"Hey, Shtel," Rick began. "How's it—"

"Don't you dare talk to me!" she cried, finding her voice.

She looked from him to his companion. The woman had a slightly sympathetic looked behind her glazed gaze that only served to further infuriate Stella.

"Don't be mad, Shtel baby," Rick slurred. "We can... make it a shreesome...."

Stella's cheeks went beet red. She'd never felt more embarrassed in her life. Anything she might have said just then got locked up tightly inside her. Wordlessly she snatched up her purse and stormed out the door, elbowing the pair of them out of her way. Once she had her car started, she squealed its rear tires backing out of the driveway and roared down Briarhill to Heron Road.

"Heads up," Mick murmured.

Ben checked the side-view mirror. "Jesus," he said. "It's the Dude."

"The who?"

"That's just what I call him—I thought he was going to put a make on me in the park back of my house yesterday afternoon. He gave me the creeps. I wonder what he's doing here."

"Well, he's sure a sharp dresser," Mick said. "Think he's a friend of Cat's?"

Ben sat up and swivelled in his seat to get a better view. "I don't know. He's not skulking. But he's going right for her door."

"Well," Mick said, "if he's got an honest reason for being

there at this time of night, we can always apologize politely and beat a hasty retreat. And if not . . ."

Ben nodded. Something hard settled in the pit of his stomach, and his heart was thumping to beat the band. His hands were sweaty as he eased open the door. Now that the moment had come, he wasn't sure he could go through with it. But then he thought of Cat, of the guy that was harassing her, and his resolve hardened.

Mick was already on the street. "Let's go," he whispered.

They jogged down the pavement, silent in their running shoes, slowing down as they neared Cat's hedge. Mick leaned close.

"Just let me do the talking," he breathed into Ben's ear. "You're big. All you've got to do is stand behind me and look intimidating—you know what I mean? You won't even have to lift a hand."

Ben nodded, swallowing with difficulty. Maybe they should have just called the cops. Sure, he wanted to help Cat, but it wasn't like he was Charles Bronson or anything.

Mick took a couple of quick steps so that he'd be the first through the gap in the hedge. Ben saw him turn in, then the figure of the Dude stepped out, one arm raised high. He had something in his hand that looked like a short club or stick. It came down with a crack as it glanced off Mick's skull.

Ben froze. Those strange eyes he remembered from the afternoon in the park—almost luminous in the dark—were tracking him. They snared his gaze, then stopped him dead as he was about to rush forward. He remembered his nightmare —the fish-scaled man with the barracuda teeth. He'd had those same eyes. Those same fucking eyes . . .

The little club lifted and fell a second time, and Mick tumbled to the ground.

Ben wanted to rush the Dude. He wanted to smash him. But he couldn't move. Couldn't even twitch. He'd never experienced such pure, simple helplessness before.

"I thought I felt spying eyes," Lysistratus said softly.

The man's voice sent a weird shiver down Ben's spine. Jesus Christ! What was going on? Why couldn't he move? What had this sucker done to him?

The Dude's eyes drilled straight through to Ben's soul, and he could feel his legs buckling under him, the pavement rushing up to meet his face. This . . . couldn't . . . be . . . real.

He hit the ground hard. All he knew was the impact—the

physical pain of hitting the pavement, and worse, the pain inside his head. Somehow the Dude had gotten inside his head. He was twisting Ben's thoughts into knots, using the pain to raise a sea of blackness in which Ben knew he would inevitably drown. He could sense more than see the Dude's approach. Just as it had happened in his nightmare, he was helpless to protect himself. Was the Dude lifting his club to use on him as well? Or was he opening his mouth to show the rows of wicked teeth . . . ?

Then, just before the final tide of darkness washed over him, he could see the face right above his own. Close, so close. The hands, strong but gentle as they gripped his head. And the eyes. Those soulless blue eyes boring into his soul . . .

Lysistratus bent over his victim, his fingers gripping the man's head tightly. He had seen this one before. In the park by Tamson House. What were he and his friend doing here? Had they somehow discovered his secret? If they had thought to become hunters, they were fools. All they had accomplished was a quick journey down the Acheron, where Hades would take them into his keeping. But first he would devour their souls. First he would rip the—

They came out of the night—two screaming furies. Before he could protect himself they were on him, spitting and clawing at his eyes. It wasn't until the pain reached his brain that he realized what they were. Cats. Cats attacking him?

He let Ben's head drop as he rose to his full height, sweeping them from him. But like rabid beasts they swarmed up his legs, clawing through the cloth of his trousers, savaging the flesh underneath. He swept them from his body again, then was suddenly aware of what set them upon him.

The impossibility of what he faced almost made him question his sanity. Before him stood a straying fragment of Cat's dreaming. It seemed she dreamed all too true.

The small being's saucer eyes were instilled with such hatred that Lysistratus took a step back. The cats pressed at him again, and again he drove them away, this time with the glittering strength that burned in his gaze. The cats fled howling. When he turned his attention back to the little man, he smiled to see the diminutive figure trembling, but unable to move.

Lysistratus stepped over Ben, blood dripping into an eye

from where one of the cats had torn a long cut across his forehead. His gaze froze Tiddy Mun where he stood. But as his hands reached for the little man's throat, the night handed him one more rude surprise.

His own small club hit him on the shoulder. Tiddy Mun drove for the shelter of the hedge as Lysistratus turned to face the new attack. His eyes blazed, but this enemy would not meet his gaze. Blood streaked his face as well.

"You sonuvabitch!" Mick roared.

He tossed aside the club and his switchblade appeared in his hand, the blade springing from its handle with a sudden snick. Lysistratus stepped back as the knife flashed toward him, but not quickly enough. Mick opened the parasite's cheek with his first slash, cut the forearm that was raised to ward the next blow with his second.

Lysistratus retreated. He could taste death in the air and knew that it might well be his own life that would be forfeit if he didn't end this quickly. But before he could launch a counterattack, the other man was upon him again. Mick feinted—left, right—then stepped in close and drove his knife into the parasite's abdomen. Lysistratus lashed out furiously and succeeded in driving his opponent back. Then, rather than following up on this brief opening, he snatched the opportunity to escape.

He hobbled down the street—not home, but where? Pulling the knife from his side, he heard it clatter to the pavement as he staunched the sudden flow of blood with the flat of his hand. If he survived this night, they would pay. Each and every one of them.

He stole a backward glance and saw that Mick was swaying on his feet, attempting to follow, but too weak from the head blows he'd taken to go far. For a moment Lysistratus was tempted to return and deal with them now, but his own wounds—especially the one in his side—were too serious. In his present condition even a child could do him harm.

Hand pressed against his side, head bowed, he stumbled on toward Riverdale.

Mick was so beat he could hardly stand. He watched his opponent flee, clutching his side as he hobbled around the corner and out of sight. Mick knew he'd cut that sucker—cut him good. But that didn't do much to help the way he was feeling just now. His vision kept jumping from double to normal, and there was a hum in the back of his head. Gingerly he felt his scalp. The skin was broken and his fingers came back bloody. The guy'd got a couple of good whacks in. The cuts were probably going to need stitches.

Retrieving his knife, he made his way back to where Ben was sitting up. Ben looked groggy. A light went on in Cat's house—upper left window. Others followed, blazing a trail down the stairs until the porchlight went on. A man appeared at the door, peering out. Bad move, Mick thought. He'd see better with that light behind him turned off.

"Your name Peter?" Mick called to him.

The head turned, eyes squinting. "Yeah." The voice that replied was wary.

"Well, I got a friend of yours out here who could use a hand. Name's Ben Summerfield—ring any bells?"

"Ben? But . . ."

Peter came down the stairs in a rush, stopping dead when he took in Mick's bloodied head. Pain was hammering in his own temples. Trying to fight it back and take in this surreal scene was almost too much for him—the stranger with the Mohawk cut, supporting Ben, who looked like Peter felt. And all the blood . . .

"Jesus! What happened?"

"We had us a little run-in with a lunatic. Say, look. I'm not feeling so shit-hot myself, and I don't really feel like hanging around out here, waiting for the man to come cruising by. I don't have many answers to the questions he'd ask, you know what I mean?"

"What? Oh, yeah. Sure."

Peter helped Ben to his feet and the three of them made their way up the porch steps. Cat met them at the door, her face haggard with the strain of her own experience with Lysistratus.

"Peter?" Her eyes widened when she saw who he was with and their condition. "My God. What's going on?"

Stella didn't let up on the gas until she reached Bank Street, and then she drove with the window down to cool her off, her fingers drumming against the steering wheel. At that moment she was almost beyond feeling hurt or being angry. Instead she felt like a fool. What made it so infuriating was that she felt like she'd just stepped into the middle of a country & western song, and she was the token innocent done wrong by her man.

She turned right onto Riverdale after crossing Billings Bridge and tramped on the gas again. The car shot around the corner. Why she hadn't broken up with Rick the first time he pulled one of his—

She almost missed seeing the man stumble off the sidewalk into the path of her car. She swerved to the left—thank God it was late and there was no other traffic—and shot a glance in her rearview mirror to see him tumble to the pavement. She stamped on the brake. If she hadn't been wearing her seatbelt she might have gone through the windshield. As it was, the belt dug sharply into her shoulder. Her head went forward, then whipped back. The car stalled.

She sat stunned for a moment, then fumbled with the buckle of her seat belt. The man was just lying there. She could have sworn she hadn't hit him, but the way he'd fallen . . . She ran back, heart thumping, high heels clattering on the concrete. He lay facedown. She hesitated, remembering something about not moving someone who'd just been hit because of possible internal injuries.

"Mister?" She swallowed, her voice a hoarse croak. "Hey, mister?"

The way he lay there, so still . . . With shaking hands she took hold of his shoulder and turned him over. Her hand came away all bloody, and she barely stifled a scream.

Oh God, oh God, oh God. I've killed him.

She looked wildly around, a hundred thoughts fluttering through her. If no one had seen the accident, maybe she could just—God, what was she thinking? Bad enough she'd run him down without adding hit and run charges.

It was all Rick's fault. If he hadn't come in like he had, with that woman on his arm, and upset her so . . .

"M-mister?" she tried again.

Two things happened. She realized that the cut on his cheek and his other scratches were too clean to have come from hitting the pavement, and his eyes snapped open. They were crystalline blue, and pinned her with their opening gaze. She was dimly aware of other wounds. One on the arm that he lifted toward her. Blood seeped through his coat, soaking his torso. His trousers were shredded in places, as though he'd been attacked by an animal.

His fingers brushed her cheek, the hand coming back to lie

against her skin. Then there was something inside her, another mind inside her own, forcing its will upon her.

"Home," he demanded in a voice that was weak, but would brook no argument. "Take me to . . . your home."

Numbly she helped him to his feet, supporting him as they approached her car. She wrestled him into the passenger's seat, went around and got in herself. A part of her screamed that this couldn't be happening, but the sheer intensity of his will was too much for her. She couldn't escape the demands it made.

The car took two tries to start. It jerked as she changed gears, ran sluggishly under her captive guidance. And all the while the stranger beside her kept his hand on her knee, and his mind inside hers. She refused to accept what was happening. But she took him home.

Sitting in Cat's kitchen, it took awhile for them to fill each other in. Peter washed out the cuts on Mick's scalp, muttering something about him going to a hospital for stitches, but the mechanic refused. Later, as they sat around the table washing down Anacin with hot tea, they tried to make sense of it all.

A lot was left unsaid because, except for Mick, they weren't sure how to describe their experiences. Mick saw it as a scuffle, plain and simple, that had come to a draw. Cat stayed mostly silent, but Peter and Ben, the terror of their helplessness still fresh in their minds, needed to talk about it. They just weren't sure what had actually happened.

"Hypnotism," Ben said finally. "That's got to be how he did it. He's got creepy eyes—I can remember feeling like they were boring right into me. That's how he got into my head."

Peter shook his head. "What about me? He was across the street when I spotted him. And I never even had eye contact with him."

No. He'd had eye contact with Cat's Tiddy Mun instead, but that *had* to have been a hallucination. Because if it hadn't been one, he was *really* starting to trip out. But then he remembered that when he'd looked out the window, he had gotten an impression of the sort of eyes Ben was describing—reaching right out at him from the shadows across the street.

"Can't be hypnotism," Mick said. "There's no way it works"

—he snapped his fingers—"just like that."

"It doesn't matter how he did it," Peter said. "What we've got to do is call the police. Let them handle it. This man's too dangerous for us to let him go on walking the streets."

"You can't call the cops," Mick said. "What're you going to tell them?"

"For God's sake! He attacked you."

"Sure. And maybe he's just this sharp-dressing dude, out taking a late-night stroll, who sees he's being followed by a couple of rough-and-readies and decides to play hero. We don't have any proof that he meant to do anything criminal. No proof at all—you know what I mean?"

"But . . ."

But nothing, Peter realized. Mick was right. They had no evidence, nothing to tell the police except that somehow this man had gotten into their heads. They could only assume he was the one harassing Cat. If they took what they had to the police, they'd be laughed right out of the station.

"So what do we do?" he asked.

"We don't do anything," Mick said. "I cut him pretty bad. He got away, but he's hurting. He won't be doing a whole lot of running around for a while."

"And when his wounds heal, and he comes back?"

"Yeah. Well, there's that."

Mick frowned into his tea mug. He looked at the small club that they'd found and brought in. It was made of a smooth hardwood, with knobs on either end. Small enough to be easily hidden under a coat. A primitive blackjack, to be sure, but the guy'd wielded it like a pro. Christ, Mick thought. He was lucky to still be up and walking around.

"There's a lot of weird shit that went down tonight that I can't explain," he said thoughtfully. "Like those cats. I never saw anything like it. They were crawling all over him, and cutting him pretty bad too. Who ever heard of cats attacking somebody like that?"

"I dreamed tonight, you know," Ben said. "The whole bit. The guy attacking me, the cats coming in like the cavalry . . ."

Mick nodded. "Weird shit. And this stuff you guys are saying about him getting inside your heads . . . next thing we'll be seeing Count Dracula hiding in the shadows, waiting to suck our blood."

He laughed, but Ben got a very strange look on his face.

"That's what it felt like," Ben said. "Like he was sucking the life right out of me." Then he shook his head. "Jesus, what am I saying? I must've taken a worse crack on the head than I thought."

But that was how it *had* felt, Peter realized. He glanced at Cat and saw that she'd gone very pale.

"Maybe we'd better call it a night," he said.

Mick nodded. "Yeah. I'd like to catch me a few hours of sleep before I have to go in tomorrow. Shit, the way I'm feeling, I may just call in sick. Wouldn't that piss Jim off. Can you give me a lift home, Ben?"

"Sure." Ben looked at Peter and Cat. "Are you guys going to be okay?"

"We'll be fine," Cat said. "And look. About tonight. I just want to say thanks. If you hadn't shown up . . ."

Ben flushed. He felt good about it now. Weird, but good. But he could still remember shitting his pants out there. Cat laid a hand on his arm.

"Thank . . . thank you for being there, Ben," she said.

"Yeah, well . . ." He shrugged, his flush deepening. "We'd better get going."

"He's stealing my dreams," Cat said when Ben and Mick had gone. "That's what he wants from me."

"You know what that sounds like?"

"I *know* what it sounds like, but that's what's happening. He's stealing my dreams. He's the . . . it was *his* presence that attacked me in the Otherworld. He's the thing that Tiddy Mun warned me against."

There it was again, Peter thought. The impossible Tiddy Mun and her other ghosts. What exactly *had* he seen tonight? Cat's imaginary gnome or . . . or what? If he accepted even a part of it, then it could all be real, and that he couldn't accept. It opened the door to bona fide certifiable insanity, and he knew that once they stepped through it, there might be no return.

He looked at Cat. By that reasoning, she was already heading for the white-jacket boys. He couldn't accept that either.

"He's the one that killed Kothlen," Cat was saying. "He's some kind of . . . of parasite. A leech. He's a vampire, Peter. That's what he is. A vampire that sucks up dreams instead of blood."

"I can't go along with that."

"But what if . . . what if it's true?"

If it was true, if her ghosts and her Otherworld were real . . . The hobgoblin's features reared in his mind's eye. It couldn't be real. But no matter what Peter's reason insisted, he also couldn't shake the feeling that what he'd seen hadn't been some sort of hallucination. And if it *was* real, then maybe Cat wasn't so far off with what she was saying about tonight's intruder. God, what was he thinking? It had been bad enough imagining him as a potential psychopath. But if Cat was right . . .

She was looking at him, gaze searching his for reassurance. He tried to find something comforting to say, but an abyss had opened inside him, and reason appeared to have fled.

"If it's true," he said softly, "then we're in more trouble than we can possibly imagine."

꒰꒱ Hounds and Ravens ꒰꒱

Father, dear father, I dreamed, dreamed a dream,
I fear it will prove sorrow;
I dreamed I was pulling heather bells
on the dowie dens o' Yarrow.

> —*from "The Braes o' Yarrow';*
> *traditional ballad (Child 214)*

10

heart of the wood

CAT LAY ALONE in her bed, staring at the shadows that crowded the ceiling above her, and tried to sort through her feelings. While it was comforting to know that Peter was sleeping on the couch downstairs, she found herself thinking more of Ben and wondering what his reaction would be to her problems. She had the feeling that, unlike Peter, he would be able to accept the enemy for what it was: a parasite. Sucking not only her creative energies from her, but her life force as well.

For that was what had been happening. How she knew it was true, she couldn't have put into words, but when Mick had jokingly mentioned vampires, the truth went through her like a shock. She just *knew* this was the reason she'd been feeling so dragged out lately. The headaches in the morning. Not being able to dream. Or write. Being more uncommunicative than ever. Was it any wonder when this . . . this thing was feeding on her?

She shivered and drew the blankets closer. She was frightened—petrified would be a better word. And very angry. This violation was worse than a simple break-in, worse even than being physically assaulted. For it was her mind that was being abused, her soul being raped. Slowly but surely the monster was consuming the very essence of what she was.

She wished there was some way she could escape. If she could just stay in her land of dreams forever. Never come back to this world. Never wake up.

She felt real in the Otherworld. It was here that she was the phantom—as much of a ghost as Tiddy Mun was. But the Otherworld wasn't a haven anymore—the enemy had penetrated her dreaming as well. If she slept and dreamed, who was to say that the dark winged shape wouldn't have her this time? And if she didn't wake up before it caught her?

Turning, she buried her face in the pillow. She had no defense against this enemy. He was gone for now, but when he'd recuperated from his wounds, what was to stop the nightmare from beginning all over again?

She could move, she supposed. To another city. Another country. But would running help? Why had she been picked anyway? Because she dreamed real and other people didn't? Surely she wasn't the only person on earth that spun her life across two worlds? Surely other people had their Tiddy Muns and their . . . their Kothlens. . . .

Maybe they did, a small voice inside her said. Maybe the monster's already fed on them.

There had to be a way out—a defense, some way to strike back. Peter couldn't help her now. He didn't believe in the very real danger she was in because he didn't—couldn't—believe in her Otherworld. She supposed she couldn't really blame him. It was as far off the wall as something from out of her own books.

Except she didn't have a Tattershank to magic her away. She didn't have a Borderlord to stand between her and the evil that threatened her. All she had was real people who couldn't see the danger for what it was, and she couldn't really blame them for that lack of vision.

Her thoughts went round and round until she felt like a Ping-Pong ball being batted back and forth across a tabletop. She wondered where Tiddy Mun was—why he continued to play his gnomish game of hide-and-seek at a time like this. But then she'd never really seen him in this world. It was always a movement caught out of the corner of her eye, a whisper of words or song that might have been the wind. Perhaps there was some law or rule that she was unaware of that forbade his manifesting in this world. Or at least something that stopped him from coming to her.

She whispered his name into the pillow. She missed him. Missed Kothlen. The pillow grew damp against her cheek. She just didn't know what to do or where to turn. She was too frightened to sleep for fear of what might be waiting for her in the Otherworld, too tired to stay awake. In the end sleep crept up on her, and once again she was dreaming.

She found herself on Kothlen's moors.

A wind blew across the hills, rustling the heather and sedge, pushing her hair into her face. It made a lonely, forlorn sound that echoed the sadness inside her, for she stood facing a cairn of stones that had never been in this place before, and she knew it for what it was.

Under those stones Kothlen slept the long sleep of his people, his soul fled to the Summer Country while his body . . . Her hands clenched into tight fists, nails digging into her palms. Dead Kothlen, laid to earth with bell heather and cowberry blossoms at his head and feet, his hands clasped across his cold chest, his eyes closed forever, his voice stilled, to speak no more.

She crouched in front of the cairn. Laying her head against its rough stones, she wept. Which was better, she asked. Not to dream, or to dream and find your loved ones dead? The thrumming pulse of the Otherworld sounded all around her, and she wondered if she could ever be happy here again. Wondered if it even mattered anymore.

For she could sense that the land was empty, stripped of its spirit as she'd been stripped of her dreams. There was nothing left for her here. Her enemy would feed on her until the hills were barren, until nothing remained except for a wasteland of bare rock and dry dusty hills.

"Oh, Kothlen," she murmured unhappily.

The wind took her soft words and shredded them. She'd missed him so much over the past few months. And now he was gone forever. Loneliness rose in a tidal swell and threatened to drown her. She stumbled to her feet and cast around

the hilltop for a stone that she could add to the cairn herself.
She found one that, when she held it up to the starlight,
proved to be seamed with quartz veins the same color that his
eyes had been.

"Good . . . good-bye," she said as she laid the stone on top
of the cairn. "Heart of my heart . . ."

Slowly she turned and left the cairn to the night and the
wind. She made her way down the hill, following the roll of
the land until it brought her within sight of Mynfel's oak and
apple wood. Before she reached the forest she turned aside,
taking the crooked path that led to Redcap Hill, where Tiddy
Mun and his people lived. When she arrived, the dun of the
gnomes was as empty as Kothlen's moors had been. But at the
top of the hill, silhouetted against the stars, she saw the proud
lift of Mynfel's antlered head.

The horned woman watched her ascend. When at last Cat
had passed the gnarled fairy thorn and stood in front of her in
the circle protected by the three longstones, Mynfel remained
silent as always. But her eyes echoed the sorrow in Cat's
heart.

Mynfel was beauty incarnate. There were twelve tines to
each of her antlers, which lifted creamy white from a high
brow. Chestnut hair spilled in a torrent down her back. Her
upper torso was that of a woman, her arms muscled but
smooth, her breasts firm, her stomach flat. From the waist
down she was a curious mixture of elk and woman. Her legs
were long, covered with a downy-soft fur, ending in split
hooves. Her honey-gold eyes dominated her face, which was
strong-featured, the cheekbones high, the mouth wide, the
nose straight.

"Lady," Cat said. "Lady, they're all gone. What can I do
now? What must I do?"

For long moments Mynfel held Cat's gaze with her own.
Then she reached forward and stroked the tears from Cat's
cheek. When she stepped back, Cat made a small sound in the
back of her throat. The shared sorrow in her honey eyes was
Mynfel's only reply. She moved from the hilltop, hooves cutting the sod, and Cat followed.

"Lady!" she cried.

Mynfel paused at the edge of the wood. Still she didn't
speak. She never spoke. Again her gaze held Cat's. Follow if
you will, her eyes seemed to say. Then she turned and was
gone.

Cat swallowed. The night closed in around her, not threatening, but no longer the same. There was a wildness in the air, a strangeness that called out to her. Taking a last look at Redcap Hill and its three dancing stones, she plunged in amongst the trees, and the forest closed in around her.

Lysistratus felt the woman recoil as she removed his shirt. So violent was her reaction that he almost lost his hold on her. The knife, while not puncturing any major organs, had cut through muscle and tissue to sever at least one arteriole. There was a great deal of blood. He firmed his grip on her mind, soothed the jangle of her nerves with false assurances.

Under his direction she swabbed the wound clean with hydrogen peroxide, stitched it closed, then applied a good measure of an antibiotic ointment before employing a dressing. Throughout her ministrations he kept the pain at bay by focusing on the four who had turned such a promising hunt into disaster.

He would return for them—quicker than they might expect. He healed more quickly than their kind did. The psychic essences of his prey accelerated his body's natural healing process. He would only have to feed more.

Not until the major abdominal wound had been treated did he allow her to work on his face, arm, and legs. The arm and legs had escaped with no more than flesh wounds. The slash on his face would leave a scar though. When Stella was finally finished, he had her sit passively on the bed beside him.

"What a night," he said.

He lifted a hand to her throat. Her pulse jumped under his touch and her whole body trembled. The flow of her thoughts ran in a constant litany of: this can't be happening, this can't be real. . . .

He had her remove the bloody sheets from the bed and remake it. Then he had her undress and lie down. She was tall and slim, her skin smooth to the touch, her strawberry-blond hair cut short and straight. He filled her mind with illusions until she forgot him, until it seemed that an old lover teased her body with knowing hands. When her body arched, he drank in her orgasm, then forced her to sleep. Her hot pleasure went through him like a healing balm.

Lying down beside her, flesh against flesh, he drew strength from her dreaming mind, though not enough to harm her. He took just enough to replenish his own dwindling re-

serves, to ease the pain and speed his recovery, for he knew he
needed her. While her mind was as soft as her body—requir-
ing no great skill to overrule and so control—she would have
to be his arms and legs until he recuperated. He would have
her bring prey home for him until he could safely hunt for
himself. A friend invited over for the evening. A man picked
up in a bar. . . .

He thought of Cat and her protectors. They expected him
to return, but they wouldn't expect this woman. Or others like
her. There might not be any need for him to go to them. Not if
he could have them brought to him.

Cat had never been this far into Mynfel's wood before—
never been very far into it at all when it came right down to it.
No one had that she knew. Not the gnomes, nor Kothlen's
people. It wasn't that it was dangerous, only that it was sacred
to Mynfel and therefore not a place for common folk to
wander. Not unless they had great need. Or they were invited.

There was scant light under the giant oaks, but Cat never
quite lost sight of the horned woman. She felt a little like a
night traveler being led astray by a will-o'-the-wisp, except
that whatever fire it was that burned behind Mynfel's eyes, it
was not fool's fire. She led, and Cat followed. The path they
took seemed to promise an end to Cat's fears. She was sure of
that. Mynfel would never lead her astray.

There was no undergrowth to impede their progress. The
oak trees—so wide in girth that two Cats couldn't have
touched hands around their trunks—reared skyward like the
supporting columns in an immense cathedral. When they
broke into a clearing, apple trees heavy with fruit appeared,
scattered the length of the glade. Between them were carpets
of pale-blue flowers, while above, the strange constellations
of the Otherworld's night skies wheeled in their solemn dance.
The forest was hushed, reverent, and in it Cat felt safe.

An undercurrent of what she'd felt when she first entered
the wood stayed inside her—that sense of wildness that she
perceived with an intuitive insight but could put no name to. It
didn't diminish the promise of safety she felt. Instead it
strengthened it. And the longer she followed Mynfel's lead—
now jogging, now at a quick walk—the more a certain *rightness* grew in her.

When they finally came to one last glade, Cat knew they'd

reached the end of their journey. Mynfel stood on the opposite side of a small pool. The water was enclosed by a low stone wall. The stones, gray and veined with dark seams, had ideographs cut deeply into their surfaces.

Cat approached cautiously, gaze darting from the pool to Mynfel, who stood silently watching her. When she reached the wall, Cat hesitated. She didn't need the horned woman to tell her what she would see in the water. She was sure she knew what would be there—an unravelling of the riddle that troubled her. On the surface of that still and dark water, her solution would be pictured. She had only to look.

She leaned forward, settling her palms against the wall. The rock was cool and dry to the touch. The surface of the water was black, reflecting not even the night stars above. It gave off a sweet scent. Kneeling beside it so that she could rest her elbows on the top of the wall, she leaned closer. The ground was soft under her knees, the stone hard against her breasts as she pressed against the wall.

At first the water stayed dark and unreadable. Then, just as Cat was about to glance questioningly at her silent companion, a shimmer rippled across its surface. She looked down into her own face, only it wasn't a reflection. The perspective was wrong. The tousled hair in the reflection tumbled back from her head instead of rising up to meet the hair that fell down toward the pool from either side of her face. And there, where the hair was drawn back from the reflection's brow. . .

Mynfel's antlers weighted down her head. She stared aghast at the reflection. Those horns on her own head lent her a look as wild and strange as the mythic being whose woods she trod. The weight was real. She could feel her head bobbing toward the water. With an effort she pulled up, stared across the pool, a question on her lips, but—

Mynfel was gone.

Fingers trembling, Cat reached up to touch her forehead, but they encountered only her hairline and a handful of curls. She looked at the pool. Its surface was a dark sheen once more.

"Lady," she called. "Lady!"

This answered nothing. It was no explanation—only another obscure riddle. She didn't have time for riddles. . . .

She circled the glade, calling until her voice grew hoarse. Again and again she lifted her hands to her brow. They encountered nothing but the memory of what she'd seen. When she finally returned to the pool, there was a deep ache inside her. Confusion mingled with fear. The sense of safety she'd felt earlier fled. Only the hallowedness of the forest remained, but now it was inexplicable. A mystery more profound than what she'd seen in the pool.

She looked into the water again, and again its surface stirred. This time it showed her Tiddy Mun creeping down a city street that she didn't recognize. She started to reach out to touch the image, but it changed, flowed into a long view of Redcap Hill. There, standing amongst the longstones as she had been earlier, was Mynfel, branched antlers silhouetted against the stars once more, her honey-rich eyes still sad, still sharing.

"Mynfel," Cat whispered.

The name rang in the glade as though she'd shouted it. The pool lost the image of the horned woman and Redcap Hill, showed Tiddy Mun once more, huddled in a driveway staring wide-eyed at a car's headlights passing him by on the street. Then the waters blackened and stilled again.

"I don't understand," Cat said.

The forest's silence was her only reply.

For a long time she sat crouched against the wall, waiting hopelessly for something to make sense of the tumult inside her, but after a while she realized that she was waiting in vain. The pool and its obscure riddles were all that she was going to be offered. She traced an ideograph with her finger, stared into the dark forest that surrounded her with a silence as still as the silence its mistress wore, then slowly stood.

She felt betrayed. Mynfel had been her last hope. Now it seemed that she'd withdrawn her protection.

"I'm not giving in," Cat told the night. "I . . . I can't."

It was fight or lose herself. The monster was stealing her dreams, sucking the soul right out of her. She *had* to fight it. The question was how.

She thought of Kothlen lying dead in his grave, and if the pool's images were to be believed, of Tiddy Mun trapped in her world. Again she touched her brow. There was nothing there. What did the antlers on her reflection mean? And Mynfel on Redcap Hill, waiting . . . waiting for what?

Cat never felt more alone than she did leaving that pool in the heart of the wood to step in amongst the giant oaks of Mynfel's forest once more.

11

❡

thursday

ELLEN HENDERSON STARED blindly at the off-white walls in the waiting room of the Civic Hospital's emergency ward. She was a sturdy woman in her mid-forties, broad-faced with black-framed glasses, her hair pulled back in a severe bun. Her husband Jack sat beside her, his usually jovial features drawn and pale. She drew strength from his big hand enclosing hers, but nothing could ease the torment inside her. The doctor's initial prognosis dropped through the maelstrom of her thoughts like a monstrous demon spinning end over end, its talons shredding everything she'd ever held dear to her heart as it went through her.

Catalepsy.

No. Not her Lisa.

The loss of voluntary motion probably initiated by a strong emotional stimulus.

Not her baby.

Cataplexy.

"Mrs. Henderson," the doctor had said. "Has your daughter appeared at all distraught recently? Perhaps she broke up with her boyfriend? Has she ever shown any severe emotional disorders?"

And Ellen, never at a loss for words, could only numbly shake her head while Jack replied to the doctor's questions.

Her baby was going to die. Her Lisa . . .

"Some coffee?" Jack asked softly, drawing her out of her inner storm for the few instants it took to register that he was speaking.

She looked at him, at the two Italian women mourning their own loss three chairs down, at the thin black man sitting across the room—his face as haggard as her own. Dimly she remembered that his wife had been in a car accident. She'd seen the orderlies wheeling her in from the ambulance, her features hidden behind the oxygen equipment. . . .

"Ellen?"

She faced Jack, remembered his question. Coffee was an alien word that didn't fit into the context of her present emotional turmoil. She started to shake her head, then saw the doctor who'd questioned them earlier fill the doorway of the waiting room. Jack followed her gaze and stood up.

"Doctor," he began, "is there some . . . ?"

His voice trailed off as he read the answer in the doctor's eyes. His daughter's death was reflected there. He saw Lisa's face in his mind's eye, her face alive with laughter, and knew he'd never hear her laugh again. Beside him, he heard Ellen moan. Turning, he took her in his arms and held her tightly in a blind attempt to ease her wracking sobs while the tears started down his own cheeks.

Linda Stinson unlocked the front door of Discount Den—a clothing shop at Bank Street near Laurier—at about five to nine. Locking the door behind her, she left her purse and knitting on the cash counter and went into the back room to open the safe. Humming to herself, she put the morning float into the till, then gathered up the green garbage bag from under the counter and took it out through the back door to leave in the alley behind the store.

As she started for the Laurier entrance where the garbage men made their pick up, something drew her gaze. She looked left, and for a long moment what she saw didn't register. The body of a wino lay there, collapsed over a suitcase, blood soaking the front of his shirt and pooling on the ground around him.

The garbage bag fell from suddenly limp fingers. She stared, her eyes feeding the horror to her brain as she fought to look away. A primal scream came surging up from her diaphragm and scraped her throat raw as it wailed forth. By the time the police were called and two squad cars had arrived, the investigating officers were unable to question her. Medics took her to the Civic Hospital to be treated for shock.

Peter woke up automatically when his inner alarm clock told him it was eight-thirty. It didn't matter that he hadn't had a decent night's sleep for two nights running, nor that he was exhausted from more than a lack of sleep. He lay for a few minutes, listening to the quiet in Cat's house, then swung his feet off the couch. He tugged on his jeans, slung his shirt over his shoulder, and padded upstairs. His reflection looked blearily back at him from the bathroom mirror. He used Cat's toothbrush and toothpaste. After washing his face, he rubbed his hand along his jawline, wishing he'd thought to bring along a razor. That'd have to wait till he got back to the store.

He paused in the hall, unsure as to whether he should look in on Cat or not. He knew she valued her privacy. If she was awake, she wouldn't take his waltzing in on her too kindly. On the other hand, he didn't want to knock on her door— waking her to see if she was awake.

After a moment of indecision, he went to the door of her room, pushed it ajar and peeked in. When she didn't stir, he crossed the room and stood looking down at her for a while. She was still asleep and seemed okay. One hand was under her pillow, the other lying on the sheet. She lay on her side, hair a wild tangle, face elfin.

In another age, considering her looks and her *sight*—if that was the right word; what she called her true dreaming—she'd probably be considered fey and persecuted as a witch. Instead she had some weirdo to contend with. Not to mention her delusions . . .

Peter sighed. He knelt down by the bed and studied her features. Where was she right now? Just sleeping like anybody else would be, or traipsing off through neverneverland, pursued by her psychic vampire? Her and a pack of Tiddy Men running across— He didn't even know what her dreamworld was supposed to look like. Like her books, he decided.

He shook his head and stood up, leaving the room as quietly as he'd entered. In the kitchen he wrote her a note and propped it up on a table at the bottom of the stairs, where she was sure to see it as she came down. After making sure the door would lock behind him, he stepped outside and pulled it shut.

He had to assume she'd be safe enough during the day, at least from the guy that Ben had dubbed the Dude. In her dreams . . . well, he just couldn't know.

When Rick awoke that morning and saw who was lying beside him in his big double bed, he knew he was in trouble.

"Oh, shit," he muttered, and stood up.

His head spun and his stomach lurched. They'd really tied one on last night. He stumbled into the bathroom and dry-swallowed three aspirin and two Tums as he relieved the pressure in his bladder which had woken him in the first place. Standing in the doorway of the bedroom once more—or rather, supported by the door frame because there was *no way* he could stand up on his own just yet—he looked at Debbie's big and beautiful body lying in his bed, vaguely remembered Stella being here when the two of them rolled in this morning, and wondered how the fuck he got himself into messes like these in the first place.

Bad enough that Bill had nixed the loan. Now he had to fuck it up with Stella as well. For a moment he tried to think of what he'd say to her. "Look, babe. It's not like what you think. . . ."

Yeah. Sure. That'd go over really big with her. And if it wasn't like what she'd think, what the hell was it? He was up the creek without a paddle, but he had to do something. He had to make it up to her. Christ, if she took her money out of the store . . .

What had possessed him to bring Debbie here anyway? How could he have forgotten that Stella was going to be waiting for him? Well, he hadn't forgotten. Not really. At the point when he'd decided to come home, he just hadn't given a shit. So now what did he do?

He went into the kitchen, brewed a pot of coffee, and managed to bring two cups—hot and black—back to the bedroom without spilling them. First I'll sober up, he thought, and then

I'll give Stel a call. He glanced at the clock beside the bed. Going on eight. She wouldn't be heading off to work for at least another fifteen minutes, and it might be a good idea to be a little more coherent than he was feeling right now before he tried to make it up with her.

"How're you doing, lover?"

Debbie was awake. To Rick's eyes she seemed none the worse for her night of heavy drinking. The way she looked, she could never look bad. She stretched languorously, aware of his gaze.

"C'mere," she purred and drew him into the bed. "Let's see what it feels like when we're not so fuzzy-headed."

Rick began a token protest, but she already had a hand between his legs and was drawing him, gently but firmly, down to her. Well, what the hell. Last night *had* been fast and furious. He might as well have something really worthwhile to make up for. He'd call Stella at work. That way she couldn't yell at him over the phone and her whole office know what was going down.

"Just like that," Debbie murmured as he stroked from her breast to the flat of her stomach to her inner thighs. "Oh, yes."

When Cat finally left Mynfel's wood behind, dawn was pinking the Otherworld sky and she was confronted with an unfamiliar countryside.

A valley lay below where she stood—a wide sweep of meadow and woodland divided by a slow-moving river. Beyond it forested hills marched on to the horizon. She'd never really thought of the Otherworld as being so broad before. That came, she realized, from always visiting one small corner of it. The moors, Redcap Hill, Mynfel's wood, the marshes to the south, the foothills of the northern mountains . . . She'd never gone westward before—not this deep into the wood and then beyond it.

Seeing the panorama spread out in front of her was like coming to the Otherworld for the first time again. What sort of people lived in this part of it? Were they hiding from the dream thief as well? Were their halls and homes lying empty?

A thin trail of smoke caught her gaze, its source hidden by a sweep of birch and trembling aspen. She watched it rise into the clear air for a long while, trying to decide whether or not to go down to it. She might be walking smack-dab into the middle of more danger, but she might also find someone who could help her where no one else seemed able or willing to. That in itself made it a risk worth taking. At last she put aside the warning tingle inside her and started down the slope.

She'd arrived in the Otherworld wearing faded jeans, a pair of rubber-soled Chinese silk slippers, and her favorite sweater —a motley-colored heather and brown affair that hung almost to her knees. She'd discovered long ago that she could choose what she'd appear in when she arrived in the Otherworld. Last night had been no exception. What she wore now was an old habit and didn't even require a decision.

By the time she'd crossed the first meadow, her slippers and the bottoms of her jeans were wet with dew. But rather than feeling discomforted, she was aware of a lightness inside her that had been missing for quite some time. If only Kothlen or Tiddy Mun were here to share this feeling of discovery with her. But Tiddy Mun was hiding, and Kothlen was dead . . . dead. . . .

She shook her head, trying to recapture the positive feeling that had dissolved as soon as she'd thought of her friends. She didn't have much success. She watched a pair of swallows chase each other across the meadow, spied a barn owl dozing high in a gray-trunked ash. She felt the sun on her face. The sky was blue above her, the air filled with bird song. Slowly some measure of that feeling returned. The ache remained, but if she just didn't think about it, it was almost bearable. By the time she'd gained the farthest end of the last field and was pushing her way through the undergrowth of the birch and aspen copse, she had almost succeeded.

It was almost as though none of the terrible things had happened. Almost, she was her old self, curiosity prickling in her as though she were one of her four-footed namesakes. Almost . . .

Becki Bones opened one bleary eye, then the other, focused them, and pulled a face. "You look like hell," she said, sitting up. "What time did you get in last night?"

Mick shrugged. "Sometime after three."

He bent down to tie his shoelaces, and Becki made a small noise when she saw the dried blood on the back of his head.

"What happened to you?" she asked.

Leaving the bed, she padded over to him and gave his head a critical once-over.

"Ben and I had a run-in with a weirdo last night. He set into us with a homemade cosh."

He gave her a brief rundown of the previous night's events. Becki sat on the bed, running her hand through her hair and bringing the spiked locks to attention while she listened. When he was done, she shook her head.

"You're not going to work," she said, more a command than a question.

"Got to. There's too much shit piled up for me to take a day off, you know what I mean? The weekend'll be here soon. I can rest up then."

"Mick . . ."

"Hey, I'm okay. It looks worse than it feels."

Becki sighed. Then she asked, "Militant cats? Was that for real?"

"Doesn't seem real now, but I know what I saw."

"And guys that can step into your head?"

"Didn't happen to me, babe. I'd rather go for the Bela Lugosi scene anyway."

Mick stuck his two index fingers along the sides of his mouth as he spoke and pretended to have a go at her with the makeshift fangs.

"Get real," Becki told him, pushing him aside.

Mick grinned. "No vampires. Just a crazy—and that's plenty, don't you think?" He finished tying his shoelaces, then stood up from the bed. "Though it'd make a helluva better story the other way."

"Was that your wife or your girlfriend?" Debbie asked.

She sat in a chair by the mirror, combing out her silvery blond hair. When she was done, it fell in a thick mane down her back. She started on her eyes then, leaning close to the mirror as she applied a dusty blue eyeliner. Her eyes were a dark gray, large and attractive. Her nose was small, mouth full. She hadn't bothered to get dressed yet, and Rick found it hard to concentrate on what she was saying.

"Was who what?" he asked.

"That woman last night—the one who stormed out as we came in. Bill's talked about her before, but I could never figure out which she was from what he told me."

"Oh, her," Rick murmured.

Debbie grinned. "Let me guess. It was your cleaning

woman—pissed because you haven't paid her this month. No! It was your cousin, just in from Arnprior for the week."

"She was my girlfriend, Stella."

"Poor Stella. I'll tell you, Rick, you're great in the sack—especially when you're sober—but you don't know shit about how to treat a woman out of bed."

"Yeah, well . . ."

Debbie laughed at his discomfort. "Maybe you can convince her that *I'm* your cousin."

"I've got to make a phone call," Rick said, and beat a hasty retreat.

Debbie had finished making up her face by the time he returned. She slipped into her bra and turned her back to him. "Hook me up, will you?"

"Yeah. Sure."

"What's the matter?" she asked as he fumbled with the clasp.

"You're not going to believe this."

She turned when he was done, found her panties lying under the dresser where she'd flung them last night, and waited for him to continue.

"Well?" she asked finally.

She turned to see him sitting on the edge of the bed, a look of confusion on his face. Maybe she'd been teasing him too much, she thought. But she did feel sorry for Stella. If she'd known Stella was going to be here last night . . . Though come to think of it, she *had* known. She'd just been too tipsy to really think about what they were doing to her. Debbie pitied any woman who tried to build any sort of a meaningful relationship with a guy like Rick. They never changed.

"Well?" she asked again.

"She's not mad." He looked up, searching her face as though he expected to find an explanation there.

"You're kidding."

"No. She sounded . . . embarrassed. She apologized for, and I quote, 'acting like an ass,' end of quote."

Hoo-ha, Debbie thought. This Stella is one bizarre lady.

"And that's not all," Rick added. "She wants us—*both* of us—over for a drink after work tonight."

Debbie shook her head. "No thanks. The thought of getting caught up in the middle of a lover's spat is not my idea of having a good time."

Rick didn't even seem to hear her. "She said going for a

threesome sounded like a good idea," he added.

"Now you've got to be kidding."

"I swear I'm not, Debbie."

"What's she like?" Debbie asked. "I mean, she's not . . . psychotic or anything, is she?"

"What?"

"Hang on. Don't get your back all up. It just seems weird, that's all. I mean, last night . . ." She shrugged.

"Maybe she thought about it when she got home last night and the idea of it turned her on."

"Maybe it did."

Debbie had to admit to herself that the whole situation had a certain implausible quality to it that appealed to her. She could see that, for all his surprise, the idea had more than a little appeal for Rick as well. She tried to remember what Stella looked like. Not quite model-slim, but an attractive lady nonetheless.

"What's she like in bed?" Debbie asked.

"Very . . . energetic."

Debbie nodded, remembering his drunken comment last night about Stella "humping like a bunny." She wondered how he'd describe her own performance, then had to ask herself— did she really want to get involved in this kind of thing? She'd never had any particular leanings toward other women, at least not of a sexual nature. On the other hand, it would certainly be something different. If you didn't try it, how would you know if you liked it or not?

"Will you pick me up after work?" she asked.

Rick nodded. The silly grin plastered on his face made Debbie laugh. Tonight, she thought, could prove to be a ver-ry interesting experience.

After fleeing the dream thief, Tiddy Mun had run as far and fast as he could, his heart pounding in his tiny chest, his big eyes wider than ever. Wherever he turned in this world, there was noise and rush. Iron dragons roaring along stone avenues. Towers of metal and glass and stone that stood taller than any tree in Mynfel's wood, taller than anything he'd ever seen before in his life, taller than the sky itself, it seemed.

The darkness hid him as he fled, but when dawn came he took the shape of a big orange tomcat and searched for shadows, for someplace to hide where a tallfolk wouldn't find him and hurt him, where the dream thief couldn't touch his soul with his eyes like hot ice.

The cat shape was the only form he could take, but it
served him well in this world. He was a friend to cats, and to
his tallfolk Cat in particular. He whispered her secret name to
himself and for a moment he felt safe, but then the fear returned, stronger than before.

He wanted to go home, but he didn't know the way. He'd
been in Cat's world before, but never so *truly* in it. Always
before it had been a shadowy place, its strangeness hazy and
ill-defined. Always before he'd had half a foot in the Otherworld. Always before he was near Cat, where it was safe,
teasing her and ready to flee into his own world if something
startled him.

But now he was lost—had been since he'd been drawn
into this world with Cat two nights past—and now he had to
spend a second day shivering and hiding, always afraid, afraid
of everything, but especially afraid of the evil stalking his
friend Cat and spreading its shadow through the Otherworld.

He burrowed amidst the refuse of an alleyway in his cat
shape, filled with a jitter of tangled nerves. He had never been
much of a thinker. He always took his little problems to Kothlen or to Cat. But now . . . Now he must think on his own,
make a plan of some sort. But he was as hopelessly lost
amidst the fears that battered at his mind as he was in this
strange and dangerous world.

He longed for the comfort of Cat's arms, for her to make
the decisions for both of them, but the evil was too close to
her. It swallowed her house, dogged her footsteps when she
left. It was too dangerous to go to her.

He remembered the men outside her house then. They had
faced up to the dream thief. They hadn't been afraid. Especially the one with the banded hair and the sharp knife with
the iron in its edge. Maybe if he found that man, he would be
willing to help a Redcap Hill gnome, lost and alone. Maybe
he would help Tiddy Mun return to Cat.

He knew the taste of that man—his smell, his look, the
essence that set him apart from other tallfolk. In fact he knew
each of Cat's three tallfolk friends now. If he couldn't find the
one with the curious hair, he would look for one of the others.
But first he would look for the knife wielder, because he had
been the least afraid, and Tiddy Mun needed to be with someone brave now.

His decision pleased him and helped hold he terrors at bay. He would wait for dark, for the safety of shadows. And if the Horned Lady meant him well, he would find his way home again.

Peter had unlocked the front door of the store and was by the window turning the "CLOSED" sign to "OPEN" when he saw Ben's cab pull up across the street. He went into the back room, plugged in the kettle, and pulled out the visitor's chair.

"Morning, Peter!" Ben called as he came in.

"Morning, Ben. What's doing?"

"Not much." Ben settled in the chair and picked up a book, idly flipping its pages before setting it down again. "I had some trouble sleeping last night, but I don't feel all that tired," he said. "You?"

Peter shrugged.

"How's Cat?"

"She was sleeping when I left. We talked some after you guys left last night, and she wasn't feeling too happy." An uncomfortable smile touched his lips. "Hell, who is? But she's got some crazy ideas about her prowler, and having you and Mick go on about vampires didn't exactly help."

"Yeah, well . . . I never told you about what happened the first time I ran into the Dude, did I?"

"Only that you'd seen him in Central Park, back of your place."

Ben nodded. "I was sitting in the grass and fell asleep while I was reading. Funny thing is, it was Cat's new book I was reading. Talk about omens, will you?"

Peter remembered something then. "You want to hear something even funnier?" He told Ben about the copy of *The Sleeping Warrior* that had seemed to leap from his bookshelf the night before Cat came into the store with her troubles.

"Weird," Ben said. "It's like we're all tied into this somehow."

"I didn't mean that there was anything supernatural about—"

"Let me finish," Ben said. "When I woke up in the park, the Dude was standing about the length of this room from me—maybe a little more—just staring."

"Ben—"

"No. Listen to me. I thought he was putting the make on

me, you know? But after he was gone, I had this empty, sort of drained feeling inside. And a headache. Now I didn't put it together at the time, but after last night I—"

"Oh, come *on*, Ben."

"Okay. It sounds crazy. But what happened last night was crazy too. What if this guy *is* some kind of . . . I don't know . . ."

"Psychic vampire?"

"Yeah!"

"Jesus, Ben. You sound just like Cat. She thinks your Dude's the reason she hasn't been dreaming lately. She says he feeds on her dreams."

"What?"

Ben sat up straight, and Peter stifled a groan. What had possessed him to come out with that? He wanted to just cut the conversation there, but Ben was waiting expectantly for an explanation. If he cut things off now, he might be killing the relationship he was hoping would develop between the two of them, the relationship that might well solve all of Cat's problems. He decided that Ben could keep what he heard to himself. Besides, Ben was trying to help Cat as well. If he and Mick hadn't shown up last night when they did, who knows what the Dude would have done?

"The reason Cat's not writing," he said, "is that she's stopped dreaming. She thinks she goes . . . someplace else when she sleeps. It's a place like out of one of her books, I think, complete with elves and gnomes. . . ." Tiddy Mun's features reared in his mind—Go away! he told it. "An Otherworld. The people there—she calls them her ghosts—are who she gets her stories from. They tell them to her and she fills them out when she writes them down."

"No shit?"

"She goes to the same place, meets the same ghosts, every night. She's been doing it since she was a kid—or at least up to about three months ago. Then the dreams stopped and her writing dried up and here we are now."

"You don't believe her, do you?" Ben asked.

"Christ, Ben. I don't know what to think."

Again he pushed away the memory of Tiddy Mun's features. He looked at Ben and thought, Cat, you picked the wrong person to come to with your problems. Here's the man you want. Ben was wearing a thoughtful expression with nothing skeptical about it.

"I believe that *she* thinks it's true," Peter added. "It's just that . . ."

"It doesn't fit into the way you see things, so you'd rather not have to think about it."

Peter nodded. "That's about it."

They were both quiet then, each following his own train of thought. The kettle started to boil. Peter got up, made them their coffees, and returned to the cash area.

"What if it's true?" Ben asked.

"That's supposing a lot."

Ben shook his head. "What the hell do we really know about the human mind anyway? What about people who claim to astral travel when they're supposed to be sleeping?"

"Those people," Peter said, "claim to astral travel in the world we know, not some place chock full of gremlins and the like."

"Uh-uh. They go to spirit realms—or at least some of them do. Like the Indians down in New Mexico or South America. And what about all the weird shit that goes down that there isn't any explanation for—at least no explanation that fits into the scheme of the world as we see it? I mean, there are enough cases of documented paranormal activity to fill this store, Peter."

"Yeah. Except not one of them stands up to scientific scrutiny. Not one of them can be duplicated in a laboratory."

"Maybe things like Cat's ghosts don't like the sterile atmosphere of a lab."

"Maybe the moon's made of green cheese and the moonlanding we all saw on TV was just another Hollywood special effect." Peter shook his head. "That argument doesn't cut it, Ben."

"Okay." Ben sighed. "But I have to consider how I'd feel if that sort of thing was happening to me—was real for me—and I couldn't share it with anybody else because they'd either laugh or have me committed. I'd feel really . . . lonely. I wonder how many unreported occurrences there are, simply because no one wants to get lumped together with the people who talk to Elvis Presley's ghost."

That hit home. Peter thought of Cat living with her secret for so many years, alienated because of it, because it made her different, but knowing if she tried to speak of it to anyone it would only broaden the gap she already felt between herself and the rest of the world. He was the first person she'd told,

and while he hadn't exactly laughed at her, he hadn't been
very sympathetic either. He believed that she believed, but
he'd made it clear that he couldn't accept it as real. That
wasn't being exactly supportive. And then there were the
things that he *had* seen. Or thought he'd seen. Like Tiddy
Mun.

He told Ben everything then, from when Cat came into the
store, straight through to when they finally went to their separate beds last night.

"She needs someone like you, Ben," he said.

Ben shook his head. "I don't know. I always wanted to
know her. To be her friend. But I never took it any further—
not seriously. I mean, what would she see in a guy like me?"
But he remembered her touch on his arm last night, and the
look in her eyes. He could feel a flush start up at the back of
his neck. "Let's talk about something else," he said.

"Like what?"

"How about this Tiddy Mun you think you saw."

Peter sighed. "Right. But I didn't just imagine it—I did see
something."

"Oh, sure."

"I just don't know if it was real or not."

"You're the one that's acting nuts now, you know that?"
Ben said.

"Yeah. That's what I've been thinking. Only..."

Peter's voice trailed off. Only what? He had to be missing
a wire or two because just talking about Cat's gnome again
brought those strange features back into his mind's eye. They
seemed so real—as though the creature actually existed. He
glanced at Ben, feeling a certain resentment. Jesus, he
thought. Ben was the one who was willing to accept it all a
few minutes ago, and now... Then he caught Ben's smile.

"See how it feels?" Ben said. "And you're not even a true
believer. Did you never think that Cat must wonder how sane
she is at times?"

Peter shook his head. "I never thought of it that way. But
what about you? How can you accept this all so easily?"

"I didn't say that I did. But I'm willing to allow that it's
possible. Did I ever tell you about my aunt who reads tea
leaves?"

"Yeah."

"It was scary how dead-on she could be. She gave it up

because she just couldn't handle the way that what she saw in the bottom of a teacup became real."

"That's not really the same thing as we've got here."

"No," Ben agreed. "What's scary here is, if Cat's dreams *are* real, then maybe the Dude really is feeding on them."

Peter sighed. "So what do we do?"

"I don't know. We've got to watch out for her. Maybe try to track the Dude down. The trouble is, we don't really know what we're dealing with. It's easy in the movies. You just look for a castle on a hill and the guy in the black cape with the long fangs—well, he's your man. But if the Dude is some kind of vampire, he's not like any I've ever heard of." Ben's hand went to his neck. "He doesn't even bite."

"In the old days," Peter said, "people used to think of blood as the life principle—a rejuvenating force. It was symbolic of our life essence."

"I follow you. So if vampires are real, the legends just mixed up what they were taking from us. Or at least how. I suppose drawing out somebody's soul doesn't make as good copy as sucking the blood from their veins—even before Hammer Films got hold of the story."

"*If,*" Peter said, "you're willing to accept that that's what the Dude is in the first place."

Ben shrugged. "The real problem is that I don't think a crucifix or stake is going to do this guy in. Sunlight sure doesn't seem to bother him. Christ, will you listen to us? Maybe we're both going off the deep end."

Peter thought about Cat and about what they all might be facing if the Dude decided to live up to their wild speculations.

"I almost wish we were," he said.

Ben shook his head. "Not me. I'd rather the world went crazy than to think it was just me." He glanced at his watch. "Gotta run, Peter. I'll see you later."

"Why don't you give Cat a call?"

"You're really turning into a little matchmaker, aren't you?"

"Whatever does the trick."

Ben thought about that for a moment, then grinned. "Well, maybe I will," he said.

The General Assignment Unit of the Ottawa Police Force

took up almost half of the third floor of the main station at Nicholas and Waller. In his office, overlooking the construction of the new Rideau Centre, Detective-Sergeant Derek Potter reread the report that had crossed his desk earlier that morning. On the surface it didn't give him much to go on. But when you put it together with one or two other items that had come in over the past few months . . .

He tapped the end of a pencil against his upper lip as he thought about it. They had a regular community of about forty winos in the downtown core. In General Assignment you didn't deal with them that much, but you became aware of them quickly enough as you made your way up from patrolman to detective. Every big city had them, though Ottawa— for all that it boasted being Canada's fourth largest city—could actually claim relatively few.

"Got your files, Potsy."

He looked up as Detective Bill McKinty sat down beside his desk, a handful of files under one arm and a coffee in either hand. Black with sugar for Potter; cream, no sugar, for himself. Bill was dark-haired where Potter was blond, beefier in the jowls and deeper in the chest. He stood an inch taller than Potter's 6'1".

Potter accepted his coffee with a nod. "Did you have a look through them?" he asked, tapping his pencil on the desk.

Bill opened the top file. "Crazy Dick, a.k.a. Richard T. Brown," he read. "The T stands for Terrance. His body was found behind Coles on the Mall at 0705 by Constable Evans on July twentieth. The coroner's report puts his death at approximately 0400. Cause of death: massive hemorrhaging due to the fact that his fucking throat was slit, ear to ear."

"Same M.O. as O'Dennehy here," Potter said. His pencil moved from the desk to the report in question.

"You got it," Bill said. "Only the rest of these files you called up don't fit in. The coroner lists them all as dying of natural causes."

"How many?"

"Four, not including Crazy Dick."

"In . . . what? Two months?"

"Closer to three."

"Something stinks here," Potter said. He lifted his gaze. "Something's killing off our street people, one by one."

"Two guys . . ." Bill began.

Potter shook his head. "Six. Not including the hooker that

Wells is working on. Same M.O. again—throat slit. She had thirty-five bucks and change in her pocket and not a penny was touched. Happened in a back alley."

"I forgot about her," Bill said. "Wasn't Wells all set to pin it on her pimp?"

"Yeah. Except it turned out she really *was* working free-lance—if you want to go with the word on the street."

"What do you think, Potsy?"

"I think she fits. I think someone's got a hard-on for low-lifes."

"So we've got three—"

"No," Potter broke in. "We've got seven. Those other four fit in."

He frowned, chewing on the end of his pencil before going back to tapping it on the report again. The same instincts that had helped him break the Hooper/Gibbs case, which got him his last promotion, were buzzing up a storm.

There was something going on, and he didn't like it. The trouble was that while there wasn't going to be a major prob-lem getting Staff Sergeant Robinson to okay their tying the three knifings together, Potter couldn't see Robinson letting them reopen the other four cases. The verdict was in on them, and foul play wasn't a part of it, not unless you wanted to try and indict Mother Nature.

No, what they were going to have to do was work on those cases when they could—a bit here and a bit there, look for connections, until they had something hard that they could take to Robinson.

"I still don't see how they fit, Potsy," Bill said. "I mean, even if we've got a slasher with a yen for winos and hookers, that still doesn't explain those other four."

Potter shrugged. "I *can't* tie them in, not in any way that makes sense. But I know they're all part of the same puzzle." The pencil beat a slow tattoo against his upper lip as he thought it out. "Are you with me on this?"

Bill nodded. You didn't back out on your partner, even if he *was* going in for some extracurricular investigating. The brass tended to frown on that kind of shit, but what could you do? It wasn't like he could just walk out on Potsy.

"Then here's what we'll do. We'll run down some of O'Dennehy's friends, like . . ." He glanced at the report on his desk. "Ron Wilson. The usual routine. At the same time we'll check on any cases in the last, say, three months that are similar to those four winos. We're looking for people who are keeling over for no good reason. Not heart attacks or shit like that, just those that died of"—he paused deliberately—"natural causes."

"I'll take Wilson and start a preliminary check with the hospitals," Bill said.

Potter nodded. "I'll start with Wells's report on the hooker case then."

Bill began to get up, then sat down again. "Just what *are* we looking for, Potsy?"

"You tell me. The boogeyman, for all I know."

"Right."

"And Bill?"

"Yeah?"

"Let's keep a lid on this."

Bill smiled. "You think I want Robinson sniffing up *my* ass?"

When Bill left, Potter stared out the window to watch a crane work its load up to the roof of the half-completed Centre, where a handful of construction workers were clustered. His pencil lay forgotten in his hand.

Damn funny business, he thought. He sat like that for a long while, then sighed and pushed the O'Dennehy report to one side. Time to track down Wells and see what he had for them.

The stranger was neither an elf nor a gnome, merely a human—as human as Cat, if appearances were anything to go by. He looked up as she stepped from the woods, one hand straying casually to the hilt of a knife stuck in the ground by his knee. There was something about both Kothlen and Ben about him that brought a lump to Cat's throat. Her natural shyness leapt to the fore and she ended up just standing where she was, waiting for him to say something.

He was dressed the way Cat always imagined a Gypsy might look: heavy green corduroy trousers, woolen yellow shirt, scuffed leather boots, a rust jacket with many pockets, and two small earrings glinting gold in each ear. His complexion was swarthy, an earthy brown, but his features were neither African nor Indian. They were finely boned, the nose slender, the cheekbones almost gaunt. His hair was black and curled to the collar of his jacket.

He was in the middle of frying flatcakes on the hot stones beside his fire. A small pot with steeping tea was perched on the rocks beside it. At his side was a traveler's pack, its contents spilled out around him. His eyes narrowed slightly as he studied her. Not until he seemed sure she was alone did he relax. His hand left the hilt of the knife.

"So," he said. "The woods sent forth their waif."

He smiled infectiously, and Cat found herself grinning back. Laughter lines crinkled around his eyes, and she saw that he was older than she'd initially taken him to be. She'd thought about twenty, what with the slender frame and the boyish tilt to his head. She adjusted that figure by about fifteen years.

"I hope you don't mind me barging in like this," she began.

"Not at all. I haven't had company for the better part of a fortnight. My name's Toby Weye. At your service. Care for some breakfast?"

"I . . . yes. Please. My name's Cat Midhir."

"A potent name."

"What do you mean?"

"I was told that these are the Katmeiny Hills. As in a multitude of cats. As in your name."

"Oh."

She made her way to the fire and smiled her thanks when he unfolded his blanket to give her a dry place to sit.

"So," Toby said as he flipped over the cakes. "Are you a native or a traveler? Or a traveling native? A native traveler?"

"A traveler. I come from"—she waved her hand in a general western direction—"back there."

"Ah. Do you want your tea plain, or with honey?"

"Honey, please."

"And are you fey?"

"I . . . what do you mean?"

"Fey. As in kin to elves and such. Magicky. Able to ride the wind and live in hills. To change your shape. To lure astray the lonely traveler. That sort of thing."

"No. I . . . I'm a storyteller."

"Ah."

Cat was finding it a little hard to keep up with him. He talked quickly, changing topics as the whim struck him. And his questions were curious, to say the least.

"What do you do?" she asked.

"I," he replied, handing her a steaming mug, "make a lovely cup of tea."

"No. I mean, I'm sure you do, but I was asking what you did for a living. Are you a Gypsy?"

"A tinker, a tailor. A Gypsy, a traveling man. You guessed by my pack?"

"Well, sort of. More from the way you look."

"Tinkerish, as it were?" Toby smiled and took a sip of his own tea.

"Yes."

"I'm afraid I must disappoint you. I *am* a traveling man, but not a tinker. And the reason I travel is that the Road calls to me—the Secret Road that wanders uphill and down, through this world and that."

He drew his flatcakes back from the fire's heat and leaned back against a stone to recite in a bardic fashion that put Cat in mind of Kothlen again.

> *What is the Road?*
> *Endless it can seem*
> *with darkness on the one hand*
> *and on the other:*
> *the Muse herself*
> *—three-faced by any name,*
> *secret as the thorns of roses*
> *and winter sharp,*
> *leaf-cloaked and older still*
> *in summer's heart.*
> *While underfoot*
> *the merry Road, the gentle,*
> *winds to where it waits:*
> *the light of an old dance,*
> *an old song*
> *—the hoofbeats of the Green Man*
> *sounding on hill and sward,*
> *his brow horned, the moon horned,*
> *the scattered notes of harp and pipes*
> *ringing wild across the hollow hills*
> *and beyond*
> *unto the moon's rim*
> *and beyond. . . .*

*And always,
there is the Road. . . .*

He cocked an eye at her and she nodded politely. "Do you know that Road?" he asked.

"I think so."

"It's the Green Man that makes it merry, for a merry fellow he is. But gentle it is too, as a place the fairies dance could be called gentle. Fey, do you see?"

"What do you hope to find when you get to the end?"

"But that's the thing!" Toby said. "It's following the Road is all. It has no end. Like Ouroborus— the great serpent swallowing its own tail. It's the doing, Mistress Cat, not the done. For once it's done, you've only to begin again, hey?"

"I think I understand now," Cat said. "I've just never heard it expressed quite like that before."

It was like her writing, she thought. Each book had its own theme, but there was one underlying thread that bound them all together, and each book took that thread—that Road—a little further along the way. If she ever got to the end, there wouldn't be anything left to write about. Maybe that was why she was having so much trouble now, what with—

"Have a cake?" Toby asked. "There's plenty. Honey or berries? Or both?" He held up a wooden bowl brimful of strawberries in one hand, a small clay honey jar in the other.

"Berries, please. You're very kind to share your breakfast with me."

"And you're very kind to stop and talk with me. That wood now." With his chin he pointed to the direction she'd come from. "Not this one here, but the one beyond the valley. It's through it that you've come?"

"Yes."

"And were there ghosts?"

Cat started. "What do you mean?"

"I was told to take the haunted wood, once I left these hills."

"That's Mynfel's wood."

Toby put an index finger along either side of his head and wiggled them. "She's one of the horned folk?" he asked.

Cat nodded.

"Then that's the way I'll be going. Pity you're heading the other way." He passed her a flatcake with berries rolling from it. "It's fingers only, I'm afraid."

"I'm not really going anywhere in particular," Cat said around a mouthful.

"Oh?" He looked her up and down. "You're not exactly equipped for wandering the wilds, are you?"

"It's a long story."

"That's right! You said you were a storyteller. I love to hear the flap of my own lips—comes from wandering about on my own so much, you see—but I like a story better, so off you go."

"Well, it's sort of difficult to explain. I come here when I fall asleep in my own world and—"

"But that," Toby said, "presupposes that *this* is a dream." He gave himself an exaggerated pinch. "I feel real to me."

"Yes, but . . ." Cat shook her head. "All I know is that when I go to sleep in the world I live in, I come here."

"As though it were a dream."

"I suppose."

"I've never heard of such a thing. Still, the Road can't be the same for everyone, or what a clutter there'd be on it. But do go on. I won't interrupt you again—at least not much."

"Well," Cat said. "It started when I was very young. . . ."

"One thing is certain," Toby said when she was done.

"What's that?"

"This isn't a dream. Because if it was, I wouldn't be real, and I most certainly am real. At least I was the last time I woke up." He shook his head. "But it certainly sounds very confusing. And not entirely pleasant. I don't like the thought of someone stealing my dreams. They're such . . . well, personal things, as it were. More tea?"

Cat nodded and handed him her cup. He filled it to the brim and spooned in a dollop of honey that made the liquid spill over the sides. Swishing the spoon about, he handed it back to her.

"This world is *like* a dream," he said suddenly. "I'll grant you that. For there are things here that fair take the breath away. Magicky things. I'm a conjuror myself, you see, but it's not the same thing at all." He held out his hand, palm open in front of her, then closed it. After tapping it with his free hand, he opened it once more to produce a small round ball. "Nothing fancy," he added. He swirled his fingers and the ball vanished. "But it's what I do."

Cat smiled. "That was very good."

"A pittance. A trifle. Merely warming up. What I really want to be is a mage. No more tricks and trickery. I want to be magic. I want to touch the heart of the world and make it smile. I want to be a friend of elves and live in a tree. Or under a hill. I want to marry a moonbeam and hear the stars sing. I don't want to pretend at magic anymore. I want to *be* magic.

"So you see, when I saw you stepping from amongst the trees—and making a dreadful racket in the brush while you were at it, I might add; a good sneaker you're not—but be that as it may, when I saw you I thought, now here's someone with magic. A fey waif if ever I saw one. And I was right, what with your hobnobbing it with elves and gnomes and such.

"But now I find it doesn't make any difference, because any moment you might wake up *there*, leaving me here with only the trees to talk to. Not exactly an inspiring proposition. Of course, I don't blame you, not one bit, but still . . . it's all rather frustrating."

He made three balls appear, juggled them for a moment, then put them away in one of the many pockets of his jacket. Next he produced a worn pack of cards, smiled ruefully, and stuck them in another pocket.

"I must sound very selfish," he said. "Here you are, with all sorts of very real problems, and here I am, playing the fool."

"Well, you've certainly made me feel better," Cat said. "*And* you're a good listener—when you're not talking yourself, that is."

"But still and all and this and that, I wish I could do something to help you. If I was a mage . . ." He leapt to his feet and struck a wizardly pose, then sat down again. "But I'm not."

"I can take you to Redcap Hill," Cat said, "where the gnomes used to live."

(Oh, Tiddy Mun—where are you?)

"Is it long?" Toby asked. "Is it far? Is it safe?"

"Yes and yes and . . ." Her face clouded. "I'm not sure. Probably not. I only saw Mynfel there, and she wasn't much help. Everybody else is gone."

"The winged shadow that dropped from the sky," Toby said, glancing up. "It's chased them all away. So safe it's not. But still . . ." He plucked his knife from the ground and brandished it. "Perhaps cold iron will stop it. Your fey friends wouldn't be able to handle iron, you see?"

"Do you think . . . ?"

"Often. But that's neither here nor there." He regarded her seriously. "We can only try, can't we?"

Cat nodded. "If I . . ." She was going to say *wake up*, but thought better of it. "If I should suddenly disappear on you . . . I'll be back. I'm not going to let him keep me away anymore. It doesn't matter who or what he is."

"Well said!"

Cat's enthusiasm came to an abrupt halt. "Why do you want to help me?" she asked.

"Why, if I help you with your dream thief, then surely in return you'll help me become magic, won't you? Shall we strike a bargain? Shall we clasp hands and cry, 'Done!'?"

Cat regarded him steadily, then reached over and shook his hand. "Done," she said.

"Then it's time we packed up and were on our way."

Detective Bill McKinty parked his car on Nepean Street and walked back to the corner of Bank, where a uniformed constable was waiting for him.

"Fredericks?" Bill asked as he approached.

The constable nodded. "He's on the bench in front of the take-out. The one in the middle."

Bill glanced across the street. There were three shabbily-dressed men sitting in front of the Friendly Corner Take-Out, their legs sprawled out on the sidewalk in front of them, their backs slouched against the back of the bench. As he watched, they passed a bottle in a paper bag from one to the other while accosting the occasional passerby for a handout.

He recognized Ron Wilson as the man turned to say something to one of his companions. Before crossing the street, Bill managed to identify the other two as well. Ralph "Redeye" Cleary was the one on the left with the rheumy eyes. The man on the right, with the smallpox scars on his cheeks, was Danny Farris.

"Thanks, Fredericks," Bill said, and started for the curb.

"You want a hand?

Bill shook his head. "I'm not taking them in. I just want to talk to Wilson."

He crossed the street and approached the trio from the rear. Leaning on the bench's wooden backrest, his hands near Ron's shoulders, he cleared his throat. Three heads turned.

"You two," Bill said, indicating Red-eye and Danny. "Blow."

Recognition dawned in their eyes, quickly replaced with guilt. Derelicts, Bill thought wearily, always looked guilty when you stopped them. All three started to rise, but Bill placed a hand firmly on Ron's shoulder, forcing him back onto the bench.

"Not you, Wilson."

Stuffing their paper-bagged mickey bottle in his pocket, Danny backed from the bench. He and Red-eye shuffled off, looking back over their shoulders as they went. Bill came around the bench to sit down beside Ron. He wrinkled his nose, but put a smile on his lips.

"I don't want no trouble," Ron began.

"No trouble," Bill agreed. "I just want to ask you a couple of questions about your late pal Farley, okay?" To ease Ron's nervousness, he dug a five-dollar bill out of his pocket and pressed it into the wino's hand. Greed overcame fear as Ron closed his tobacco-stained fingers around it.

"What'cha want to know?" he asked.

"You know how Farley died?" Bill began.

"I don't know nothing 'bout —"

Bill cut him off with a quick motion of his hand. "Ease up, Ron. Listen to the question before you answer it — got it?"

"Yeah," Ron mumbled, looking at his feet.

"What I want to know," Bill continued, "is whose bad books was Farley in? Who did he cross that likes to cut people up?"

Ron glanced sideways at the detective, then back at his feet. "Everybody got along with Farley," he said. "You know that. You must've checked his record, talked to a couple of the uniforms on the beat."

Bill nodded. "Okay. Farley got along just swell with everybody. That's why someone took out his throat with a knife."

"He's not the first," Ron said softly.

"Meaning?"

"Hell, you know Crazy Dick got it the same way in July. Somebody's out to get us — that's what I think. Somebody's trying to clean up the city. But we don't hurt nobody. You know that. What do they want to hurt us for?"

"Who's they?"

Ron shrugged. He looked past the detective to the end of the block, where Red-eye and Danny were hanging around, trying to look casual. Christ, Ron thought. He could use a shot of what was sitting in Danny's pocket.

"Farley ever talk about anybody out to get him personally?" Bill asked. "Did he sound at all nervous or scared lately?"

Ron started. "He was scared," he said, looking the detective in the eye. "He picked up a bad case of the heebs a couple of nights back. Kept talking about snakes. Or men with snake heads. I can't remember which."

"Snakes?"

Ron nodded.

"And that's it?"

"Yeah." But then Ron remembered something else. "There was this guy in the park yesterday—up by Tamson House. We were sitting around, taking it easy, when he walks by. Young fellow—maybe thirty, tops—blond hair, good-looking, wearing a real sharp suit. When Farley saw him, he damned near shit his pants. Looked like he'd seen a ghost or something. Damned near spilled the whole bott—er, the coffee we were drinking."

Bill ran Ron through the incident twice more, but couldn't get any more details out of him. "Anything else?" he asked, standing up.

Ron shook his head.

"Well, thanks, Ron. You take it easy. If I were you, I'd find someplace else to sleep at night—off the streets."

Ron shrugged. "I'm thinking of moving on. I got a cousin lives down in T.O. Maybe I'll give him a visit. I don't know."

"Okay, Ron. Thanks for your help. We'll see you around."

Ron looked down at how his fingers trembled where they gripped his knees. Not if I can help it, he thought. Not if I can fucking help it.

After Ben left, Peter tried to keep himself busy. He walked about, straightening books on their shelves, dusting, writing out a couple of checks and one order, rearranging his display tables. When he sat down behind the cash once more, he

found he'd killed no more than an hour. Business was slow—
business was invariably slow during the week—and he had
the store to himself for the most part, which left him with too
much time in which to worry and think.

He considered calling Cat more than once, but he'd left her
the note and knew she'd call when she got up. He tried to
read, but Tiddy Mun's face kept looking up at him from the
pages of the book. He thought about the way both Cat and
Ben took this vampire business so seriously.

He could almost understand Cat's embracing the theory—
no matter how outlandish it might seem in the light of day.
From what she told him, she'd already spent the better part of
her life flitting between the real world and the one of her
dreams. What was one more supernatural wonder to
her? Though horror might be a better way of putting it. But
Ben . . .

The way he and Ben had sat around this morning discuss-
ing the whole problem so seriously really bothered Peter.
What it was, he realized, was not really knowing for sure. It
was having to sit around and wait while doubt gnawed away
inside him. It was knowing, when he managed to muster his
beleaguered reason, that it was all crazy, but being afraid that
maybe it wasn't. For there was what he'd seen himself, and
what Ben had felt last night and in the park, and Cat and her
ghosts. Allowing Cat's prowler supernatural powers only
complicated an already confusing situation.

Sighing, Peter picked up his book once more.

"Where are you from, Toby?" Cat asked.

They were in Mynfel's wood, the oak trees towering high
above them as they walked through a green twilight. Toby
glanced at her and shrugged.

"From another world again," he said, "though when I came
here, I thought myself finally come home. My homeland is a
mountainous place called Ayrn and I lived in its Luckenhare
Dales. I did this and that for many's a year—from digging
graves to digging potatoes—but was never happy with what I
did. I was living in Kerr-on-the-Water, a town famed for its
cheeses and clockmakers, when I met up with a band of traveling folk and first took to the road. With a small *r*, I might
add.

"They were a merry company, and I lived with them for the

better part of five years. We had a juggler, a mime, three
acrobats, a strong man, and Elsie Telfer, who read fortunes. It
was Elsie who told me about the Secret Road—about the
borders between the worlds and how there were some places
where the Gentle Folk were to be found, and every third tree
hid a wizard."

When Toby spoke of borders, Cat thought of her own book
and its central character, Aldon, the Borderlord. Kothlen had
told her of him, antlered-browed and tall. "There are borders
between the worlds," Kothlen had said, "and each has its
guardian, its protector. They keep the unwary from straying,
and guard the magicks of the borders from those who would
put them to ill-use." From that her novel had grown. From a
tale of Kothlen's. A story. And now. . .

She stopped the turn of her thoughts. If there was an
Otherworld, why not several other worlds?

"What are these borders?" she asked.

"They're the places where the Road touches a world. Like
a gate, as it were. They can be tricky to find, but Elsie showed
me one outside Rosdun—that's on the way to Killydown-
fair. . . ." He paused and gave her a quick smile. "I don't
suppose the names mean anything to you, so I don't know
why I mention them. Still, be that as it may, the border Elsie
showed me was on a low hill just off the road outside Rosdun.
'Walk straight in betwixt those longstones,' she told me,
'and if you've the way set in your mind, and your heart
yearns strong enough, sure and you'll find the Road just
beyond them.'

"Well, I did just that—upped and came, and here I am, as
it were. I've been here the better part of a fortnight, just walking with only the wide open land and me. Then I came to the
hills. The last time I heard a voice, other than yours or my
own, was that same fortnight ago when I shared my supper
with a raggedy man on the Road who claimed to be a warden,
set there to warn folk from this very world."

"Why was he doing that?" Cat asked, feeling a sense of
déjà vu. It was like *The Borderlord* coming to life for her.

"Well, I think he was part mad and the other part fey,
myself. 'Too many magicks abroad,' he told me. 'But that's
why I've come,' I replied. And then, when he saw I would be
going whether he said no or not, he gave me what few directions I have. Named the Katmeiny Hills for me. Warned me

not to talk to strange waifs who popped out of the woods at breakfast time."

Cat laughed. "He didn't!"

"Ah, well. Perhaps not in so many words. But he was full of warnings, that one was, with his wild hair and tattered clothes and eyes like they'd looked once too often into the unknown. Gave me a proper fright he did, at times. If it wasn't for Elsie's foretellings, I might have turned back, there and then."

"What did she tell you?"

"That if I wanted real magicks, I must go to where magicks are real. That there was danger on the Road, but great joy as well. That I would arrive in the place I sought, but would not return." He gave her a wink. "Suitably nebulous, of course, but promising enough to send me packing and—"

"Here you are," Cat finished for him.

"Exactly. A wee touch older than when I left, but not a great deal wiser—though that doesn't worry me overmuch, for: 'If you wait long enough at the ferry, sooner or later you'll cross the river,' or something like that. Isn't it time you told me another story?"

"I suppose. What sort would you—"

But before she could finish her sentence, forest and companion were gone and she was crossing the borders between one world and another, as quick as a hawk dropping from the sky.

Cat woke up and regarded the familiar confines of her bedroom with a certain amount of regret. She should have felt exhausted from all the running around she'd done in her dream. Instead she felt rejuvenated. Newborn. She hadn't had a dream like that in so—

Kothlen's death stabbed through her. Kothlen. Gone forever. Tears brimmed her eyes. Tiddy Mun lost. Mynfel's lack of help. And Kothlen . . . Kothlen . . .

She rubbed at her eyes with her knuckles, trying to keep the tears at bay. Don't think about it, she told herself. Don't remember. She tried to concentrate on Toby Weye, on how meeting him helped to soothe her heartaches. Slowly the pressure eased into a dull ache. She had to go on. It was as simple as that. Otherwise she'd sink into a downward spiral from which she'd never escape.

Toby, she thought, holding on to her recent memories of the Otherworld as though they were a lifeline. What a character. Surely there was a story in her meeting him? If she could just get working, try to put the worries aside long enough to feel real again . . . But her brief stay in the Otherworld had been just an interlude. The troubles hadn't gone. Kothlen wouldn't come back. But if she tried, *really* tried . . .

She wondered if Peter was awake yet. Glancing at her bedside clock, she saw that she'd slept away the better part of the day: one o'clock. Peter'd be long gone. Slipping out of bed, she padded downstairs to make some coffee and found his note waiting for her at the bottom of the stairs.

Dear Cat,

Duty called and all that. Why don't you call me when you get up? Here's hoping you dreamed, and dreamed true.

best,
Peter

She read it through on the way into the kitchen and thought about how lucky she was to have some friends in *this* world finally. She liked Peter, but thinking of him brought Ben's features to mind. She remembered him sitting in her kitchen last night, all big and shy. She liked him too, only in a different way, and was pretty sure that he liked her—she had seen it in his eyes.

Thinking about him gave her a warm feeling inside. She was sure that a relationship with someone like him would be so much better than the disasters her others had been. The sudden urge to call him came then. She sat down at the kitchen table and pulled the phone over. Peter would know his number.

She picked up the receiver, ready to dial, then slowly set it back down again. What would she say to Ben if she *did* call him? What if she had just imagined that look in his eyes last night? What if he thought she was just some flake who happened to write books that he liked?

God, things could be confusing.

She stared at the phone for long moments, building up her

nerve. I'll just get his number from Peter first, she thought. Then I can decide from there. She reached for the phone again, but it jangled just before she touched it, almost lifting her from her seat. Feeling as though she'd been caught in the act of she didn't know what, she picked it up before it could ring a second time.

"Hello?"

"Uh... hello, Cat. This is... uh... Ben—uh, Ben Summerfield, and I was... uh..."

"I was just thinking about you."

There was a moment's silence on the other end of the line, then Ben asked, "You were?"

For some reason the surprise in his voice and his shyness made Cat feel less shy herself. "I was just going to call Peter to ask him for your number."

"You were?" Ben repeated, then he seemed to catch himself. "Jeez, that's great. I mean, well, what I was calling for was to, uh, ask you if you'd maybe like to go to a movie or something with me tonight, maybe."

The warm feeling that Cat had felt thinking about him earlier seemed to blossom inside her. "I'd love to."

"You would? That's great! Would you like to go for dinner before the movie?"

"That'd be really nice, Ben."

Cat could feel him grinning from the other end of the line, which made her smile.

"I guess I'll pick you up around six," he said. "Would that be okay?"

"Sure. Six would be fine. I'm glad you called, Ben."

"Me too." He seemed about to say good-bye, but then he cleared his throat. "I was talking to Peter this morning," he said, "and he inadvertently let out this thing about your dreams."

Cat thought she'd die. Her pleasure at talking to him went cold inside her. "He... what?" she asked in a small voice.

"He didn't mean to," Ben said quickly. "We were just talking about the Dude and last night and stuff and—well, I just wanted to let you know that, while I'm not sure I understand it all, I'm backing you all the way. And I'm not just saying that to humor you, Cat."

"I..." She didn't know what to say.

"I thought it was important to let you know that I knew—just to be, you know, up front about it all." He hesitated, waiting for her to say something. When there was no reply, he went on. "Look, if you, uh, want to call off tonight, I'll understand."

"It's not that," she managed finally. "It's just . . . I don't know . . ."

"You're not mad, are you?"

Cat thought about it, and realized that what she felt was relief, mixed with a certain amount of embarrassment, but relief all the same. "No, I'm not mad," she said. "I'll see you tonight, okay?"

After they said their good-byes, Cat put the receiver down and stared at the phone. Strangely enough, everything did feel fine. For all her embarrassment, the pressures inside her had eased as though someone had just pulled the plug on the tension that had been winding her up so tight. Peter . . . Thinking about him now, she had an inkling of where he was coming from. He hadn't betrayed their friendship. No. He'd just decided to play matchmaker.

Shaking her head, she reached for the phone again and dialed the number for the store.

Peter looked across the store after he hung up and thought, Doesn't that beat all? Imagine Ben telling Cat about their talk this morning. But that was Ben, always up front about everything.

Had anyone asked Peter how Cat would react to the news that someone else knew about her secrets, someone she hadn't told, he would have said that she could very easily withdraw into her shell again. He wouldn't have taken the chance of mentioning a word to her about it himself—not until she brought it up first. But Ben . . . well, he had to be doing something right. Instead of being mad, Cat had actually sounded happy. And it was obvious that she was looking forward to her date with him tonight.

Peter smiled, relaxing for the first time all day. Maybe they'd soon be seeing an end to ghosts and Otherworlds—and to weird guys hiding in the shadows, waiting to steal peoples' dreams. Christ, he hoped so.

"Snakes?" Potter asked.

Bill was sitting across the desk from him, filling Potter in on his interview with Ron Wilson. The pencil in Potter's hand beat its inevitable tattoo against the pad in front of him. Bill looked up from his notes and nodded.

"That's what Wilson said. Snakes, or a man with a snake's head."

"Shit. What's that supposed to mean?"

"Only thing I can think of is voodoo," Bill said.

Potter grinned at him. "Right."

"C'mon, Potsy. You think I buy that? But what I *am* thinking is, if we've got a wacko, or a bunch of wackos that *do* believe . . ."

"I see what you mean. They can do as much damage as the real thing. We got anything along those lines?"

"It's being run through Ceepik right now," Bill replied.

"What about this guy in Central Park?"

"I was getting to that. I did some checking around the hospitals, and the first place I hit, bingo! A young woman was brought into the Civic late yesterday evening by the name of"—he consulted his notes—"Lisa Henderson. She was found in a catatonic state in Dundonald Park last night, and died early this morning. She had no history of emotional disorders or that kind of thing. The doctor I talked to said it was like her body just shut down."

The pencil went still in Potter's hand. "And?"

Bill smiled. "I went up to the park and had a look around, talked to a few people. A"—he checked his notes again—"Mr. Winters remembers seeing Henderson in the park last night with a young guy —"

"Blond-haired, well-dressed . . ."

"Not exactly. Winters was out walking his dog at the time. Says he didn't get all that good a look. Henderson's companion was dark-haired, casually dressed. What Winters remembers is his eyes—forceful, he called them. A piercing blue. Said the guy just glanced at him and he felt like those eyes went right through him. Gave him a creepy feeling like"—Bill read from his notes—"he'd 'put his hand in a nest of snakes.' That's what made it click for me."

Potter frowned. His instincts were buzzing up a storm. "What do you think, Bill? Is it worth putting an APB out on him?"

Bill shrugged. "I don't know, Potsy. We'd need both descriptions. Wilson didn't say anything about weird eyes, but—"

"I've got a feeling," Potter said.

"It's not a hell of a lot to go on."

"Don't I know it? But what else have we got? At least we can have the uniforms keep an eye out for him."

12
⤫

the hunt begins

DEBBIE FELT OVERDRESSED when they arrived at Stella's apartment. Where she and Rick were dressed for the office—he in a summer-weight light-brown suit, she in a knee-length slitted skirt, designer blouse, nylons, and high heels—Stella looked enviably comfortable in a pair of hip-hugging jeans and a dusty rose T-shirt.

"Hi," Stella said brightly, stepping aside so that they could come in. "Glad you could make it."

She closed the door and locked it. Rick mumbled something, and Debbie thrust out her hand to Stella.

"Hello, yourself," she said. "I'm Debbie Mitchell."

Stella shook without any firmness to her grip. "Nice to meet you," she said.

Something about her made Debbie pause. It was in her eyes. They had a not-quite focused look about them. Maybe she'd been building up her nerve by smoking a joint or starting early on the drinks. She could do with a drink herself, Debbie decided. Then she saw that a fourth person had been added to their cozy threesome.

"Rick and . . . um, Debbie," Stella said. "This is Lucius Marn."

Gorgeous was the first word that Debbie came up with to describe him. But then, just as Stella's eyes belied the cheerful hostess image she was trying to put across, this man's eyes radiated cold, raw power. There was a fresh scar on his cheek that lent him an even more fiendish air.

She sat down on the couch across from Lysistratus and nodded hello. She could hear Rick ask Stella in a stage whisper, "Who the hell's he?" Lysistratus ignored him, and Debbie missed Stella's reply. She was too busy watching Lysistratus watch her. All his attention was focused on her, and she was beginning to feel more than a little uncomfortable. She was used to being stared at—liked it, in fact, so long as it didn't get too weird. *This* was getting weird.

She tugged her skirt hem down to her knees, but couldn't concentrate on what she was doing. Those blue eyes, crystalline and compelling, seemed to draw her right out of herself. She felt as though she were falling into darkness. The last thing she heard was Rick's voice, edged with concern.

"Debbie? Hey, Debbie? Are you all right?"

No, she wasn't all right. But she couldn't answer because her vocal chords were paralyzed and every bone in her body had turned to jelly. Her head slumped back against the couch's cushions.

Lysistratus was in a good mood.

The woman was remarkably well-endowed, but she had an appeal beyond her obvious physical attractions. There was a vitality in her that promised strong dreams. She had a defined sense of self as well, though it was weakened by a willingness to care for others. The potential for too much loyalty—to her friends, to the human race in general—lay inside her. Such attributes were liabilities for what Lysistratus had in mind. Regrettably, she would be useful for nourishment only. But her companion . . .

He was an excellent specimen. A strong sense of self ran through him, a loutish concern for himself above all others. He lived for sensual gratification, which made him a perfect subject for Lysistratus's uses.

Debbie was quick to fall under his influence, unconscious moments after he'd made eye contact and touched her mind.

Later he would make her sleep and dream. Later she would gratify his needs in ways that Rick could never imagine. But first he must deal with Rick.

"Debbie? Hey, Debbie? Are you all right?"

Rick bent over her worriedly, then turned to look at Stella. She regarded him blankly, as though her mind had shut down. Frowning, he turned to Lysistratus. The parasite was waiting for him, eyes flaring with power, a thin smile on his lips.

What's with this guy? Rick thought. He looks like he wants to—

Pain exploded in Rick's skull. A cold fire spun through his body like a vortex, centering in his groin. His mind flooded with apocalyptic visions that ranged from Miltonesque hellscapes to the final horror of his own death. He saw his face deteriorate with age, his body become frail and brittle. Death came to him, moment by inexorable moment, until he was nothing but bones and a mouldering skull fit only to house maggots and worms, until bone became dust, and no trace of the man he'd been remained at all.

In the lifespan of the universe he was shown to be less than a mote, his life as pointless and inconsequential to the overall order of things as some one-celled microscopic organism's life was to his. The truth settled in him and he fled screaming deep inside himself, desperate to escape it.

But wait, a voice called softly in his head, drawing him back to view other possibilities. *It doesn't have to be like that.*

New imagery cascaded through his wounded soul. He saw life unending, saw himself wielding power over others until he was godlike in his stature. He learned how the life essence of his fellow men could feed his own immortal soul. He saw himself savagely coupling with overpowered partners, debasing them as he took and took, giving nothing in return, leaving them as less than nothing, while he grew stronger still.

Imagine the pleasure, the voice whispered to him, *of loosing your seed into a victim as you feed on their soul.*

Lysistratus knew Rick, knew just what was needed to play the man like a marionette.

The apocalypse inside Rick lay forgotten. Aging and his own inevitable death faded until all he could see was the proffered power. Greedy, Rick reached for it, understanding that it lay dormant in each and every human soul. It was a dark core of self, fueled by the primal instinct of self-preservation above all other considerations. An evil that needed only a key to be unleashed inside him. A key that he was now offered.

But remember, the cold voice inside him warned. *What I have given, I can take back.* Then slowly the presence withdrew from his mind.

Rick staggered, staring wildly about as his eyes came back into focus. The dark knowledge, the power seeded in him, muttered sibilantly in the back of his mind. He stepped up to Stella, lifting trembling hands to cup her face. The power reared inside him. A pulse fed through his hands like liquid fire as her energies filled him, roiling inside him, lifting him to a crescendo that he could no longer bear.

He dropped his hands and stared stupidly at them while the stolen strength rushed through him—ambrosial, a sweetness that made him want to weep with the pleasure of its taste inside him. He regarded Lysistratus with tears blurring his gaze.

"Jesus fuck," he mumbled. "It . . . I . . ."

Lysistratus smiled. He had felt that same blind euphoria when he had come into his own power. His mentor had been Agis, a scholar of Delos whom he met in the agora of the Delians in the same year that the island broke free of neighboring Naxos—Agis, who would still be alive today if he hadn't had a falling out with an actor in Athenae and been stupid enough to drink wine laced with hemlock when it was offered to him.

The actor had thought himself a good friend of Lysistratus's before he died.

The parasite had rarely shared his gift with anyone else in the ensuing years. He knew too well how easily it could backfire on him. But sometimes it was necessary—though in each such case, the favors had been taken back once their recipients had served their purpose. Lysistratus had learned the lesson that Agis never had.

"What . . . what do I have to do to . . . to keep this?" Rick asked.

Lysistratus laughed. "Nothing you won't enjoy."

More images filled Rick's mind—faces, thought patterns. Coupled with them was the information he would need to track them down. A feral light glittered in Rick's eyes as he turned to leave. He paused at the door as Lysistratus called after him.

"You can do what you want with the others," the parasite

said, "but the woman's mine."

Rick grinned. "Sounds like a good deal to me."

"Oh, it is," Lysistratus said as the door closed. He turned his attention to the two women—Debbie lying slack on the couch, Stella weaving where she stood, eyes blind though they were open and staring. "It's a real bargain."

Tiddy Mun crept out from under the refuse he'd been hiding in all day, changing from cat shape to gnome then back again. His every nerve was stretched taut as a bowstring. The night had come, and it was time for him to begin his search. But now that the moment was at hand, he wasn't sure he could go through with it.

The shadows surrounding him were dark—more so because of the pools of too-bright light just beyond them. Anything could be lying in wait for him. There was too much noise beyond the alleyway, too many iron dragons, too many shadows. Too much of everything and not enough of him. He was only one very small and frightened gnome.

At length the alleyway itself became oppressive, and he ventured out beyond its mouth, onto the street. He cast back and forth, trying to find the one mind among the many that he was looking for. He pictured the banded hair, the knife blade, the courage. . . . When he found it at last, he hurried off, hugging the walls of the buildings. He threw many a backward glance over his shoulder, his little heart pounding hard in his chest through the whole nightmare journey.

The ending went as perfectly as either Cat or Ben could have hoped it would.

They had a leisurely dinner at Tramps—one of the many trendy restaurants that were slowly taking over the Old Market area. Both of them enjoyed the decor—which consisted mainly of floor-to-ceiling bookcases loaded with old, leatherbound volumes—and their roast beef. From there they drove to the Westgate Shopping Mall and waited in line with a hundred other people to see Spielberg's *E.T.* They laughed and cried in all the same places and came out holding hands, feeling the warmth of a shared experience and a new closeness.

On the way home to Cat's house the conversation turned to her dreams, and she found herself talking more freely to Ben about them than she could have to anyone a week ago. Maybe she was just getting used to it, she thought, seeing how often she'd talked it through in the past few days.

"I had a lovely time, Ben," she said when Ben pulled the cab up in front of her house. "I'd like to do it again."

"Me too. Are you going to be okay? Are you sure you don't want someone to stay with you?"

Cat nodded. "After the beating he took from your friend Mick, I don't think he'll be coming around for a long time."

Without talking about it, they seemed to have both come to the same decision to take things slowly. Cat put her hand on the door handle, then paused to look back at Ben.

"Are you free tomorrow night?" she asked. "I thought maybe we could have dinner at my place, if you'd like."

"I'd like that a lot."

Cat hesitated a moment, then leaned forward and kissed Ben's cheek. Before he could react, she whispered a quick good night and was out of the car. Ben sat for a moment, watching her go up the walk to her front porch. A silly grin spread over his face as he pulled away from the curb.

Cat turned at the door, not stepping inside until his taillights winked out of sight. As she closed the door, she was welcomed by Ginger and Pad, weaving in and out between her legs and crying for their elevenses snack. After feeding them she puttered about the kitchen awhile, then finally went upstairs to her study, where she sat down to reread the twelve pages she'd written that afternoon.

Twelve pages! And they were still good, all these hours later.

She smiled as she laid them aside. Putting out the light, she started to get ready for bed, but a creepy feeling stole over her. She felt as though there were eyes on her. The feeling got so bad that she didn't want to even undress for bed.

This is stupid, she told herself. But the feeling wouldn't go away. She should have asked Ben in, she realized. But it was too late for that now. She padded into her study and peered out the window at the street. Surely he couldn't be back—could he? Mick had really hurt him.

Yes, a small voice said inside her. But if he's really the creature you think he is, would that stop him?

She couldn't see anybody out on the street, but the feeling persisted until she had to go downstairs into the kitchen. The cats were already flaked out for the night on the couch in the living room. Great company. She paced back and forth, peered out the kitchen windows, then out the front. Every creak and noise of the old house made her start. Finally she gave in.

She went to the phone, thought of calling Ben. She dialed Peter's number instead. When he came on the line she had a moment of complete paralysis—this was so dumb—but then she managed to speak.

"Is your . . . is your couch free tonight?" she asked.

Peter's voice immediately sounded worried. "What's the matter, Cat? Is he—"

"No. It's just nerves—I hope. Do you mind?"

"Not at all. C'mon over."

By the time she was sitting in Peter's living room, she felt more foolish than ever, but it was better than going bonkers in her own house, she told herself firmly.

"How was your evening?" Peter asked.

For a moment Cat didn't say anything. She took a breath, let it out, then leaned back on the couch.

"It was good," she said finally. "Really good. Ben's . . . well, he's a little old-fashioned, but then so am I. We had a really good time."

"How come you didn't call him? Not that I mind, but . . ,"

Cat sighed. "It just all seems so stupid. I mean, there couldn't have been anybody there, but I just got the creeps. I thought of calling Ben, but I didn't want to come across as a complete flake. Not if we're going to . . . not if anything's going to come of this."

"You really like him?"

She nodded.

"That makes me feel good," Peter said. "You're both good folks. I'm glad you hit it off."

"You mean old Mr. Matchmaker likes to see a job well done."

"Now you sound like Ben."

Cat laughed. "He's got a name for everybody. You know what he calls you?"

"Peter Baird, the Bookstore Laird."

"I wonder what he'll come up with for me."

"Cat the Brat," Peter said.

Cat laughed harder, and Peter joined in. When they caught their breath, he looked at her for a long moment.

"Things are going better now, aren't they?" he asked.

Cat nodded. "I've started writing again—twelve pages

today. And except for a bad case of nerves tonight, I guess things are looking up."

They talked some more, neither of them bringing up the man that Mick and Ben had chased off last night, then Peter finally stood up and called it a night.

After he'd gone into the bedroom, Cat changed her clothes for an old flannel shirt that she liked to sleep in, and got into her makeshift bed on the couch. She lay awake for a while, thinking of Ben, then wondered if she'd dream tonight, and if she did, whether she'd find herself back at Redcap Hill or in the part of Mynfel's wood where she'd left Toby. She drifted off, still wondering.

Mick stretched out full-length on his bed, leaning his head against the headboard with a pillow propped under him. Christ, he was beat. And his head. He had a headache that just wouldn't quit. One of Honey Bane's early punk singles, "Boring Conversations," was playing at low volume on the stereo.

"Want me to turn that off?" Becki asked as she came into the room.

Mick shook his head, grimacing as the movement set up a new wave of pain.

"You look like shit, you know that?"

"I feel like shit," he replied.

Becki came to sit on the side of the bed. She pulled a bent joint out of the back pocket of her jeans, straightened it, and regarded it critically. When she was satisfied that it had survived her pocket, she offered it to Mick.

"Want some?"

Mick thought about it for a moment. It was either going to help his headache or make it worse. "Fuck it," he said, and reached for the joint.

Becki gave him a light and they passed the joint back and forth until the roach was too small to handle.

"Well?" Becki asked.

"Got any more?"

Becki produced two more from the same pocket and Mick grinned. Already he felt better.

Ben was still beaming by the time he got home. He was too wound up to go to bed right away, so he spent a couple of hours poring over various books he'd picked up at the library that afternoon. They dealt with vampiric lore—both fictional-ized accounts and supposed fact—but he didn't come up with anything that related to his own experiences with the Dude, didn't come up with anything even vaguely useful.

By then he was tired enough to hit the sack, and he fell asleep thinking of Cat and the evening he'd just spent with her. And dinner tomorrow night . . .

It was close to two in the morning when he woke up, not really sure if he was still asleep and dreaming, or if he had indeed woken up. There was a steady rhythmic pressure on his pillow, like a cat kneading it with its forepaws, except—

I don't have a cat, Ben thought.

He turned with a sudden movement. An icy chill started up his spine. There was nothing there. He put out a hand and gingerly touched the pillow. It lay there unmoving and very pillowlike. He stared at it for long moments. Slowly the prickle of fear subsided and he breathed easier.

A dream. Not as weird as the one the other night, but still just a dream. Thinking too much of a different kind of Cat.

He was about to lie down once more when a soft golden glow rose up from the pillow. It swirled into a ball-like shape, hung suspended before his stunned gaze for a few shocked moments, then shot down the hallway into his living room. A cold sweat broke out on him as he watched it go.

Ghosts of the evening's reading preyed on his nerves. What he'd just seen had nothing to do with what he'd been reading, but it belonged to the same realm—that of the impossible. It was one thing to suppose that these sorts of things might be real. Quite another to experience them.

Then he heard a sound from the living room. A scratching noise, as though something was worrying at his window screen. He stared down the hallway, every night fear he'd ever had choosing that moment to return to him. It wasn't a loud sound. More a spectral whisper. As though something was trying to get in.

He waited for it to stop, praying to a God he'd abandoned in public school. The Dude's features rose in his mind's eye. Last night's helplessness returned in a rush. He was out there. The monster was real, and he was out there. Trying to get in. And neither a locked door nor his screened windows were going to keep something like him out for long.

He shot a glance at the phone. He could try to call someone—Mick, the cops—but by the time they arrived, he realized, it'd be all over. He could try to sneak out the back way, but that would leave him exposed and alone in the middle of the park, dressed in his skivvies, with nowhere to hide.

"Jesus," he whispered into the cloying darkness. "What am I going to do?"

There was an umbrella that someone had left in his cab, leaning in the corner by his dresser. Taking a deep breath, he eased out of bed and fetched it. With the umbrella clutched in his sweaty hand, he started down the hallway—better to face his fears becoming real than to just lie there, waiting for it to come to him. The scratching sound grew louder with each step he took. His bladder threatened to release the liquid it had stored while he slept. As he neared the darkened doorway that opened into the living room, it was all he could do to keep moving.

I'm going to die, he thought.

Holding the umbrella so tightly that his knuckles went white, he edged forward. He raised his makeshift weapon in front of him and entered, gaze snapping to the window. For a long moment he stared at the silhouetted figure outlined by the streetlights. Then slowly his fear ran from him.

"A cat," he said, "A frigging tomcat!"

He crossed the room and tapped the handle of his umbrella against the window beside the screen.

"Shoo!" he cried. The umbrella went clack, clack. "Bugger off, you!"

His attempts at chasing it off only increased the cat's scratching. It rose on its hind legs, caught its claws high in the screen and hung like it was being crucified. Ben shook his head and went up the stairs to the door. There was no accounting for some animals. Especially cats. Did it think it was going to earn a saucer of cream for this performance?

He opened the door and waved the umbrella at the animal. "Go on! Get out of here!"

The cat pulled free from the screen with the calm assurance of never having been actually caught in the first place, and faced Ben. The reflective layer behind its retinas glowed red as they caught the glare of the streetlights.

"I mean it!" Ben cried. "Go on!"

It leapt off the low windowsill, straight up at him. For a moment Ben flashed on his dream, on last night, on cats attacking—

He jumped back, startled by the animal's unexpected move, and it dodged between his legs, darting down the stairs and into his apartment. Ben swung the umbrella at it—a half second too late.

"Shit! Look," he told it as he followed it down into his living room. "You can't stay in here, okay?" Christ, what if it was rabid or something? "Why don't you just go back to whatever alleyway you crawled out of and . . ."

His voice trailed off.

The big tom was up on its hind legs again, but this time there was no screen for it to claw. Instead its body shimmered. A ripple ran through it the way an image reflected on water undulates when it's disturbed. Then the cat was gone, replaced by a small skinny man with large watchful eyes and a wild mat of hair.

The change left Ben staring slack-jawed. The umbrella fell from a suddenly limp grip and clattered to the floor. He wanted to bend down to pick it up, but didn't dare take his gaze from the strange manifestation in front of him, wasn't sure he'd even be able to get back up because his legs were feeling so shaky. . . .

"Please," the little man said. "I mean no harm. I am Cat's friend."

Cat's friend. Jesus. A minute ago it *was* a cat! But then what it had said sunk in. Not *a* cat's friend, but Cat Midhir's friend. Jesus H.! This was her little gnome from the Other-world that Peter had told him about.

Ben felt as though his world was tumbling down around his ears. This was too much. Never mind his telling Peter to keep an open mind. This . . . He realized suddenly that the creature standing there in front of him was as scared as he was. While it didn't make him feel any braver, it did make him feel marginally better.

"You're . . ." Ben searched for the name. "You're Tiddy Mun?"

A small hopeful smile touched the little man's lips. He nodded eagerly. Slowly Ben sank to the floor and leaned back against the stairs. Another moment and he would have toppled over.

"What're you doing here?" he asked. He was probably still dreaming. He'd only *thought* he'd woken up. "What do you want from me?"

"I've come to warn you," Tiddy Mun replied. "Your

friend . . ." He spread his thumb and index finger and move his hand along the top of his head, going from the point of hi hairline to the nape of his neck, aping Mick's Mohawk. "Wit the banded hair. He is in danger."

They were going to play charades now? Ben thought "Who?" he asked loudly. "Mick?"

The little man shrugged. The name meant nothing to him He repeated the motion of his hand.

"He was with you last night—he had the knife of colc iron. Tonight the evil stalks him. I . . . I would have warnec him, but I'm too scared." He pointed to Ben. "You're strong. Big. You can help him."

Rick cruised the streets after leaving Stella's apartment, trying to come to grips with what he'd experienced. It was like being high all the time, but a better high than any he'd ever had before. It was like a coke rush, but it was a constant thing, without the numbness. And Christ, did it feel good. With this kind of power . . .

Look out world, Kirkby's on prowl. Lock up your babes, 'cause as sure as Santa Claus likes his milk and cookies, this dude likes his tits and nookie.

It was well past midnight when he got down to some serious business. First stop was a bistro in Hull, where he used his new moves on some sweet young thing. She was outside, in the back of his car with her dress up around her neck, almost before he could snap his fingers.

That's the way I like it, he thought, driving back into Ottawa after dumping the girl in the parking lot—dazed, but relatively unhurt. No point in making waves. Not when a man's got work to do. But later . . . He pulled the rearview mirror down so that he could check himself out. Looking good. Time to really boogie now.

It was going on two when he pulled up at the curb about a half block down from his first stop. This was where the punk lived—the one that had knifed Lucius. With rudimentary skill he reached out with his mind as Lucius had shown him, reassuring himself that the punk was there. Humming to himself, he stepped onto the pavement and headed for the house.

With a pair of wire cutters he snipped the phone lines where they entered the building. Glancing back to the street, he saw that he remained unobserved, and headed for the back of the house. The wire cutters went back into his pocket. He'd get the knife he was going to use in the asshole's kitchen.

He was still humming under his breath—Paul Anka's "My Way"—as he moved down the laneway that separated the punk's house from its neighbor.

Help Mick? Ben thought. If Tiddy Mun had been the Dude, Ben wouldn't even have been able to help himself.

"We have to hurry!" Tiddy Mun urged him.

"Yeah. Sure."

Think, he told himself. What do I do? Call Mick. He headed for the bedroom, getting dressed while he dialed. All he got was a busy signal.

"Shit."

Now what? Call the cops? And tell them what? You see, there's this vampire loose and he's going to kill my friend. Well, not a real vampire, this guy sucks out your soul instead of lapping your blood, but you're dead all the same when he's done with you. Right. That'd go over just great. Okay. How about there's this prowler? He shook his head. They'd only ask how *he* knew. Mick's apartment was on Third Avenue, south and across Bank Street from where Ben lived. About a block from Bronson. That was a good mile at least. So how did he know there was a prowler loose way the hell over there? Well, you see, this little gnome told me. . . .

He dialed again, but still got a busy signal. What if the phone was off the hook? Or the line had been cut? Did vampires think about things like cutting phone lines? He rubbed his temples, trying to relieve the tension headache that had started up. He glanced at his uninvited guest. He had trouble believing any of this was real.

He rang Mick's number a third time, but knew as he was dialing that he was just putting off the inevitable. When it came right down to it, he had to go himself. No intermediaries. When the busy signal came on the line again, driving the point home, he slammed the phone down and hurried down the hall. Jerking open the door to the hall closet, he scrabbled around through a mess of winter boots, stacks of magazines, and old coats until he found his baseball bat. Hefting it, he started for the door, not even wanting to think about what he might have to do with it.

"Are you coming?" he called over his shoulder.

But Tiddy Mun was already following at his heels.

* * *

Rick came to a window and peered in. A bedroom. Illuminated by a light on the floor somewhere. Lying on the bed was the punk he'd come for. And lying beside him . . .

Well, now, Rick thought. We might have us some real fun here. Got to kill 'em both, no question about that. But a babe like her deserves a bit of a send-off before we stick the old blade in. She deserves to be stuck with something else first, and Rick had just the thing to do the job. He was getting hard just thinking about it.

He continued on to the back door. Just knowing he could do anything now—any fucking *thing*—made him want to try it all. He'd thought about killing someone before, wanted to a time or two, but it just wasn't something you did. They locked you up and threw away the key for that kind of shit. But now . . .

Oh, man. I can do anything. And I'll be doing it forever.

Mick was high, plain and simple. He held Becki loosely in his arms and drifted in a pleasant limbo that owed nothing to the reality that scratched away at the four walls that sheltered them. He had to have a leak, but couldn't summon the energy to get up from the bed. His headache was gone now. Everything was gone but the buzz.

Dy-no-mite weed, he thought. Just what he'd needed.

Turning his head slowly, he saw that all Becki was wearing was a T-shirt—one of his. He looked down at his own body. He wasn't even wearing that much. He remembered their lovemaking and smiled. He touched one of her nipples and felt it harden through the material of the shirt.

"Mmm," she murmured, snuggling closer.

"Love ya, babe," he said softly, brushing her forehead with his lips.

The back door was a pain, but Rick managed to jimmy its lock without too much noise. Easing it open, he slipped through, making sure it locked again behind him. Got to lay it on them with the eyes, he reminded himself as he moved carefully through the darkened kitchen.

He found the knife sitting on a breadboard and hefted it, enjoying the weight of it in his hand. He could feel the excitement build up inside him. It was like nothing he'd ever experienced before. He was so hard now he thought he'd drop his load right there in the kitchen.

* * *

Ben slammed the door to his apartment and ran for his cab. Tossing the baseball bat onto the front seat, he started the car with a roar. Tiddy Mun, who'd been approaching the vehicle nervously, lunged for the bushes beside Ben's apartment at the sound.

"It's all right," Ben called to him. "It's just . . . just a wagon without a horse."

Tiddy Mun sidled out of the bushes, saucer eyes wider than ever. A wagon? It was an iron dragon. He'd seen these monsters on the streets, swallowing and disgorging tallfolk, and feared their metal hides almost as much as he did the evil that stalked the Otherworld.

When he'd crept to within a few feet of Ben's door, Ben reached down, and grabbing him under the arms, hauled him in. Tiddy Mun shuddered at the proximity of so much of the cold metal. His teeth chattered against each other. He perched on the seat, trying hard not to touch anything but its vinyl covers, eyes blinking furiously.

Shoving the gearshift into first, Ben peeled away from the curb. Tiddy Mun moaned beside him.

The door to the bedroom slammed open, shredding Mick's contentment as though a bear's paw had just raked across his chest. For a long moment of drug-induced stupor, he just stared at the intruder. The suit and short hair registered, the clean-shaven cheeks and the knife, the eyes. . . . The eyes were like the Dude's had been last night, icy and glittering. They pulled him down into their depths, turning everything inside him into jelly.

He was dimly aware of Becki rising from the bed, of the intruder striking her. She staggered across the room and brought the stereo down when she landed against it. As she rose again, the intruder hit her with the hilt of the knife closed in his fist. Her head struck the side of the bed as she tumbled to the floor.

Mick tried to get up, but the eyes held him immobile. He fought their influence, but now they were inches from his face, impossible to avoid, fish cold and penetrating. Mocking him. There was a weight on his chest. He remembered the knife, tried to call up the rage, the anger he needed to fight the spell of the intruder's eyes, but all that replied was a vast darkness without relief.

* * *

The tall and stately giants of Mynfel's wood reared all around Cat, hallowed in their green silence. She knew instinctively that this was where she'd left Toby yesterday afternoon. Before she had a chance to look for him, she heard something stir behind her.

"Mistress Cat!" a now-familiar voice hailed her.

"Hello, Toby." She turned and smiled to see his cocky grin. "Have you been waiting all this time?"

"Indeed, indeed. I could only hope you'd return from wherever it was that you'd gone. How was your day?"

"Fine. No, it was great. The first really good day I've had in a long time."

"I'm happy for you," he said. "But happier to see you back. This is a strange wood, no mistaking it, and I've not felt quite . . . well, *right* the whole time I've been waiting."

"This from a man who wants to find real magic?"

"Ah, yes. Well, there is that. Shall we walk while we talk?"

Cat stood quietly for a moment to get her bearings. She always knew the way to Redcap Hill; it tugged at her, as though an invisible thread bound them.

"I've had a thought or two," Toby offered once they'd started walking. "About what you were telling me before you left. It was a curious tale, all things considered, and if I hadn't seen you vanish with my own two eyes, I might well have discounted the whole thing as I waited for you to get back. But be that as it may, once you did disappear—without so much as a puff of smoke—it put a whole new light on to an already incredible tale."

"You didn't believe me?" Cat asked.

"Now I didn't say that. I was merely stating that I had one or two reservations—very small reservations, mind you, but there they were all the same. I knew your being here couldn't be a dream, because that would make me nothing more than a figment of your imagination—a rather dismal prospect, you'll have to admit yourself. At least from my point of view. What I did consider was that this other world of yours might be a dream."

He shot a glance at her to see how she was taking it all, but the poor light made it hard to gauge her reaction.

"Of course," he added, "then you upped and vanished—clinching your story, as it were. So then I thought, with my back up against these old and magic trees and the better part of a day and the evening to think in, that you were in the unenviable position of trying to exist in two separate realities. I tried to imagine what it would be like, and decided it would be confusing."

"It hasn't always been easy," Cat admitted. "I tend to concentrate on one world at a time, to the eventual harm of the other. It's hard to balance what I want to put into them. Sometimes I want more of one, sometimes more of the other."

"I can see how that might happen. Have you ever tried to stay in just one?"

"But I don't want to! They're both equally important to me."

"Ah."

"Besides, I don't think I could. I don't think it works that way. I don't even know how it *does* work. I've never really had any problem existing in both—nothing serious, that is—until whatever it is that's been stealing my dreams showed up. That weird man. He's the one that's spoiling it all."

"When I think of him," Toby said, "I feel a cold chill run up my spine."

"Me too. But I have to deal with him somehow. I just don't know where to begin."

They walked in silence for a while, letting the peace of the forest settle the uneasiness that both of them felt when they thought of the dream thief.

"Another curious thing," Toby said suddenly. "The horned lady whose wood this is—you said her name was Mynfel?"

"Yes. Why?"

"I just find it odd, that's all. I would have thought she'd be named Derowen, for the oaks. Or even Avallen, for the apple trees in its glades."

An unsettling premonition started up Cat's spine. "What . . . what *does* Mynfel mean?" she asked.

Toby glanced at her. "Why, yarrow, of course. In the old tongue of the herbalists, that is."

Cat stopped in her tracks. She could hear her heart thundering in her breast and thought there was an answering thrum

that ran through the forest, earthy and root deep. She could
see Kothlen standing before her, hear his voice so clearly he
might be with her now, instead of lost in the years-old memory that had surfaced.

"Everyone has a secret name," Kothlen told her then.
"Every *thing* has one. It's the using of names that lends spells
their strength. You must always guard yours, sharing it only
with those you trust."

"What's yours?" Cat asked. She was eleven then and full
of the optimism of youth.

Kothlen regarded her seriously, then smiled. "Foxmoon,"
he said.

Young she might have been, but she was old enough to
understand what this moment meant. By giving her his secret
name, Kothlen had sealed their friendship forever. Then she
felt terrible.

"I don't know mine!" she had wailed. "I want to tell you
mine, but I can't."

"Why yours is Yarrow," he said.

"How . . . how do you know?"

"Because I have given it to you just now. Someone must
gift you with it, must see to the core of what you are and pluck
that secret forth for you."

"How do you know it's right?" she'd asked. But she already knew that it was because it fit her as though she'd been
born to it.

"I looked at you, looked in you, and it rose up from
here"—Kothlen tapped his chest—"unbidden."

She had looked up into his handsome alien face then, shy
in that moment, when she hadn't been shy with him for years.

"My name's Yarrow," she'd said so softly it was almost a
whisper.

Yarrow. Mynfel. Yarrow. The horned woman and the
horned image in the pool. Oh, God, Cat thought. What does it
mean? Kothlen—what had he known? Why had he given her
the horned lady's name?

"Mistress Cat?" Toby said, tugging at her sleeve. "What's
the matter?"

"I . . ."

Understanding hovered just out of reach. She felt that if
she could just push far enough, it would be hers. But the more
she concentrated, the more it eluded her. Then the song of the

forest, the deep thrum of its roots reverberating like harp-strings against the loam, faded from her mind and the moment was gone. All that remained was a tangle of riddles, more vexing than ever. She shook her head slowly.

"I just felt . . . strange for a moment," she said. She tried to keep her voice light. "But I'm fine now. Come on. We should get going."

They went on. Toby chattered, relating one impossible story after another, but Cat was only half listening. She worried at the riddles, trying to separate one from the other, but they were all so entwined that the tangle just got worse instead of better. Then they arrived at the wood's central glade and Cat paused again, staring across the moonlit grass.

"The pool," she said.

"Will you look in it again?" Toby asked.

"I don't know if I should. Or if . . . if I even can."

Not with what she knew now. But the mystery reared up inside her, the riddles demanded to be solved. The dark water called to her. She found herself walking toward the pool, leaning against the low stone wall, knees on the grass once more, breasts pressed against the cool stone. She looked down at her reflection, but it was no more herself looking back than it had been the last time.

The horns lifted from her brow like the bare limbs of an autumn tree, and in her eyes was an unfamiliar light. Inside the light . . . there was the roll of Kothlen's moors, swelling in rounded waves; Redcap Hill, fey and hallowed, Mynfel standing there amidst the stones, silhouetted against the moon. Mynfel whose name was the same as Cat's own secret name.

Yarrow.

Some of the riddles began to unravel. *She* must be Mynfel. And so the Otherworld was her creation—its denizens, companions forged out of her own longing for company. And when they had gone, she'd shaped another companion out of her loneliness—a small man, old and young, like Kothlen and like Ben, but not the same as either, his eyes holding both foolishness and wisdom. He had a knife at his belt and a pack on his back.

She saw the two of them walking through the oak wood, perceived the shadow that overhung all of her dream world. But she didn't see the shadow as a manifestation of her dream thief's power. Instead she saw it as the terrible realization that none of this, not the vision, not the pool, not the Otherworld itself, was real. The shadow was reality intruding on her delusions.

A shudder went through her. Truth or lie? Which was it? Another riddle, or did the reflected images mirror the truths that she must always have kept hidden from herself? But that meant—

She tore her gaze from the visions and stared wildly about her. How could it all seem so real? For all these years . . . Her gaze fixed on Toby—he was a stranger now. Not dangerous, just not real.

"Who are you?" she demanded.

"Nobody important. Just me. Toby Weye. A traveling man, remember? Why are you looking at me like that?"

She shook her head. "You're not real. None of this is real. I just made you up because everybody else was gone. But none of it has ever been real."

"Cat . . ." Toby began, but his voice started to fade. His body took on a certain translucence. For a moment she could see right through him. Then he was gone.

"No!" she wailed.

But everything was fading. The trees grew insubstantial. The whole world was disappearing right before her eyes.

"No!" she cried again.

Blackness came spinning up inside her. She lost her balance, fell to the ground, but never felt the impact because she was already—

—awake.

"Cat? Cat!"

She snapped her eyes open to find Peter crouching by the couch, his features worried.

"It's all right," he said. "It was just a dream."

"But that . . . that's just . . ."

Tears welled up in her eyes and were loosed in a flood. Her throat grew thick with emotion, trapping the words inside her. The truth settled like a hard knot in the pit of her stomach. That was all it had ever been. A dream. Many dreams. Years of dreams. She'd been conspiring against herself, slowly but methodically driving herself insane.

Peter held her, awkwardly patting her back. She buried her face against his chest, her shoulders heaving as she cried her heart out. She kept trying to explain herself, but the words wouldn't come out.

"Don't try to talk," Peter murmured. "Just take it easy. You're going to be all right."

Eventually the sobs subsided. Peter got up to get her some Kleenex. Leaving her alone for the moment, he went into the kitchen to make them both a cup of tea. He knew that he had to give her the time she needed. If he pressed her, it wouldn't do any good. It might just alienate her again. Christ, he wished Ben were here. He'd probably be able to handle this better. Peter thought of phoning him, but by then the tea was ready and Cat had joined him in the kitchen.

She sat down at the table and accepted the steaming mug gratefully. Cupping her hands around its warmth, she waited until he'd sat down across from her, then haltingly began to relate what had happened in her dream.

"So it was you with the cats last night?" Ben asked.

Tiddy Mun nodded. They were just turning down Third Avenue now and the little man was still shivering uncontrollably. Ben gave him a sidelong glance.

"Scared?" he asked.

"No. I mean, yes. That is . . ." Tiddy Mun turned panicky eyes to Ben. "It's the iron of your . . . your wagon."

Well, that figured, Ben thought. Didn't the old stories always make mention of the fact that cold iron was anathema to fairy? The little guy was lucky that Ben had Fiberglas screening on the windows of his apartment. He wondered how Tiddy Mun would have gotten him to open the door if there hadn't been, then he realized the way his thoughts were going and shook his head.

Christ! Here he was going off to do battle with one of Dracula's cousins—his only ally a munchkin from Cat's dreams who was probably more scared than he was—and he was thinking about window screens. What he should be doing was trying to come up with some sort of a plan of action for when they got to Mick's place. The trouble was, every time he started to think about what they were getting themselves into, everything just blocked up inside him. It was like last night all over again. He just wasn't cut out for this kind of stuff. But then again, who was?

He pulled the cab over to the curb a block east of Mick's

apartment and killed the engine.

"Well, *I'm* scared," he told his diminutive companion.

Tiddy Mun regarded him mournfully.

"No," Ben added. "I'm not backing out. But if there were any other way to handle this . . ." He shook his head. Picking up the baseball bat, he opened the cab door and stepped out. "Come on, little fella. It's time to get this show on the road."

Wary of the car's metal, Tiddy Mun joined him on the street. Third Avenue was quiet, untouched by their mounting terror. Ben's shirt stuck on his back in the warm air. His legs were starting to tremble, and he knew that if they didn't get moving soon, he just might not be able to make it at all.

"The evil is near," Tiddy Mun murmured.

Ben nodded, his face pale and drawn. "Are there any cats around that you can scare up for us?" he asked.

"Only Cat's two will listen to me," Tiddy Mun said. "Because they're my friends."

"Just thought I'd ask," Ben muttered. "Let's go."

He led the way down the block. Mick's building loomed in the glare of the streetlights. It was a three-story brick and frame structure that had been divided into five apartments— two on each side and one on the top floor. Narrow driveways separated it from its neighbors on either side. Mick's apartment was on the lower west side of the building. Ben glanced at Tiddy Mun, and the little man nodded.

"It's already inside," he said, replying to Ben's unspoken question.

"Great."

Debbie awoke with a splitting headache. She was lying on a strange couch in a strange room and it took her a few moments to orient herself. She felt drained, as though she'd fainted or . . . or what? There was an emptiness inside her, a sense of violation that made her look down at her body. She was surprised to find that she was still fully clothed, because the way she felt . . .

Then it all came back to her. This was Stella's apartment. She and Rick had come here for an after-work drink. And there'd been someone else here. Lucius . . . Lucius somebody-or-other. With the scar on his cheek and . . . and his eyes. Compelling eyes. Those eyes—they had stolen something from her.

She sat up, but too quickly. The room spun in her sight and

the throb in her temples quickened. When her vision settled to
normal and the pounding in her head became a little more
manageable, she took stock of the apartment. Neither Rick nor
Lucius were in sight. But Stella . . . She lay sprawled in an
armchair, her head slack against her chest.

Oh, God, Debbie thought. I've got to get out of here.

Whatever was going on here was too much for her to han-
dle. Gingerly, she rose from the couch. She paused near
Stella, uncertain whether she should try to rouse her or not.
What if she were dead? She was lying so unnaturally still.
What if—

Get out of here! Debbie told herself. Now. While you still
can.

She hesitated a moment longer, then crossed the room,
stepping carefully, one hand pressed against a temple. She
never reached the front door.

"Debbie."

She turned to see him standing in the doorway that led to
what she supposed was the bedroom. Her pulse hammered.
His eyes, she thought suddenly. Don't look into his— But she
warned herself too late.

"You're not thinking of leaving, are you?" Lysistratus
asked softly.

Against her will she shook her head. She could feel him
inside her, moving her body as though it was a puppet and his
mind was the hand inside it. He made her return to the couch.

"Are you unhappy?" he asked.

Debbie could make no reply. She stared blankly into noth-
ingness, her mind devoid of thought. Lysistratus joined her on
the couch, sitting close. He took her hand between his and
caressed her slack fingers.

"I can make you happy," he said as he began to unbutton
her blouse. "Happier than you can begin to imagine."

Ben and Tiddy Mun ducked down the nearest driveway so
that they could approach Mick's apartment from the rear.
Once off the street they plunged into deep shadow, tall dark
houses rearing up on either side of them. There was a '78
Accord parked in the driveway that Tiddy Mun gave a wide
berth. He squeezed himself against the nearest building, teeth
chattering at the proximity of the metal.

Once in the backyard they crept towards their goal. It'd be
just their luck, Ben thought, to get spotted as prowlers them-

selves. When they reached Mick's back door, Ben hesitated. Now what? Smash their way in? That'd be sure to rouse the neighbors—though that might not be such a bad idea. They'd call the cops and the whole problem would be out of his hands. Except that the noise would warn the Dude, and there was no way the police would get here in time.

The baseball bat was slippery in his hand. He transferred it from right to left, wiped his palm dry, then took it up again. With the bat gripped tight, he tried the door with his free hand. The knob wouldn't turn. Okay, Ben thought. I've seen enough cop shows. This I can handle.

He glanced around, then holding the bat between his knees, dug out his key ring. The key holder had a long slender piece of plastic at the end embossed with an orange tree and the words Souvenir of Florida on it in gaudy lettering. With his heart pounding wildly, he slipped it into the crack just above the lock's face plate and brought it down, jiggling as it went, until it caught the angled bolt latch. He gave the door a push and it swung open.

Shoulda been a thief, he thought. His hand shook as he replaced the keys in his pocket and took up the bat again. Right. Sure. He took a last look about the backyard, then pushed the door farther open and slipped in. Tiddy Mun was right behind him.

They found themselves in Mick's kitchen.

"Where's the Dude?" Ben whispered. "Can you tell what room he's in?"

"The Dude?"

"The. . . the evil you sensed."

"Very near. Not in the next room. Perhaps the one beyond."

Ben swallowed. As he started to step into the hall, Tiddy Mun tugged at his arm. Ben turned.

"The eyes," the little man warned. "Beware of its eyes."

Remembering his own experience the previous night, Ben nodded. He stepped into the hall, every nerve screaming. The moment of truth was at hand, and he didn't think he was going to measure up. He'd gone into a funk last night. What was going to make tonight any different?

The bat was a leaden weight in his hand. He'd been in this house a hundred times before, but right now it was all alien territory. Mick's bedroom was the second or third door on the right. First there was the bathroom, then a small room Mick used for storage, the bedroom, and finally the living room at the end.

Ben paused, hearing something. Tiddy Mun bumped into him and he almost died of fright. Terror lanced through him, white and hot, before he realized what had happened. He was about to turn to warn his companion to be more careful, when he heard the sound again. It came from down the hall. From the bedroom. It sounded like a quiet laugh.

Ben edged forward nervously, the bat held out in front of him. When he reached the doorway to the bedroom, he stepped in.

Diffused streetlight spilled through the bedroom window, mixing with a small lamp on the floor. The light illuminated all Ben's fears come to life. His gaze took in a swirl of details at a glance. Becki lay sprawled on the floor by the bed, wearing nothing but an oversized Clash T-shirt. Beyond her Mick's stereo lay smashed. Records spilled across the room. An armchair lay overturned by the window. And at the bed, rising from it, was a man in a light-colored suit. Mick lay nude on the bed. Unmoving.

As the man turned to face him, Ben froze with shock. A stranger faced him. Not the Dude. Not the vampire. A stranger. But the same intense light glittered in his eyes. Feral. His eyes were . . .

Ben tore his gaze away. He'd almost been caught again. For a long moment the tableau held. Then Ben's fears drained and rage leapt through him.

He charged forward, the bat held high. The man spun from the bedside, a knife in his hands. Its blade gleamed with a wet glisten as it caught the light. Swinging the bat, Ben hit the man's arm and knocked the knife flying. Before he could regain his balance to swing again, the man lunged at him. His shoulder struck Ben, sending him across the room, where he hit the wall hard and slid to the floor. The bat flew from his slippery grip. The stranger picked up the wreckage of Mick's turntable, but before he got a chance to pitch it at Ben, a hissing, clawing fury leapt onto the man's back, talons digging deep into his shoulder muscles.

The turntable fell to the floor with a crash. The man cried out in pain as he fought to dislodge the big tomcat from his back. When it clawed its way to his head, he got a purchase on a forepaw, tugged the beast free and flung it at Ben. Ben was scrambling to regain his weapon when the cat struck him. As it rolled from him to land spitting on the floor, Ben's fingers closed on the handle of his bat. He rose, weapon in hand, but his attacker had fled down the hall.

Ben followed to see the stranger reach the front door, fling it open, and escape into the night. By the time Ben reached the open door, the man was getting into a car about a half block from the house. The engine roared, the car tore away from the curb, and the man was gone.

The last few minutes' action settled on Ben as he stood breathing heavily in the doorway. Adrenaline had sent his heartbeat accelerating until it seemed his heart would burst. It lay sour in his stomach now. The full realization of what had happened hit him. That hadn't been the Dude. There was more than one of the creatures! Then he remembered Mick and Becki.

He started for the bedroom, his footsteps lagging in fear of what he'd find there. Tiddy Mun met him in the hall. The little man limped and favored one arm. Ben brushed by him. He took a deep breath in the doorway, then flicked on the overhead light. The glare blinded him for a moment.

He knelt first by Becki. A bruise was starting to discolor the skin above her left eye and the cheek below it. Ben lay the bat aside and awkwardly put his fingers against her neck, searching for a pulse. He could feel one, but inexperienced as he was, he couldn't tell if it was normal or not. At least she was alive. He tugged her T-shirt down over her hips, then went to check on Mick.

When he reached the bed he looked once, then turned away. Bile came roiling up his throat. He didn't want to look again, but he couldn't stop himself because he just couldn't believe what he'd seen. Mick's throat had been cut from ear to ear, the slit gaping like a macabre grin. Blood soaked the bedclothes.

Ben went white and tumbled from the bed. He only just made it to the toilet bowl, where he threw up the contents of his stomach, heaving long after it was empty. He pressed his face against the porcelain, his mind numb with shock. His vision blurred with tears.

"It wasn't even the Dude," he said in a strained voice. He turned to face Tiddy Mun, who was standing in the doorway watching him. "It wasn't even the fucking Dude!"

He got slowly to his feet and forced himself back into the bedroom, keeping his eyes averted from the bed. He leaned weakly against the door jamb. He had to call an ambulance, the police. He had to—

"For Christ's sake," he told Tiddy Mun, who'd crept into the room after him, "how many of those creatures *are* there?"

His gaze locked on the little man's, pleading for answers. But Tiddy Mun didn't know what to do either. This wasn't his world. He shivered, hugging his hurt arm to his chest.

"If . . . if there are more than one of them—" the gnome began in a small voice, then broke off, unsure of how to continue, unwilling to complete the thought that rose fearfully inside him.

Ben caught the unspoken fear. "Cat," he cried. "Oh, Christ! Peter and Cat!"

Death lay on the bed, filling the room with its presence. Its smell was heavy in the air—blood and the stink of fear. Was it reaching out at this moment to strike the rest of his friends— hitting them all at once? Was there one of these monsters breaking into his own apartment right now? He shivered, torn between fear and a need to act. To warn Cat and Peter. To call the police. To do *something* before—

Becki moaned, drawing his gaze like a magnet. As her head moved, shifting slowly from side to side, her eyes fluttering open, Ben was galvanized into action. He reached her before she could sit up and look at the bed. She stared at him with a glazed expression, as though she was finding it hard to focus on him.

"B-ben . . . ?" she asked uncertainly.

He knelt by her, helped her up, keeping her face from the bed.

"There . . . there was this guy," she said slowly. "He . . . he had a knife, Ben . . ."

"You're okay," Ben said. His throat felt tight, like it was clamping shut.

Becki regarded him strangely. She lifted a weak hand to touch his cheek. "You . . . you're crying," she said. "Ben, why are you— Mick!"

She tried to pull away from him, but he held her close.

"You . . . you don't want to see," he said in a choking voice. Fresh tears stung his eyes and ran down his cheeks.

She fought his hold on her, panic skittering in her eyes. "Mick!" she cried. "What's happened to Mick?"

"He's dead, Becki. He's...the guy cut his...He's dead...."

She went slack in his arms, her face white as his words sank in. "No," she moaned softly. "Please, no."

They had to get out of here, Ben realized. If she saw what was on the bed...if he didn't want the same thing to happen to Peter or Cat...They couldn't stay. He had to find the strength to step past his grief. Warning Cat and Peter, getting Becki out of here—if he concentrated on those things, really tried, he might get through it. He'd never get rid of the horrific memory of Mick's throat and all the...all the blood....

He forced his feet to move. With Tiddy Mun's help he got Becki out of the room. Don't look back, Ben told himself. Jesus, don't look back. He discovered that the phone was dead, so he couldn't even call Cat or Peter. They'd have to go to their houses. Becki let herself be led from the apartment to Ben's cab. She sat meekly in the passenger's seat, never even giving Tiddy Mun a second glance.

With shaking fingers, Ben got the key into the ignition. He kicked the engine over, put it in gear, and pulled away from the curb. His knuckles were white from the force with which he was gripping the steering wheel. He kept seeing Mick's face, then Cat's or Peter's features superimposed over it. Now it was *their* throats that were cut, *their* blood soaking the sheets.

The car seemed to inch its way to the corner of Third and Chrysler. It took every measure of concentration that Ben could muster just to keep going. South on Chrysler, down to Fourth. Peter was closest, so he'd go there first. It wasn't more than six blocks to the store. He just had to get there in one piece.

Please, he begged the faces rolling through his head, their throats gaping and fountaining blood. Please, go away.

13

the hounds are loosed

PETER LISTENED TO Cat's story with mounting apprehension. This abrupt about-face worried him almost more than the initial supposition that there actually was an Otherworld—a place of dreams that was real, or at least real to Cat, if not to him. To see her now, huddled in the chair across the table from him, feet on the seat, knees pulled up to her chin, her face like a mask, rigid, expressionless... The sharp pain in her eyes told him all too clearly what she was going through.

"Cat," he said softly. "You're letting things get to you, that's all."

"You don't understand," she said. "Don't you see what this means? I *am* insane. I've *always* been insane. Not dangerous, maybe, but right off the deep end all the same."

She caught the shrillness in her voice and looked away. Taking a deep breath, she spoke again, her words deliberate. "It's like all those stories about the autumn of the elves and their magicks failing. It's autumn for me now and *my* magicks are failing. My magicks never even were."

"You never lost your ability to write," Peter began. "Not really. You just—"

She cut him off. "I'm not talking about writing! I'm talking about dreaming. I'm talking about living my whole life all tangled up with fantasies and ghosts that never existed."

"Cat—"

"And what about Ben? Here I thought I'd found myself a guy that maybe things could work out with, but he's going to find out all too soon just what a lunatic I am. Psychic vampires, for God's sake! I can't believe that *any* of us could even pretend to take that seriously."

"Ben's not—"

"It won't make any difference, Peter, though thanks for trying. Ben'll leave, just like every other guy I've ever gone out with once they get to know me."

"That's not fair."

"Fair? Don't talk to me about fair. How about being a crazed writer who can't even tell the difference between what she writes and real life—you call that fair?"

For a long moment their gazes held, then Cat shook her head. She got up from the table and went into the living room, where her clothes lay. She put on her jeans, leaving the over-sized shirt hanging out, and stuffed the rest of what she'd been wearing when she came over into her bag.

"What are you doing?" Peter asked.

"I can't stay here. I'm going home."

"What about your prowler? Your dream th—"

"There *is* no dream thief—can't you see? There aren't any dreams for him to steal in the first place. *He's* not real, because the *dreams* aren't real."

"And what about last night?"

"God, I don't *know.* There's enough weirdness in the world as it is without having to give it supernatural trappings, don't you think?"

Peter shook his head. The sudden role reversal was throwing him off base. He didn't know if Cat was insane or not at this point, because he was seriously beginning to doubt his own sanity. Nothing was making sense anymore.

"Did you ever think," he asked, "that maybe those other relationships didn't work out *not* because those guys couldn't handle you, but because you couldn't handle *them*? Maybe you didn't so much drive them off as ran away yourself?"

She stared at him, face paling. Shut up, Peter told himself, but the words came boiling up from inside him.

"It's like someone just trying to be your friend," he went on. "You say you want friends, but you don't really. As soon as someone gets close, you drive them away. You don't want anything to be real. Just your ghosts. And now that you think they're gone, you've got nothing left, have you? Only where does that leave the people who care for you?"

He knew he was hurting her. A reverberating echo of her pain tightened in his own chest. But the words all came out in a rush, almost before he knew what he was doing. He was angry with her, more angry at himself. For playing matchmaker, for dragging Ben into this, for the pain it was going to cause Ben—never mind that hurt Cat was feeling right now. Everything was a mess. Cat, Ben, himself . . . He looked at her, suddenly sorry he'd said anything at all. But the words hung between them and couldn't be taken back.

"Oh, Jesus," he tried. "I'm sorry, Cat. I didn't mean—"

"No, Peter. Maybe you're right. Maybe . . ." She couldn't finish. Turning, she caught up her shoulder bag and ran for the door.

Peter stood frozen, watching her go. He cursed his own blundering stupidity, then ran to follow. "Cat!" he called from the top of the stairs.

She turned, the front door open in front of her, tears streaming down her cheeks. "Just . . . just leave me alone, Peter. I'm everything you . . . you said I was. I can't . . . even handle reality. . . ."

Then she was through the door and gone.

Peter plunged down the stairs, taking them two at a time, stopping at the front door when he realized he wasn't wearing anything but a pair of boxer shorts.

"Cat!" he cried again.

She ignored him. Maybe she didn't even hear him. He watched her get into her car, heard the door slam, the VW's engine kicking over, catching. The headlights came on and she pulled away from the curb. He watched her make her way down the street until all he could see were the two winking taillights, then he ran back upstairs to put on a pair of jeans.

When he reached the porch again, he never even got a chance to lock the door behind him. A Blue Line cab was pulled up in front of the store. Peter hesitated, hand on the doorknob. A premonition ran like a wild spark through him.

He saw Ben get out, then . . .

He saw Tiddy Mun. He stared at the little man, unable to accept the image that his eyes were sending to his brain. It . . . just . . . wasn't . . . possible.

He never saw Becki slouched in the passenger seat. Never glanced at Ben who was moving toward him with the somnambulant steps of a sleepwalker. His entire attention narrowed to focus on the small figure of the gnome. Tiddy Mun. One of Cat's ghosts. Real. But if he was real . . .

At last he turned to Ben, his eyes pleading for an explanation. Ben looked back at him with a panicky gaze.

"Peter," he said numbly. "Oh, Peter. We're in deep shit."

By the time Rick parked near Cat's house he was feeling good again. Okay, so maybe he'd panicked back there. But it had all happened so fast. The guy had been big, and hadn't let Rick get a bead on him with the old magic-eyes routine. And that fucking cat . . . He'd forgotten all about the power, about what *he* could do. But, hell, he was new to this game. He'd get back to that dude—him and the other one Lucius wanted. Right now he had other business.

He regarded the dark bulk of Cat's house, the stolen strength of Mick's psychic essence still rushing through him euphorically. That last moment, just when he cut the punk's throat and the soul's final essence had fired through him . . . Rick shivered, reliving it. Never thought a dude could make me feel so good, he thought with a grin.

He got out of his car and moved toward the house. He could tell the building was empty, but he had already decided to wait for the woman to return. She was the one Lucius wanted the most. When he brought her in, maybe Lucius wouldn't make too big a production of the way he'd fucked up earlier. Wouldn't be smart to get in *that* sucker's bad books.

He heard the sound of a car then, and stepped into the shadows of the cedar hedge. Wouldn't do for a cop to spot him right now, not with all this blood on his suit. Some of it was his own—that damned cat!—but most of it came from the punk when he'd cut his throat. Christ, he sure had a lot of blood in him. Rick glanced up the street and relaxed. Cops didn't drive VW's. Fact was, nobody drove bugs much these days.

When the car kept coming closer, a tingle of anticipation started up in him. Maybe he'd made a mistake in not going after the other two first. Just thinking of the driver of this car started the juices running in him again. Guess you could never get too much of a good thing. Then the car pulled into his victim's laneway and forced the lust from him. It was her— and she belonged to Lucius. He flexed his fingers at his sides, waiting for the engine to die, for the car door to open.

Hey, Lucius. Look what I got for you.

When the car engine shut off, he reached into the vehicle with his new abilities to see what made this woman so special. Tasting her, he almost lunged out of the hedge, lust overriding responsibility. There was so much inside her, and it was so fucking pure.

Saliva built up in his mouth and he trembled. His hand went down between his legs to touch the hardness swelling in his pants. No wonder Lucius wanted her for himself. She—

He shook his head, forcing reason to assert itself. Anyone that could give him this kind of power wasn't someone you fucked around with. This one belonged to Lucius. But there'd be others like her. Others that he would find and keep for himself.

When the car door opened, he moved forward from the shadows of the hedge.

Peter couldn't take his eyes from the little man. Ben's jumbled account of the night's events barely penetrated his consciousness. He stepped from the porch and moved close to Tiddy Mun, one trembling hand reaching out to touch the gnome. The little man stood still, saucer eyes wide as he watched Peter approach. Physical contact broke Peter's spell.

Real. The little man was real!

He snatched his hand away. His gaze shifted from the gnome to Ben, his mind awhirl. If the gnome existed, then so did Cat's Otherworld. And if *it* existed, then there really *was* a thief of dreams, and that meant— Cat! She was out there in the night, alone. And the vampire was out there hunting her.

Suddenly what Ben was saying broke through the rush of his own thoughts. He realized there was a woman in the cab, took in Ben's state of shock and what he was saying.

"Dead?" Peter demanded. "Who's dead?"

"Jesus, Peter. Were . . . weren't you listening? One of those vampires killed Mick. Cut his . . . throat . . . cut it with a knife. . . ."

"What do you mean *one* of the vampires?"

"The guy that . . . that killed Mick wasn't the Dude. I never saw him before. And that means there's more than one of them! We've got to warn Cat."

More than one. The words went through Peter like a fire. He stepped closer to Ben, saw that his friend was on the edge of a complete breakdown. After what he'd been through . . .

"Who's she?" Peter asked, pointing to the cab.

"Becki. She's . . . was . . . oh, shit. She was Mick's girl-friend, Peter. There was so fucking much blood, and he was just lying there. . . ."

The woman was in worse shape than Ben by the looks of her. Reddish-blue bruises discolored her face. She sat in the passenger's seat, staring blankly out the windshield. He had to get both Ben and her to a hospital. But first he had to warn Cat. He turned to Ben, gripping him by the arm.

"Get in the cab, Ben," he said softly.

Ben just stared at him. "His . . . his throat was cut," Ben said wonderingly. "From ear to ear—you know how they say that in the detective books? Jesus! I just can't . . . believe . . . The blood . . ."

Tiddy Mun came to Peter's aid. Between the two of them they got Ben into the backseat.

"They're going to kill us," Ben said. "They're going to kill all of us, Peter, one by one. . . ."

Peter shook his head. "It's okay, Ben. No one's going to get us. Not you, not me—not any more of us."

"You don't understand," Ben said. "You didn't see him. I . . . I don't know why he took off. He could have had me right then. If Tiddy Mun had . . . hadn't jumped him . . ."

"Look, Ben. I—"

Ben gripped Peter's arm fiercely. "Don't look in their eyes, Peter. That's how they get you!"

His grip faltered and his gaze turned inward, replaying the horror of what he'd found in Mick's bedroom. Peter closed the door and moved to the driver's seat. Bending down to get in, his gaze went from Becki to Ben. He was forgetting some-thing. He was . . . Turning, his gaze settled on Tiddy Mun, who was standing mournfully on the pavement.

"You," Peter said softly. "What are you? And what're you doing here?"

He shook his head as the incongruity of what he was doing hit home. The little man shouldn't even exist. But he did. And he was standing there. And he was talking to him. . . .

"I'm Cat's friend," Tiddy Mun replied. "That's all."

Cat. He had to get moving.

"I . . . still can't believe you're for real," Peter said.

"I want to help," the little man said, not understanding Peter's talk of realities. To Tiddy Mun things simply were. Some were nice and some terrified him. But he never questioned their existence. "Cat's my friend," he repeated. "The evil seeks her. I'm very afraid, but I want to help."

Peter nodded. Whatever it was that was out there hunting, it *was* evil. And it wanted Cat. It was his fault that Cat was out there. She'd come to him, looking for help, and he'd driven her away. He slipped behind the wheel of the cab, then leaned across the seat to speak to Ben. Ben's eyes had a lost look to them.

"I couldn't help him," Ben said. "I just . . . just didn't get there in time. And Cat . . ."

"We'll get there in time," Peter promised, but Ben wasn't listening anymore. His eyes had gone unfocused again. Peter glanced at Tiddy Mun, who stood just behind the door of the cab.

"Are you still coming?" he asked.

The little man nodded, hands clasped in front of him to keep them from trembling. "The metal . . ." he said. "The cold iron . . ."

Peter rubbed at his temples. Then, reaching down, he helped the little man up. Tiddy Mun scrambled across his lap to sit between Becki and Peter, his limbs shivering.

Oh, Cat, Peter thought as he shut the door and turned the engine over. I'm so sorry. If we get out of this, I'll believe anything you tell me. Any damn thing.

All the way home Cat thought about what Peter had said. Couldn't he see what all this was doing to her? Maybe he couldn't have understood, but couldn't he at least have tried a little harder to see things from her point of view? It wasn't just the suspicion that there might be something wrong with her— not anymore. Her whole life had been lived as a lie. A delusion.

She'd been something of an elitist, believing she could see more than the plebian hordes with whom she shared the planet. She was special. She dreamed true. But the truth of the

matter was, she wasn't so special at all. The psychotic wards
of hospitals were filled with people just like her.

Her tears dried up, but not her grief.

Now she didn't have only Kothlen to mourn, she had all of
them. Kothlen's kin. Tiddy Mun. Mynfel, whose name she
shared. The Otherworld itself. They weren't dead. They
weren't gone. They'd never existed anywhere but in her own
imagination in the first place.

How did you mourn what never was?

She'd never felt so lost or so alone as she did on that drive
home. The route from Peter's store to her own house stretched
to impossible proportions—a night journey that promised no
cleansing at its completion, no catharsis. She was used to
being alone and not feeling alone. But now, inside her, desolation lay bleak for wasted miles.

There were no landmarks, nothing familiar to reach out for
in that wasteland. No hope. Just the barren expanses. Dreamless. Self-pitying. The late-night streets echoing the emptiness
inside her. No escape possible. Not to an Otherworld ruled by
antlered Mynfel, because it didn't exist. And in this world?
Did she dare take a chance with someone as kind as Ben? Did
she want to mess him around? He deserved more than someone like her. And Peter, just trying to be a friend . . .

Crossing Lansdowne Bridge, she considered pushing the
gas pedal to the floor and sending the car through the railings
to the canal below. But that wouldn't solve anything. Then she
was over the bridge, nearing Sunnyside, and the moment was
gone.

She turned right on Willard. Home was just a couple of
blocks away. A big empty house, filled with books and
records. Two cats. It wasn't what she needed right now, but it
was all she had. Pulling into her driveway, she sat still for a
few moments, hands gripping the steering wheel.

Home is where the heart is, she thought. Was that what was
wrong with this house? That it wasn't where *her* heart was?
Her heart lay in the woodlands and rounded hills of the Otherworld. The remote home of her dreams. Of emotion. More
recently home might have worked out to be where Ben was.
But not in this empty house.

Tomorrow, she thought as she killed the car's engine, I'll
apologize to Peter and talk to Ben. He's coming over for din-

ner, anyway, so I'll just talk to him. I'll try to be real in this world. Maybe he can help me do it.

A hesitant whisper of hope stirred in her. She stepped out of the car feeling less lost for the first time since she'd woken earlier and realized her dreamworld was a sham. It was time to make a turn around. It was time to stop pretending and be real. If it wasn't too late already, she had to—

Something slammed her hard against the side of the car, spinning her shoulder bag and car keys from her hands. A big hand gripped her jaw, forcing her to look up. Eyes like ice stared into her own. Cold fear shoved panic through her like a knife. The eyes glittered with their own inner light, drawing her into them. A jackhammer pounding started up behind her temples. She could feel herself falling into those eyes, as though they were sucking her in.

She struggled in her assailant's grip. He slammed her hard against the car again. Spots danced in front of her eyes, a whole kaleidoscope of tiny sparks that pulsed and spun in an incoherent rhythm. And beyond them, feral as a nightmare, the eyes bore into her—demanding, taking, ripping her consciousness from her.

This wasn't happening to her, her reason told her. There was no one out to get her. No dreams for a dream thief to steal.

She wished someone would tell her attacker that. Then a black wave came washing over her and she went limp in his grip.

Rick shifted Cat's weight and slung her over his shoulder. Success danced inside him like the shifting reflections from a mirrored disco ball. It was so fucking easy. With this kind of power what could stop you?

Nothing, he thought as he wrestled his burden to where his car was parked.

When he gave Rick the power, Lucius had shown him the way things went. You had to lull your prey. You had to deceive them with shifting lies so that they never had a chance to believe that the threat to them was real. That was how Lucius and his kind survived.

Lucius played it slow and easy, but Rick was beginning to realize that you didn't have to sneak around in the shadows.

You could just step out, bold and easy, and if anyone got in your way, just squash them. Otherwise what was the point of having this power? You didn't hide, you got right out there. On a talk show maybe, or set yourself up like one of those TV evangelists and get yourself a few million followers with just a snap of your fingers.

He dumped Cat unceremoniously into the passenger's seat and closed the door on her. Rounding the car to the driver's side, he realized that Lucius simply didn't understand the potential of what the power had to offer. His values were centuries out of date. You didn't have to go out looking for prey. These days people were so stupid, they'd line up to have their souls sucked out of them. It all depended on your PR. Hell, look at the Moonies. Or L. Ron Hubbard's people. *They* knew where it was at.

Starting the car, Rick was already planning his campaign. If he could sell computers to people who neither wanted them nor could afford them, this'd be a piece of cake. He'd set it up as a self-awareness gig and just watch the suckers and their money come pouring in.

"It's a whole new ball game," he said, patting Cat's limp form. "A whole new ball game. And I'm going to make the rules. Too bad you're going to miss out on it, babe, 'cause it's sure gonna be some show."

Peter pulled into Cat's driveway behind her VW and was out of the cab almost before it had stopped. The bug's door stood ajar. Cat's shoulder bag lay on the gravel. A half dozen feet away her car keys lay glinting in the glow thrown by the car's interior light.

"Oh, Jesus . . ."

Peter picked up the shoulder bag and turned it over in his hands while his gaze went from the car to the darkened house. They were too late.

"It has her," Tiddy Mun whispered, edging from the car. Tears glistened in the little man's eyes.

Numbly, Peter turned to face his companion. "How could we be too late?" he demanded. "The cavalry's never too late. We're the bloody cavalry, aren't we?"

Tiddy Mun shook his head, understanding only the words "too late."

"It can't end like this," Peter said. He dropped the bag,

hen hit the roof of the VW with his fist. "How can it end like
his?"

The vampire—the enemy, whatever the hell he was—had
stymied them at every turn. He was always one step ahead of
hem. Mick was dead now. Ben and Becki were sitting in the
car like a couple of zombies. And now he had Cat.

"If we could only find him," he muttered.

If the vampire meant to kill Cat, he'd have done it here.
The way he finished off Mick. But he wanted Cat for something else. For what? To feed on her some more? To steal her
dreams? What would happen when he stole all her dreams?
Would there be anything left that was still Cat? Or would there
be just a husk with her face, her body, but no one home inside?

Can Cat come out to play?

Sure, Peter. At least what's left of her. . . .

Christ, he wasn't going to make it through the night. Not in
one piece. Not with any level of sanity left.

Think, he told himself. Where would he have taken her?

Just look for the castle on top of the hill. . . .

A small hand plucked at his sleeve, and he looked down
into Tiddy Mun's features.

"You'd know!" he said before the gnome had a chance to
speak. "You knew he was going for Mick. You can take me to
where he's got Cat!"

Tiddy Mun nodded. "But he's too strong for us. We
need—"

"The hell he's too strong for us." Peter pushed the little
man toward the cab. "You just show me where he is."

"We need more help," Tiddy Mun said.

"Where do we get it?"

The little man trembled. "This is your world," he began.

"There's just you and me," Peter said. "She hasn't got anybody else right now. In the time we'd spend trying to convince
somebody we're on the level, Christ knows what he'll have
done to her."

Peter backed the cab out of the driveway. "Which way?"

Tiddy Mun pointed north.

Measure by measure the blackness cleared.

Cat sat up, putting a hand to her head. A headache
drummed steadily between her temples and her head still rang

from where it had struck the car. But as awareness returned to
her and she saw where she was, she shook her head slowly,
setting up a wave of nausea.

"Please, God," she murmured. "Just go away."

But her surroundings remained, firm and real.

She lay in the middle of the circle edged by the three
standing stones on Redcap Hill. In the Otherworld. The place
of her dreaming that didn't exist. But she could see the top-
most branches of the fairy thorn from where she lay. There
was Mynfel's wood. The sky above was studded with the constellations of the Otherworld. The familiar wind of Kothlen's
moors lifted and tugged at her hair.

"You're not real," she told her surroundings. "Not anymore. Just go away. Please!"

She willed the illusion to leave her. She might be crazy, but
at least let her be crazy in a place that was real, where a doctor
might help her or . . . or something. Then she remembered her
attacker, and suddenly she wasn't so sure that going back was
such a good idea. He was so much stronger than her, handling
her like she was a toddler. Maybe the delusion was better.
Because his eyes . . . in his eyes . . .

Nothing made sense anymore.

"Mistress Cat?"

No, she told herself when she heard that voice. I'm drawing the line. I saw right through him like he was made of . . .
of glass. He's an illusion, just like everything else around me.
If I lie very still and ignore him—ignore everything—it'll all
go away. I'll wake up in my own bed and find that I was never
attacked in my driveway, there was never a prowler or . . . or a
dream thief, or whatever he was.

Toby Weye squatted in front of her. She looked away from
him, staring down at the grass, and refused to speak.

"Mistress Cat . . . ?" he tried again.

A hand—God, it felt real—reached out to touch her.
Numbly she lifted her head to look into his face. He regarded
her with a strange, guarded expression, snatching back his
hand once he saw that he'd gotten her attention.

"Go away," she said softly.

"I can't."

Of course he couldn't, Cat realized. He'd be here for as
long as she projected the illusion that he existed. You're not

real, she thought at him. You don't exist anymore. Time to go *poof* and vanish. Bye-bye.

He stayed right where he was, still watching her. "One moment," he said, "we were by the pool in the forest, and in the next I was here. Alone. You told me I wasn't real, that you'd made me up, and then"—he snapped his fingers—"I was here." He leaned closer. "I *am* real, Mistress Cat."

"Okay," she said. Is this how it happened? Illusion and reality blended together until you couldn't make head or tail of it? Phantoms that expounded on their existence, that you had to accept or they just wouldn't leave you alone? "Okay. You're real. Now go away."

"I can't," he said again.

Cat sighed. Maybe if the pounding in her head would let up for a few moments, if things would just slow down for her . . .

"Why not?" she asked.

Toby pointed down the hill. She looked, and saw what she hadn't noticed before. She'd been too busy disavowing the existence of the Otherworld to bother with all of its details.

Around the hill, just beyond the protection of the stones, shadows . . . capered. There was no other word for it. There were dozens of them—sly, liquid shapes that conducted some cabalistic dance she could only watch for a few moments before she had to look away. They drew her gaze and repelled her at the same time. There was something in their movement, like the gliding gait of a reptile, that awoke primal terrors deep inside her. She couldn't watch them without becoming nauseous.

"What . . . what are they?"

Toby shook his head. "I've never seen their like. They were here when I arrived—not many at first, but enough to keep me penned at the top of the hill. Their numbers have grown since."

"But what *are* they?"

The creatures wove a sinuous dance just beyond the stones, trapping the eye. More than anything else they convinced her that, imagined or not, there was more to the Otherworld than what she could have created. Those things *couldn't* have come from her. But if they had . . . God, if they had . . . She couldn't follow the thought through. Better to pretend that the Otherworld was real on its own.

"I've had a thought," Toby said.

She dragged her gaze from the weave and dip of the shadows, glad to concentrate on him, on his face, on what he was saying, even if she had made him up.

"They belong to your dream thief," he said. "They're his power . . . manifesting in this world."

Like the time the black shape had dropped out of the sky a few nights ago. These things left Cat with the same impression. They lacked something. They hungered. They wanted her.

"Why don't they attack us?" she asked. But she already knew. The longstones on top of Redcap Hill were protecting them.

Toby shrugged. "My iron blade?" he ventured. "The hill's magic? You said it was hallowed, didn't you?"

"To Mynfel," Cat replied. "But she's . . ."

What exactly *was* the antlered woman? A manifestation of Cat's, just as those capering shadows were the dream thief materialized in the Otherworld? Or was she a being who belonged to this world, one who had withdrawn her favors? Cat had never truly understood just what it was that Mynfel represented. Mynfel had always been the silent companion, the sense of peace that Cat could draw strength from, the deepness that underlay the whole of the Otherworld.

"What can we do?" she asked.

"Try to break free?"

Cat shook her head. She couldn't bear the thought of being touched by one of those creatures, to have them crawling over her, clutching at her hair, the shadowy smoothness of them clammy against her skin.

"And go where?" she asked.

Toby nodded. "Then we can either wait, or take the battle to your enemy."

"You don't understand," Cat said. "I'm not in control of . . . of any of this. Ten minutes ago I was convinced it didn't exist. Even now I . . . I'm not all that sure. . . ."

"But—"

"I'm not even sleeping right now! The last thing I remember is some maniac attacking me in my driveway."

The memory of her assailant's eyes floated up in her mind, chilling her. She tried to explain it to Toby, but the words came out in a jumble. The confusion was too complex to unravel in a few easy sentences. How could she explain it when she wasn't even sure herself what was real anymore? But Toby drew one fact out of her story.

"He wants you," he said. "He hunts you on both worlds, Mistress Cat. Now he has your body on one, your soul trapped here on another. You must wake up and face him."

"Wake up? I'm not even sleeping!"

"Wake, or you doom us both."

"You don't understand." No one understood. *She* didn't even understand.

"Wake!" Toby cried. He grabbed her by the shoulders and shook her forcibly.

"I'm not a hero!" Cat cried. "Going back won't do any good."

But it was already too late.

The drumming headache between her temples took on the rhythm of Toby's shaking. The Otherworld began to dissolve around her. The smell of grass and moor wind was replaced with the stale odor of old car leather and aftershave. She had a dim impression that she was underground somewhere. In a car and underground. The car wasn't moving. Her face was pressed against a man's leg that shifted as she moved away from it.

"Oh, no, you don't," an unfamiliar voice said.

She struggled, but she was in too confined a space. An arm went around her neck, cutting off her air as it dug into her windpipe. A hand grabbed her hair, twisting her head back so that she was looking up into her assailant's face. The eyes caught her gaze and she started to plummet again, falling into their depths. Desperately, she tried to look away, but only managed to squeeze her eyes shut.

"Look at me!" the man demanded. "It'll only hurt forever."

She clawed at him. The arm around her neck tightened. The hand in her hair twisted with a new grip. The moan of pain that roared inside her died somewhere between her diaphram and her vocal chords. She desperately needed air.

Her eyes popped open, pleading. The power of his gaze leapt out at her. Mercilessly he battered at her will. Falling. She was falling again. Blackness, compassionate and peaceful, wrapped itself around her. Falling. She dropped like a stone into the darkness.

She felt his grin all around her. His mind was inside hers, toying with her most private thoughts. That was the ultimate violation. As her defenses collapsed under the sheer ferocity of his attack, her sense of defilement allowed her one final recourse. He was too strong. She couldn't fight him physically. So . . .

Falling into the darkness, she locked onto his will. Using the force of his assault to fuel her own need, she drew him down into the void that was swallowing her.

The shadows bleeding into his own mind were Rick's first intimation that something was wrong. But by then it was too late and he was falling with her.

14
⌘

the ravens feed

LYSISTRATUS HAD BEEN amused with Rick's performance as he monitored him throughout the evening. He admired the flair with which Rick made use of his gift, but knew as soon as Rick's mind turned to its grandiose schemes that this relationship would have to be terminated before the night was ended.

It wasn't simple fear that made the parasite live as he did on the fringes of society—it was plain common sense. He knew through experience what Rick had yet to learn, that no matter how many hundreds one could dupe with the power, there would always be those like the shaman who could *see* beyond it to its threat. And it was the ones with such *sight* that were the most danger to his kind. Lysistratus had long ago decided that it was better to live on the fringe and still have all you could wish for, than to be dead.

No, Rick would have to go.

Besides, he made mistakes. His killing of the punk had been sloppy, and then, excited as he'd been by the sudden influx of the dead man's soul mingling with his own, he'd been unprepared for the subsequent attack and rout from the apartment.

Lysistratus was troubled as well by the recurring presence of that straying from Cat's dreams. What was that inexplicable creature? He saw again the diminutive being's saucer eyes, the war of fear and determination reflected in their depths. It was a creature from a fairy tale, from . . . from a dream. It had physical presence, yet whenever he reached for it with his mind, it slipped from his approach as though it were something that couldn't be grasped. He could sense its whereabouts, but he didn't seem to be able to snare its thoughts. And whenever it was near, things went wrong.

Lysistratus sighed, leaving the puzzle aside to ride Rick's thoughts to Cat's house. Anticipation rode high in him as he shared the wait in the hedge, peaking when Rick captured Cat and started back to Stella's apartment with her. As the car pulled into the underground garage below the highrise, Lysistratus rose from his chair.

Soon, he thought.

He gazed out the window. The panorama of Ottawa's night skyline paled before his anticipation. The Human League's "Don't You Want Me" came to mind, as it often did when he thought of Cat and her narcotic sweetness. The Europop beat sounded to the rhythm of his pulse. She wanted him, only she didn't know it. But soon . . . He could already taste her dreaming strength—

Her rousing from Rick's control came as a rude shock, cutting through his pleasure. A vague aftertaste lingered, swiftly faded. He turned from the window.

"Don't you dare lose her," he commanded, his eyes cold.

But she fought Rick with a desperate fear. When she drew Rick down into the darkness with her, his body slumping across hers in the car, Lysistratus lunged for the door of the apartment. The abrupt motion pulled open the wound in his side, and he staggered at the sudden pain. Blood grew in a widening stain on his shirt. He moved resolutely down the hall. Her strength would heal him.

He reached the elevator, stabbing the Down button with a stiff finger. He wouldn't let her escape him again.

The second time Debbie regained consciousness, she didn't move. She was naked—she could feel a chill on her exposed skin—but she'd learned enough the last time not to move even though she could sense Lucius in the room with her. She knew it in the way a sleeper wakes, knowing that she's being watched. But she didn't dare open her eyes to pinpoint his position in the room, not when she remembered how easily he'd dealt with her the first time she woke.

She concentrated on keeping her breathing even. She had to get by him—get her clothes and get out. God knew what he planned to do with her. But her previous attempt had ended in such a dismal failure that she didn't know what to do.

There was something in his eyes. . . . It was like hypnotism —the way a snake mesmerized a bird—only it worked faster than any kind of hypnotism she'd ever heard of. All he had to do was zero in on you with his eyes and he had you. Zap! Just like that.

So she had to move quickly and *not* look in them. Screw her clothes. Better to be naked than dead. She'd just go. Once she got out the door there was no way he'd stop her. Not without a chase.

She heard him move and everything went still inside her. The muscles of her stomach drew tight. He'd gotten up from a chair and moved . . . where? She couldn't remember what he'd done to her the last time he'd knocked her out, but if he touched her again, she knew she'd scream. She wanted desperately to open her eyes, but all she could imagine was his face about six inches from her own, and those eyes boring into her own. . . .

Move, damn you! she thought. She had to know where he was.

She was so caught up listening for another movement that when he suddenly spoke, she almost jumped.

"Don't you dare lose her."

Lose who? Who was he talking to? Stella? Rick? Someone she hadn't even seen yet? God, the pressure was getting to her. Her head ached. And when she thought of all those newspaper headlines about strange cults and mass murderers, she just wanted to throw up. Was she going to end up as a thirty-second video clip on the six-o'clock news?

Her mind filled with footage of sheet-draped bodies being taken out of the building in stretchers and the announcer's excited voice speaking over the picture: "While the police have not officially released the names of the victims, pending notification of next of kin, a reliable source has informed us that one of the women was Deborah Mitchell, late of—"

She stifled a moan. She *had* to get out of here.

She heard Lucius move across the carpet, shoes whispering on its thick pile. The front door of the apartment opened, and she stole a peek. The door was behind her. There was no one in her range of vision. If there wasn't somebody standing right behind her, she could get up, grab something—that vase—

The door clicked shut. She pushed herself up from the couch, hand scrabbling for the vase. Turning, her makeshift weapon lifted and ready to be thrown, she faced an empty room. He was gone. Where? For how long? And what did she do now? Get the hell out of here and chance meeting him in the hall? What if he had a gun?

He didn't need a gun. He had his eyes. Those eyes . . .

She found her clothes puddled at her feet and hurriedly slipped them on, underwear first, blouse, skirt. Her nylons she stuffed in the pocket of her skirt. Holding her high heels in one hand, the vase in the other, she decided to check the apartment before doing anything else. Lucius might have Rick tied up in one of the other rooms.

She tiptoed to the bedroom, vase ready in her hand. The door was half open, and she pushed at it with her foot. Her headache throbbed behind her temples. The sick, twisted feeling in her stomach worsened with each inch the door opened. Anything could be in there, from horribly mutilated bodies to one of Lucius's confederates, waiting for her with those same cold eyes. . . . What she found was Stella sitting up on a big double bed, eyes dazed, hands clutching her head.

Debbie's grip tightened on the vase. She looked into the other woman's eyes, remembering Lucius's power too late, but before she could tear her gaze away, she saw the undisguised shock registering in Stella.

"You," Stella said numbly, hands falling away from her head. She grabbed fistfuls of blanket to cover her nudity. "You . . . you're here. Oh, my God! Then it's all real!"

Debbie stepped into the room, and Stella backed up against the bed's headboard with the look of a trapped animal about her. Another victim, Debbie thought. Then she remembered that she still had the vase uplifted in her hand.

"I'm not with . . . him," she said, setting the vase on a dresser. She put her shoes beside the vase, then held her hands open in front of her, trying to appear non-threatening. Stella wore all the panic that Debbie was fighting down herself.

"Where's Rick?" Debbie asked.

"R-rick . . . ?" Stella's gaze went past Debbie's shoulder.

"There's no one out there," Debbie said. "Not right now. Have you got a phone?"

Stella nodded, pointing. Bringing it to the bed, Debbie sat beside her. Before she dialed, she indicated the door.

"Keep watch."

Stella swallowed and nodded again.

Don't say anything about his eyes, Debbie told herself as she dialed. She and Stella needed help, not to have their sanity questioned.

"Hello, operator? I need the police. This is an emergency."

Tiddy Mun pointed to the high rise and Peter slowed down.

"That tower," the gnome said. "In the caverns underneath it."

Peter turned onto Lees Avenue, then steered the cab down the ramp that led to the underground parking. Sensors caught the cab's bulk and the garage door slid upward. Peter tramped on the gas. Fired up as he was, the entranceway reminded him too much of the gaping maw of some monstrous beast that was swallowing them.

"Ahead," Tiddy Mun said.

The little man spoke no more than he had to. Fear of the parasite, combined with his prolonged exposure to so much iron, left him barely able to give the directions Peter needed. Inside this cave it was worse than ever. There were so many metal dragons. . . .

Peter nodded. He didn't ask how Cat was doing, or if she was still alive. He wasn't even sure that the gnome could tell him if he did ask. What Peter had to do now was concentrate on getting them to wherever she was. One thing at a time. That was the only way he could handle this. If he started to think, he knew he'd just fall apart.

He glanced in the rearview mirror, saw Ben's drawn features, and shook his head. Peering ahead, he tried to catch a glimpse of Cat in the jungle of cars that the headbeams lit up in a rapid-fire flicker of glare and shadow.

Rick arrived on Redcap Hill moments after Cat. He stood stunned, his mind desperately trying to assimilate what had happened to him, where he was. One moment they were struggling in his car, in the underground lot under Stella's apartment building, and now . . . now . . . His gaze settled on Cat, and he moved toward her. It was all her fault.

Cat backed away. She was still unsteady on her feet. The simple act of breathing had never seemed so sweet. She sucked in lungfuls of air.

Rick moved deliberately forward. He seemed all the more menacing because of his slowness. Cat caught a glimpse of Toby regarding the two of them, his hand on the hilt of the knife in his belt. Beyond him the shadow things had multiplied. There appeared to be over a hundred of them now, leaping and writhing, icy eyes turned to watch her. A low gibbering ran through their ranks, building steadily in volume.

Cat looked away. She wanted to block her ears. Her head and chest hurt. Her vision spun.

"Don't know . . . how you're doing this to me," Rick muttered, "but it's not going to work. No way, babe. I've got the power with a capital P."

His advance, her retreat—they made a macabre dance. If he got hold of her . . . His eyes glittered menacingly, but she refused to be lured into them, refused to meet his gaze. His entire attention was focused on her. He was trying to draw her to him by the sheer force of his will. The need to meet his gaze grew stronger with each passing moment. But there was no other world to draw him into. No other escape.

Cat backed away from him until she was brought up short by one of the longstones. She sidled along the rough surface of the standing stone, eyes downcast, but watching Rick close in on her all the same. Now he was a half-dozen paces away. Now five. Her head pounded. A sibilant whisper that grew from somewhere inside her mocked her.

Meet his gaze, it said, *and it will all be over. Peace will come then. In the end. Peace will come.*

No! she told it.

Rick lunged for her and she darted under his arm. His hand came down, snagging her hair as she passed him, bringing her up short. She fell in a tumble, head lifted from the ground as he held her up by the hair. Pain seared through her skull. She flailed her arms. One wild blow caught him in the crotch.

He let go of her hair and she rolled free. He bent over in a half crouch. When he straightened, the fire in his eyes had grown. He shouted something at her, but it was lost in the wailing roar of the shadow creatures that encircled the hilltop.

He took a step toward her and she couldn't move. She watched him come, willing herself to get up, to fight, but she just wasn't strong enough. Only the eyes she refused to meet. She had that much strength left. She focused on his chest, watching it grow larger in her vision, step by terrifying step. Then he stopped and something blossomed in the center of his chest.

A knife hilt protruded there. Fresh blood ran down his shirt, joining old stains. Cat could only stare. Nothing really registered for her yet. Rick looked down at the knife, his eyes going blank. He lifted a hand to pluck weakly at the weapon, then pitched onto his side. Cat watched him fall, but she still couldn't move. In a moment he'd get up. The unfocused eyes would grow clear and center on her again, drawing her down and down. . . .

She flinched as a hand touched her shoulder. Slowly she turned to find Toby standing behind her.

"I wasn't sure," he said. "Not at first. Didn't know if he was friend or foe. Then, when I did know, you were too close to him to give me a clear throw. Mistress Cat?"

"Is he . . . is he dead?"

Toby nodded.

"Then it's over . . . isn't it?"

"Ah . . ."

She followed his gaze. All around the hill, just beyond the perimeter guarded by the standing stones, the creatures stood, silent and watchful. A hundred black shadow shapes, motionlessly eerie. Their eyes reflected the same light that had been in her attacker's eyes, only in them it appeared older somehow. More evil.

"There's so many. . . ." she murmured.

Toby nodded grimly. He bent to retrieve his knife. It would do little against such a horde, but it was all they had. His hand froze halfway.

"Mistress Cat?"

The body was gone. Only the knife remained on the grass.

"Oh, God." The words escaped Cat in a rush.

Gingerly, Toby reached for his weapon. He prodded it with a finger. When nothing happened, he picked it up turned it over in his hand. If he hadn't seen the man, his attack . . . seen him fall . . . Had they been fighting a phantom? But there was blood on the knife's blade, still glistening, wet. There *had* to have been someone there.

"How . . . ?" he began, then shook his head.

He plunged the knife into the ground to clean the blade. Cat moved closer to him. The circle of shadow shapes tightened until there was no clear way through them—if there ever had been. Here and there a slit mouth opened in the parody of a grin. The creatures appeared to be waiting.

"What do we do now?" Toby asked.

Cat shook her head. Fear tightened everything inside of her. "I don't know," she whispered.

Lysistratus reached the car just as the last spark of life sped from Rick. He stared down at the man's slack features. How had she killed him? What was there inside her that had such power? Her dreams were strong, but dreams didn't kill.

He rolled Rick's body aside and pulled Cat up so that she lay lengthwise on the car seat, her head close to where he stood. For long moments he studied her. Pain lanced his side from his reopened wound. He was somewhat light-headed. What he needed was the woman's dreaming strengths to ease his pain. He needed it now, before he got any weaker.

Hands spread, he reached down to cup her face, then hesitated. She had drawn Rick down into herself and killed him there. That spoke of something inside her that lay in wait for him. A danger that he couldn't ignore.

Be careful, he told himself. But her scent filled his nostrils, her very proximity seeped into his every pore. . . .

He was stronger than Rick could ever have been. He was old, perhaps the last of his kind. No longer mortal. No longer human. Except for physical violence, humankind had no defense against him.

He reached forward again and unbuttoned her shirt. Her skin was warm to the touch, her breasts soft as he closed his hands around them. At the instant of contact he had a momentary sensation of seeing her through myriad pairs of eyes. The power of contact broadened to encompass sight and smell and sound. He was inside her, she inside him. The rush that filled him as he tightened his grip on her made him dizzy.

Dimly he heard the sound of a car entering the garage, but he was already sinking into the sweet balm of her dreaming. The world around him lost meaning. Only her dreaming strengths existed. Filling him. Pouring into him. She was his. Finally, she was his.

* * *

Peter stepped on the brakes.

"There!" Tiddy Mun cried, pointing a trembling finger.

The cab's headbeams caught the shape of a man hunched over the open door of a car, too intent on whatever he was doing to pay them any mind. Cat! Fear for her went through Peter like a banshee's wail. The man had her.

He jumped out of the car and started for them at a run, pausing when he realized that he was empty-handed. Turning, he almost bowled Tiddy Mun over. The little man handed over Ben's baseball bat, his hands shaking. Peter glanced back at the cab. Becki leaned against her window, oblivious to her surroundings. Ben was stumbling from the backseat.

Turning, Peter started forward again, weapon in hand.

Cat staggered, fell to her knees. Instantly Toby was beside her, putting an arm around her shoulders.

"Mistress Cat! What—"

Her hands went to her stomach, ran up to her neck, down again, tearing at her sweater.

"I . . . I'm burning . . . inside. . . ."

She pushed away from him and fell forward, fingers digging convulsively into the earth. Toby dropped his knife and took hold of her shoulders, trying to turn her over. A chill draft struck his cheek and he turned to look at the shadow creatures. To his horror they were dissolving, one by one, swirling like dust devils as they rushed into the area that had been protected by the standing stones. The wind of their passing was cold and clammy on his skin. Ice formed in the marrow of his bones.

"Burning!" Cat shrieked.

He took hold of her hand. Her fingers tightened like a vise around his. Her skin was hot with an intense fever. Ice and fire: the dervish whirling of the shadow creatures as they spun into a frozen wind that passed between him and Cat . . . the heat of her skin as fierce as though she really were burning up from inside . . .

Her voice was no more than a ragged moan now. "Burning . . . the fire . . ."

Something consumed her. Toby gathered her up in his arms and held her close. He felt so helpless. If there was only something he could *do*! By now half the shadow creatures had vanished—vanished inside of *her*, Toby realized in shock. A cold that burned. The remaining creatures surrounded them, dancing once more, so close that they brushed against him.

The stones had kept them out before—why not now? By the stars, *why* not now?

Because, he understood suddenly, she had allowed them in.

The shadowy smoothness of the creatures' touch made Toby cringe. His limbs grew leaden and cold. The shadows danced more slowly now, in a ritual movement rather than their earlier wild caperings. One reached for Cat. Toby hugged her closer, to no avail.

Like the others had, the thing dissolved, passing through clothes and flesh until it was inside her. Torn between wanting to help and needing to push her away from him, Toby forced himself to hold on. Low gibberings started up once again, and he wasn't sure if they came from the creatures or himself. Another came close, reached for Cat, then froze.

Peter hauled the man out of the car and slammed him into the side of a nearby station wagon. He caught one glimpse of Cat—lying still . . . so still—then he turned to face the parasite. Lysistratus had hit the car with the side of his head. His eyes were unfocused, his step uncertain. Peter swung the bat and caught him with a glancing blow.

The parasite went down, hitting the ground like a dead weight. Peter bent over him, the bat raised for another blow. Lysistratus's eyes snapped open, sought Peter's gaze, trapped it.

The bat spilled from suddenly numbed fingers to clatter on the concrete. Peter took a step back and Lysistratus rose smoothly to his feet. Cat's dreaming strengths, stolen and firing him, kept the parasite from toppling over. His head rang, but her sweetness eased the pain. She filled him, her psyche as rich and golden as the legendary wine of the gods.

He moved for Peter, hands outstretched to cup his face, then sensed Tiddy Mun's attack. The gnome came at him in the shape of a big tomcat. Lysistratus remembered cats . . .

He met it face on. The cat tore at his hands and wrists, trying for his eyes, spitting and hissing. Lysistratus ignored the runnels it cut in his flesh. Grabbing it by a shoulder, he flung it at a concrete support.

The cat struck the pillar with a dull thud, landed on the hood of a car. The cold metal seared it. It tumbled to the ground and the smell of burning flesh and fur filled the air. On the pavement the cat became a little man and lay very still.

Lysistratus turned to face Peter once more. The woman's dreaming was everything he'd imagined it would be. It made the wound in his side seem like nothing. The deep scratches on his hands and wrists were a joke. How could he have waited so long to take the full power of what she carried inside her? He had the strength of a thousand in him now.

His eyes blazed with power, but Peter knew enough not to look into them this time. He dove for the bat, tearing long scrapes from his skin on the rough pavement. Lysistratus glided toward him before he could regain the weapon. The parasite caught his hair and pulled him away from the bat. A second hand found purchase on Peter's shirt.

Lifting him from the ground, Lysistratus's eyes bored into Peter. They demanded that Peter face him. Peter shook his head, trying to free himself of the need to look, to be lost again, but a darkness came washing up through him, primal and absolute. . . .

"No!"

Lysistratus turned, dropping Peter to the ground. Peter fell in a limp bundle of limbs. Ben faced the parasite. He was half blind with tears, the bat in his hands.

"I won't let you hurt anybody else!" Ben roared.

Lysistratus moved forward and Ben swung the bat. The parasite lifted an arm to ward off the blow, but it struck true. The two bones of his forearm snapped under the impact. The arm hung useless. Pain seared through him until Cat's stolen strengths swallowed it.

Before he could raise his other arm, before he could step in and grasp his enemy's flesh, trap his will and suck him empty, the bat was up again, swinging for his head. The blow cracked the temporal bone of his skull. He spun back against Rick's car, falling in a twisted sprawl of outspread limbs. One hand snagged in Cat's hair. The fingers scrabbled to make contact with her skin.

Ben stepped forward. He was horrified at the damage he'd done, but more determined than ever to finish the monster off, once and for all. He lifted the bat, hesitated when Lysistratus's eyes snapped open once again, their gaze locking onto his. Fire ran through Ben like a knife.

There's no way it can live with that kind of damage, Ben

thought numbly. One half of the parasite's head was matted with blood, the skull obviously cracked. It *couldn't* live through that.

But the gaze gripped his, the will leapt forth to grapple with his. The bat fell from nerveless fingers for a second time, and Ben toppled to the ground to lie near Peter's unconscious form.

Toby held Cat in the crook of one arm, beating at the shadow shapes with the other. They reached for her, many of them at once, three and four joints to each gnarled finger. The wind stirred the tattered tissue on their heads that passed for hair. Their features became individual, and as they did, the sameness of their eyes appeared all the more horrifying. It was as though one being watched him through many pairs of eyes.

They tugged and pulled at him, but he only gripped Cat tighter. His shirt was wet and cold against his sweaty skin, his hair plastered to his forehead. He shrugged off the grasping fingers with stiff movements, but knew he couldn't last much longer. Talons were beginning to form at the ends of their fingers. They snagged in his shirt, pierced his skin. There were so many of them—and all those eyes watching him with the same expression, slit mouths gaping and grinning.

Abruptly Cat trembled in his arms, where she'd lain as still as death before. As he looked at her, she pushed him away with a sudden strength. She screamed and her body bucked spasmodically. A cloudy gas rushed forth from her mouth, swirling and taking shape in the air between them.

Toby moaned as something began to materialize in the midst of that ragged cloud. It gathered vapor about it like a cloak, solidified. The suggestion of glittering blue eyes—like azure lights blazing in ice—pierced Toby to his soul, numbing the last of the fight left in him.

Cat lay still, her features white. The apparition, now complete, drew the remaining shadow creatures into it. One by one it swallowed their dark lanky shapes, its own body becoming more corporeal with each of the creatures that it drew into itself. At last it stood alone, tall and handsome. The grass withered at its feet. The hilltop grew darker, as though the stars themselves withdrew their light from where he stood. But the Otherworld shape of Lysistratus burned with its own inner light.

Finally the parasite understood Cat's strength, the power of her dreaming. Unlike the ghostly lies that most humans realized in their sleep, her dreams took her to a realm, the very foundations of which were the stuff of dreams. Little wonder that what he stole from her fulfilled his needs so completely. Here the world itself would feed him. Here he would never lack for sustenance.

He glanced at the guardian longstones. They had protected her from his tracking senses. They would have kept her safe if he hadn't come to this world through her. And what a world!

His gaze went to her still form. She stirred under its power. His voice drew her awareness back to the hilltop. Bleakly she looked up at his tall form and knew his power. She felt ravaged. Drained. Pain thudded behind her temples. She was like a shell with nothing of herself left inside, no *her* left anymore —or so little that it hid in a dark corner of her soul, skittering and frail.

"Don't you want me?" Lysistratus asked her mockingly.

Her gaze lifted to meet his. God help her, but she did.

She knew who he was immediately. Compared to him she felt like a child. He was the invader, but he ruled simply by his presence. He stood on Redcap Hill as though it had always belonged to him. He was power incarnate, and he exuded a magnetic attraction that couldn't be denied. Beside him even Mynfel would be overshadowed, would be no more than a pale reflection of his radiant strength.— strength he had stolen, but it was no less real because of that. No less his to command.

The other man, the one she'd drawn down with her, through her . . . he'd been bad enough. But he was nothing compared to what she faced now. It wasn't just the power— knowing the parasite could play her like a puppet, knowing he could lay the Otherworld to waste. It was knowing, sickly, that some part of her *wanted* to go to him, to feel his touch, to give herself to him.

"Come to me," Lysistratus said.

His power pierced her. His will slipped inside her, meeting no resistance. Dazed, she forced herself up. She got as far as her hands and knees, but couldn't rise any farther. A small part of her remembered the vision in Mynfel's pool. Her terror then was a joke compared to what paralyzed her now. She would welcome those branched antlers weighting down her

brow, if having them endowed her with enough power to
break the hold her mocking captor held her with.

But that vision had been a sham. What did it matter if her
secret name twinned Mynfel's? It proved nothing. Meant
nothing.

Bound to the parasite's will, she had to obey him. She
began to crawl in his direction. Her hand landed on Toby's
knife. She gripped it reflexively, closed her fingers around the
sharp blade and opened a deep slash in her palm. The knife
fell free, and she stared numbly at the blood welling from her
hand. She watched it drop and soak into the earth. She didn't
even feel the pain.

Lysistratus drew her in like a hooked fish. He had her so
completely overpowered that eye contact was no longer necessary. She moved forward again, setting her bloodied palm
down on the earth to pull herself along. As the open wound
ground into the dirt, a sudden shock went through her, stealing
the last of her ebbing strengths.

She sprawled forward on the ground, her mind ablaze with
a kaleidoscope of sound and images that twisted and churned
in a maddening blur. Incongruously, tattered remnants of the
real world made themselves be known. Words leapt through
the maelstrom—words torn from the pages of the books that
she'd spent the better part of her life immersed in.

*A rotund figure, narrow-framed glasses in the midst of a
frizz of charcoal-gray hair . . . a high-pitched voice crying
over the droning sound of a harmonium . . . Allen Ginsberg's
primal* Howl *. . . speaking of a generation destroyed by madness. . . .*

Cold fire ran up her hand. Her head was too heavy to lift.
She sensed Lysistratus standing directly over her.

*Blake's 'Mad Song': "Like a fiend in a cloud, with howling
glee. . . ."*

The ground heaved under her.

Toby, forgotten, his sanity spilling from him in a rush,
watched golden-green sparks leap from the craggy tips of the
standing stones. When his gaze alit on Cat, his jaw went
slack.

*"No future!" Sid Vicious fronting the Pistols . . . the crash
of discordant music warring with his angry voice. "No future. . . ."*

The horned head lifted from the ground. The pulse of her
lifeblood mingled with the energy stored in the longstones—

ancient batteries awaiting a key to unlock their mysteries. She saw herself reflected in Lysistratus's eyes. She shook her head. She didn't understand what she saw—not the weight on her brow, nor the cold fire that filled her palm with more than pain and sent it speeding through her abused body.

She was aware of it all on a subliminal level. Far clearer was the knowledge of the parasite's hands reaching for her, the Otherworld as a wasteland and herself lost in—

Milton's 'Paradise Lost': "The seat of desolation, void of light. . . ."

An emptiness from which there would be no return. A banishment that was ultimate. Final.

Lysistratus gripped her by the throat and lifted her, his face inches from her own. Her lungs begged for air. His gaze drove into hers. He ignored the sprouting horns, the potential for power that was dying stillborn with each passing moment. He had her. She was his. That was all that mattered. And not all the transformations in this world or any other were going to save her now.

Tattershank, the wizard from her own Cloak and Hood, *forcing Meg to her feet to face the demon: "I am dying. Save at least yourself. Your world. . . ."*

She lifted her arms to strike at Lysistratus. Her blows were ineffectual, but blood sprayed from her wound, momentarily blinding him. The blood burned where it struck his eyes and skin.

His grip faltered, and she tore herself free to stumble across the withering grass. She forced air through her bruised windpipe with deep rattling gasps. When she fell, it was against one of the three standing stones. She pressed her cheek against its bruising surface. Strength surged through her from the stone. She turned, her back to it, her head still heavy with the unfamiliar weight on her brow.

Half blind, Lysistratus moved toward her. His eyes no longer had the power to bind her, but there was the undeniable pull of his radiance that made her want him almost as much as she needed to destroy him. And there was still strength in him—enough to suck her empty, enough to bleed the Otherworld barren. . . . Her world . . .

She braced herself against the stone and met his outstretched hands with her own. Beyond fear, she joined her gaze to his. The buffeting power of his will pounded against her own. She fought him as best she could, awkwardly, the raw power filling her, but spilling uselessly from her untrained mind. He battered aside her clumsy defenses as soon as she erected them, drove into her with the skill of centuries at his command.

His feral eyes blazed. His hands were locked around hers, crushing bone, drawing her out of herself. . . .

But she heard only—*Tattershank: "Save at least your world. . . ."*

The Otherworld a wasteland, bowing under Lysistratus's fierce hunger. . . .

"Save at least yourself. . . ."

He was too strong. She couldn't keep him out of her. One traitorous part of her commanded her to let him have his will. The effort of holding him back was a monstrous, gibbering pain. He loomed over her—in height, in skill, in strength. She was a frail leaf ravaged by the force of his gale, an ugly smudge compared to his radiance. She was falling into a—

". . . void of light. . . ."

The longstone rasped against her back as she was forced to her knees. With success so near, Lysistratus laughed. The sound bled into her—

". . . with howling glee. . . ."

Mynfel, help me! she pleaded to the night skies. There was no reply except for the endless jabbering inside her own head.

"No future!"

". . . destroyed by madness. . . ."

"Save at least your world. . . ."

There was no deeper Otherworld to draw Lysistratus into, as she had with her first assailant. No Toby waiting there with knife in hand to help her. There was nothing. Only—

". . . desolation, void of light. . . ."

A darkness inside her like a prison rose steadily upward through her mind, drawing into it all that made her who she was. It stilled the cacophony, swallowing the voices one by one. It was a black cage steadily consuming her.

No! she cried as it threatened the very core of her being. That's all I have left—that's all that's me!

Mine, the blackness demanded with Lysistratus's voice. Sibilant. Triumphant. *Come to me and be mine.*

"No!" Cat screamed.

Despair towered in her. She lifted her face. Her horns struck the longstone behind her. Sparks of witchfire flew about at the contact. Blind rage stabbed through her. Power swelled.

"You go into it!" she cried. "It can't have me!"

She was unskilled. Her use of the power was awkward. But her desperate fury, her final need, overcame her lack of knowledge. The Otherworld itself came to her aid, feeding her the strength she needed through the standing stone that supported her. The dark prison meant for her enveloped Lysistratus in a cloying, unbreakable web. Down it plunged inside her, dropping as though all the fiends of hell pursued it, drawing the parasite with it, locking him deep inside her with no escape, no reprieve, no mercy. . . .

Lysistratus's hands loosened their grip on hers. She saw the fading light in his eyes. The blue fires in the depths of their pupils dimmed. He gave a wailing cry that echoed deep inside her.

You were mine. . . .

His body fell across her. She shrunk from the contact, pushing at him, rolling the body away. With stunned eyes she watched it dissolve until no trace of him remained. Only a distant moan—but that came from inside her . . . from the shadow prison . . . the blackness. . . .

"Oh, God. No."

She couldn't live with that inside her. What if it broke loose, spread cancerously through her, made her into what he had been. . . .

Would that be so wrong? the treasonous part of her that had been attracted to the parasite asked.

She couldn't live with it—live with it and know how close she came to giving herself to him.

There was no other way, her reason told her flatly. This is the price she would have to pay if she wanted the Otherworld to be preserved, if she didn't want him loose, feeding on the dreaming minds of her own world, if she didn't want to take his place.

"But I'm not strong enough," she whispered.

Her fear of dying was nothing compared to what she felt now. She would always have to be on guard against him—against a part of herself as well. She would always feel that pinprick of evil inside her, knowing that it would be loosed again if she ever dropped her guard, knowing how close she came to welcoming it. . . .

"M-mistress . . . Cat . . . ?"

She turned a dull gaze in Toby's direction.

"Did . . . did we win?" he asked.

Submerged, faintly, she felt Lysistratus stir inside her. "I don't know," she said tonelessly. "It . . . it doesn't feel like we won. . . ."

She lifted a hand to touch the heavy weight on her brow. The antlers grew insubstantial, just as Lysistratus's body had, fading under the touch of her fingers. But though they were gone, she could still feel their weight. She looked at her hand. The cut on her palm was a white scar. The blood that had woken the bond between her and the Otherworld was gone. The wound was healed, but the bond remained.

A sense of vertigo came over her. The hilltop spun in her sight. She was tired . . . so tired . . . drained. . . .

Toby touched her shoulder and she toppled over.

"Mistress Cat?" she heard him say, then she was—

—looking into Ben's face.

"Cat? Jesus, Cat—are you all right?"

"Ben . . . ?"

She was back. In her own world. The rest was all a dream. The Otherworld and— She felt the faint stir deep inside her, and shuddered. No. It had been real. God. How could she live with that . . . that thing inside her? And when she thought of how she'd almost just given herself up to—

"Everything's going to be okay," Ben said. He glanced at where the two bodies lay sprawled—one on the floor of the car, the other outside on the concrete. "It's over now, Cat. They're both . . . dead."

But it's not over, she wanted to tell him. Not when the creature was still inside her. Not when she'd almost let him seduce her to his side. Not when she could still hear that traitorous part of her, whispering and sibilant—its voice a combination of the parasite's and her own.

But she didn't have the strength to speak. She heard the sound of approaching sirens. Ben helped her to her feet and kept an arm around her shoulders for support. The physical contact was comforting. She saw Peter leaning weakly against the side of the car. Both Ben and Peter looked like they were just barely holding themselves together. She knew just how they felt.

"Somebody must've called the police," Ben said.

Peter nodded. "When we talk to them," he warned, "let's just keep it straight. No dreams. No vampires. No little magic —" He glanced over to where Tiddy Mun had been flung, but there was no sign of the little man. "No little magic people. Okay?"

"Whatever," Cat said dully.

"*We* believe you, Cat," Peter said, "but we've got to leave it at that, or they're going to lock us *all* up."

"Okay," Cat whispered. "No . . . no dreams. No ghosts." Just a monster imprisoned inside her.

Ben wrapped his arms around her and drew her close. Peter lowered himself down to the pavement and leaned against the wheel of Rick's car, staring at his shaking hands. That was the way the policemen in the first patrol car found them.

The ringing of the phone jarred Potter out of a sound sleep. He reached blearily across his wife and hooked the receiver with a hand, bringing it to his ear. The side of his face was pressed against his pillow. His voice was muffled when he spoke.

"Whazzat?"

"Potter."

The authoritative tone of the voice dissolved the muddiness in his head. "Yeah."

"Got us a hot one. Tag-sheet says you want to be buzzed if we pick up another slasher victim."

Potter was fully awake now. He sat up. "What've you got?"

"You better get down here—underground garage at the corner of Main and Lees. The Marquis—you know the place?"

"Yeah. Who's the victim?"

"The body's not here, at least not that one. Listen, Potter. It gets real complicated. It'd be a lot easier if you'd just get down here."

"I'm already there," Potter said.

He hung up and started to get dressed.

Yarrow

May I be an island in the sea,
may I be a hill on the land,
may I be a star when the moon wanes,
may I be a staff for the weak one:
I shall wound every man,
no man shall wound me.

—traditional Scots charm

15
❄

friday morning

THE FOUR OF them sat in a special waiting room at the Riverside Hospital, waiting for the plainclothes detective who had questioned them earlier to return. Peter and Ben's minor wounds had been treated, and like Debbie, they had both refused sedatives.

Cat had come through her ordeal physically unscathed, except for some bruising around her throat. Her real wounds lay inside, still open and raw. But while she had refused to be treated for shock as well, her reasons were radically different from those of the others. She was afraid of the balm that the sedatives promised, afraid of finding herself back in the Otherworld and having to go through it all again.

Becki and Stella were both in another room under police guard, after having been treated for shock.

There was no conversation amongst the four as they waited. Ben held Cat's hand. Peter sat on the other side of her, staring at the floor. Debbie was in a chair across the room. They all looked up when the door opened and Detective-Sergeant Potter returned.

"Okay," he said. "Forensic's come up with a set of prints that match Kirkby's." He pulled up a chair and sat down in front of Peter, Cat, and Ben. "I just want you to go through how you ended up under the Marquis again."

"We've already told you," Peter said.

"So humor me. Tell me again."

Peter glanced at Ben, then shrugged. "Okay. Ben arrived at my place, told me that Mick had been killed and that Cat was in danger."

"And you thought she was in danger because of this prowler, the one that you"—he indicated Ben—"and this Jennings had a run-in with a couple of nights ago?"

Ben nodded.

"And then?" Potter prompted.

Peter sighed wearily. "We got to her place just in time to see this Kirkby guy pulling away from her place. We saw that her car door was open, her purse on the ground, so—"

"You gave chase. Who'd you think you were? Clint Eastwood? Why didn't you call us then?"

"I . . . we . . . I told you before," Peter said. "We just weren't thinking straight."

Potter regarded him for a moment. They were hiding something. He knew it. All four of them. But whatever it was, he couldn't put his finger on it. The Mitchell woman's story corroborated theirs, the prints on the knife were Kirkby's. . . . It nagged him that he couldn't get it out of them. But this was the fourth time he'd taken them through it, individually and in a group. He couldn't hold them any longer. He didn't have anything on them.

"Okay," he said with a nod. "I guess you can go. Just make sure you get down to the station later today to sign your statements. Nicholas and Waller, third floor. Ask for Detective-Sergeant Potter. Got it?"

"Yeah. Thanks."

"There's going to be an inquest," Potter added. "You'll have to appear at it. Maybe a court appearance. It all depends on the Crown Prosecutor, but I doubt it'll get to court."

"Sure." Peter stood up.

"Your cab's down in the lot," Potter told Ben. "I had one of the patrolmen drive it over for you."

When Ben didn't say anything, Peter nodded his thanks to the detective. "You guys coming?" he asked.

Cat waited for Ben to get up.

"I'm thinking about Becki," Ben said. "Maybe someone should be here when she . . . you know, comes around."

"The doctor said they'll both be under sedation for most of the day," Potter said. "You might as well go home."

"I guess . . ."

"Oh, Ben," Cat said. "I'm so sorry about Mick. If it hadn't been for me—"

Ben shook his head. "It wasn't your fault. It's just . . . just the way things turned out, I guess." His eyes brimmed with tears. The rage that had allowed him to strike down the parasite had long since fled, replaced with a sense of despair that he could be driven to do such a thing. And losing Mick . . .

Peter put his arm around Ben's shoulders and Cat took his arm on the other side. Cat understood what Ben was going through. The ache of losing Kothen was still fresh inside her.

Across the room, Potter approached Debbie. "You're free to go as well, Miss Mitchell."

Debbie sighed. She looked across the room to where Cat and Peter were comforting Ben. It's funny, she thought. She knew so many people, but after hearing their story, what they'd gone through for each other, she was just realizing how superficial her life had become. Where was the person she could call a friend? A person that could be counted on like these people counted on each other? Where was the person who could count on her?

"If you could just come down to the station later?" Potter was saying to her.

She nodded.

"Do you need a lift home?"

Debbie stood wearily. "Please."

"Anybody else need a ride?" Potter called over to where the others stood.

Peter shook his head. "We'll be okay. Thanks."

"Suit yourself." The door closed quietly behind Debbie and the detective.

They sat in Cat's kitchen, just the three of them now, too tired to move, too tired to sleep, police and hospital far from their thoughts. Dawn was finally streaking the eastern horizon.

"Cat?" Peter said after a while. They'd spoken no more

than a few words to each other since leaving the hospital. "What really happened to . . . to him?"

She looked up, her eyes haunted. "I . . . trapped him." She tapped her chest. "He's here. Inside me."

Haltingly she tried to tell them what had happened in the Otherworld, watching their faces to gauge their reactions. But the disbelief she'd half expected to see never came. Both Ben and Peter had seen and experienced enough to accept just about anything at this point.

"Jesus," Ben said when she was done.

"I'm scared," she told them. "Scared to sleep, because of what I might dream. Scared he's going to get loose. Scared that he's going to turn me into whatever he was. Scared that some part of me *wants* to like him. . . ."

Ben reached across the table to take her hand. "Nothing's going to turn you into what he was, Cat."

"We can't know that. We don't even know *what* he was. Or how he got to be that way."

Peter shook his head. "Ben's right, Cat. There's no way you're going to become what he was. If you were strong enough to . . . to trap him like you did, you're strong enough to keep him there."

"Do you really think so?" she asked in a small voice.

"I know so." Peter glanced at Ben. "And if you need any help, we're going to be around—for as long as you can stand us."

He said it lightly, but she knew he meant it. Ben tightened his grip on her hand. For a moment she felt good, thinking that there'd be people to share this awful burden with her, then she realized that it just couldn't be that way. She pulled her hand from Ben's and folded her arms so that neither of them would see how she was trembling.

"It won't work," she said.

"Don't push us away, Cat," Peter said.

"I don't want to!" Her eyes brimmed with tears but she refused to cry. "You just don't understand, neither of you. I'm not me anymore, not . . . not with this *thing* inside me."

"That doesn't matter to me," Ben said.

Peter nodded. "Or to me."

"Well, it should. I couldn't stand becoming what he was and maybe . . . maybe finding myself feeding on *your* dreams. . . ."

Ben tried to reach for her hand again, but she backed away in her chair. He started to say something, then paused, looking helplessly at Peter.

Peter found it hard to meet his gaze. He was remembering how Cat had fled from his apartment last night. He didn't want to get into another argument with her. He didn't want to tiptoe around her, but he figured that after all she'd gone through, after the things that had seemed to prove her to be crazy had finally been validated, it wasn't his place to try to force her to do anything.

Ben read something of Peter's thoughts and nodded, almost to himself. "Okay," he said to Cat. "I'm here if you want a friend, but I won't push."

"It's not that I don't care about you. . . ."

"I understand, Cat. Really I do. Look, maybe you should try to get some sleep."

She shook her head. "I can't, Ben. I just can't."

"You're going to have to sleep sooner or later. It's either go to sleep on your own, or keel over from exhaustion."

"We'll stay, if you want," Peter added. "Downstairs. You need something—anything—just call down to us."

"But I can't let you just—"

"No more arguments," Peter said. He gave Ben a quick glance.

Ben blinked, then came around the table and helped her to her feet. This close to her, it was hard not to just gather her in his arms, but he fought the impulse.

"I'll go to the glade," she said as Ben left her at the door to her bedroom. "I can't go back to the hill. I want to know if Tiddy Mun's all right, but I just can't go there yet."

"You do that," Ben said. "Just try to find some peace, Cat. That's what you need. Some distance between what happened tonight and the future. And it'll come."

He stood there and for a moment Cat thought he was going to kiss her, but then he turned and went back down the stairs. She watched him go, torn between wanting to call him back and knowing that she had to be alone. She didn't think she'd be able to sleep, not all wound up as she was and knowing that they were downstairs waiting for her to do just that. But the pillow was so soft against her cheek when she lay down, and she was feeling so drowsy. . . .

* * *

The glade was deserted. Slowly she walked under the apple trees, pausing when she was a few feet away from the stone wall of the pool.

"Mynfel?" she called softly.

There was no reply. Morning had stolen into the glade. Sunlight gleamed on the surface of the pool as she drew near it.

"Please," she said. "Come to me this one last time. I have to understand. What's real? Am I a dream, or is it this place?"

Though she needed a voice to answer her, the quiet of the glade soothed her. She closed the remaining distance between herself and the pool and knelt down by the wall. Looking into its water, she knew she had to accept that the riddles would stay unanswered. Her own face looked back at her—without the antlers, without the strangeness in her eyes.

She wasn't sure when the wood's mistress came, but suddenly she looked up and Mynfel was standing across the pool from her.

"This world is real," the antlered woman said. "You and I are the strangers in it, but only one of us is real as you use the word. We are two sides of the same tree, dear heart. I was here because you needed me. But you do not need me anymore."

The horned woman had never spoken before. Her voice was low and throaty. Like one unused to speaking.

"I need you now more than ever," Cat said.

"Yours is now the strength."

"But that thing's inside me. I'm not strong enough."

"You are strong enough. Did Kothen not name you Yarrow? Heal-All?"

"Yes, but—"

"Then heal our world of its hurts, dear heart. Heal yourself of the shadow that worries you from within."

"Did . . . did I just make you up?"

"I was always your reflection." Mynfel smiled her smile of old. "As you were mine."

Cat looked back at the surface of the pool. Again there were antlers on the image's brow, but Cat couldn't feel their weight.

"Set me free," Mynfel said.

Their gazes met—Cat's searching, Mynfel's warm and full of riddles to which there could never be answers. Slowly Cat lowered her gaze. She leaned over the pool and stirred the reflection with her hand, the white scar on her palm shining through the water.

When she looked up again, Mynfel was gone. But Cat didn't feel alone. She knew she *was* strong now. Not just because she had to be, or because Peter and Ben and Mynfel said she had to be, but because she was.

She felt the thing that had been the parasite stir inside her. Rather than fighting it, she sent down peaceful, soothing thoughts. The shadow withdrew, deep and deeper, fleeing.

Cat stood up and smiled.

Years had been crammed into the past week. So much pain and sorrow. But at last she knew her own peace. Not borrowed from ghosts or the Otherworld, or lately from Peter and Ben. But a peace of her own. And because of it she had something more to offer them than just her need. She could be Peter's friend. And Ben . . .

She left the glade and headed west through the forest. Shafts of sunlight dropped through the giant oaks, giving the wood its cathedral effect again. The air was invigorating, and she began to run. In no time at all she was out of the forest. She saw Redcap Hill in front of her, the three standing stones stark and gray on its summit, the fairy thorn on its slope. She heard a shout and turned to find Tiddy Mun hobbling toward her, with Toby at his side, supporting him. It was because of them that she'd come.

Tiddy Mun waited for her to drop to her knees and hold open her arms to him, then he hugged her tight with his one good arm. "I missed you," he murmured in her ear. "I was so afraid. I couldn't get home. Whenever I tried to, I couldn't find the way. The darkness was everywhere. But then in the cave of the iron dragons, when you washed the darkness away, suddenly I could see the borders again and step my way home."

"Peter and Ben both told me how brave you were," she said. "You're the bravest gnome that I ever knew."

The little man blushed and hid his face against her shoulder. When she squeezed him, he winced and Cat held him at arm's length, worry plain on her face.

"You were hurt," she said.

Tiddy Mun nodded. "The iron in . . . in the metal dragon. It burned me. . . ."

"Oh, Tiddy!"

She turned him around and pulled up his tunic to examine his back. Her face paled. The skin on his back was raw in places, inflamed from the tops of his shoulder blades to the small of his back and all along his right side. She imagined how much it must hurt. The chaffing of cloth against the wound alone . . .

"The bravest gnome of all," she murmured.

She wanted to help, but didn't know what she could do. She lifted a hand, hesitated. Mynfel's words returned to her.

Yarrow. Heal-All. Heal our world of its hurts.

If only she could.

If she could be like some biblical healer and cure such afflictions by a laying on of her hands. . . .

Her palm throbbed, and she looked down at the white scar. Again she felt the weight on her brow. Perhaps in her own world she'd be helpless, but here, in the Otherworld . . . If what it took was wanting to, wanting to so bad . . . caring so much . . .

She laid her palm gently against the little man's back and felt the hotness of his wound run into her hand as she willed his pain away with all her heart. Before her eyes his skin cleared, the inflammation dying, whitening, healing. . . .

Tiddy Mun let out a long sigh of relief as Cat stepped back. She stared in wonder at her hand, his back, her hand again. The scar on her palm flamed red—a bright slash against her skin—then dulled and was white once more. The throbbing stilled. Her brow was light again, the weight gone, and she understood at last what it was that she had become in the Otherworld.

A warm brightness rose inside her. Mynfel, she thought. I think I understand. This Otherworld *is* our world, but you were only here until I could take your place. It was in your care, and now it's mine—mine until it's time for me to go on.

The warmth she felt inside, she realized, was her own acceptance of her responsibility. Not borne as a burden, but as a gift, a deepness of spirit, a kinship with all that made this small corner of the Otherworld hers to care for. She was like the raggedy man that Toby had met on the Road, like the Borderlord in her own book.

That was why Mynfel hadn't—*couldn't* have—helped her. It was a lesson that Cat had to learn for herself. The lesson she should have learned long ago. But she'd been too busy taking—from Kothlen, from Mynfel, from the Other-world itself—to understand that she had to give as well. Otherwise she was no better than the dream thief.

It was because of this bond between the Otherworld and herself that she was a part of two worlds, just like Mynfel must have been before her. She'd been brought here so that the horned lady could go on. To where? It didn't matter. She'd find out when the time was right, when it was *her* turn to go on. When she'd found someone else who could live between the worlds, learning the same lessons, finding that same strength inside herself.

And it was, Cat realized, a lesson that couldn't be handed down in words. It couldn't be taught. It had to rise up from inside one's own self. It was a self-realization that had to be truly and instinctively understood to be valid. And it would have come sooner or later—even if there had been no dream thief—beause Mynfel and she *were* reflections of each other.

She turned to face her friend with shining eyes. Tiddy Mun regarded her with undisguised love, Toby with a bewildered smile. Her sudden good humor was infectious.

"A few hours have done wonders for you, Mistress Cat," Toby said.

She nodded. "Do you still want to learn magicks?" she asked.

"Of course. I'm still on the Road, as it were. The Secret Road—"

"'. . . while underfoot the merry Road, the gentle, winds to where it waits,'" she quoted.

Toby's smile grew broader. "The very one," he said.

"When I come back," she said, "I think I'd like to go a ways with you."

"You're going away already?" Tiddy Mun asked, his disappointment plain.

"But I'll be back soon. And if I'm not, you can always come and fetch me."

"I will," he assured her very seriously.

She kissed him on each cheek, then stepped back. "Good-bye," she said.

"Good-bye," they chorused back, and then she was gone.

Cat padded barefoot down the stairs and entered the living room. Ben was the first to notice her.

"Cat, are you . . . ?"

"I'm fine, Ben."

Peter stood up from where he'd been slouching on the couch. "Things worked out then?" he asked.

"Thanks to both of you."

There was a long moment's silence, then Ben stood as well.

"We should get going," Peter said. "I'm dead on my feet."

Cat nodded and followed them to the door. Peter went on ahead, but Ben paused in the doorway. They both had losses to deal with, Cat thought. She had Kothlen and he had Mick. But if they could face their losses together . . . She put her hand on his arm as he went to follow Peter.

"Will you stay with me, Ben?" she asked.

"I . . ."

"We did have a date for dinner tonight, and dinnertime's not that far away."

Ben looked at Peter, who just smiled and closed the door on them.

Peter whistled as he went down the walk, pausing when he saw a big orange tomcat watching him from the far end of Cat's veranda. It wasn't Ginger or Pad, because both of Cat's pets were flaked out in the living room.

He and the cat regarded each other for a moment, then Peter gave it a brief salute and continued on down the walk. Just before going through the hedge, he looked back. The cat was gone, but there was a sound in the air. It could have been a snatch of song, or perhaps it was only the wind.

Smiling to himself, Peter went on home.

AUTHOR'S NOTE

The preceding novel is a work of fiction. All characters and events in this book are fictitious, and any resemblance to actual persons living or dead is purely coincidental.

I'd like to stress that, while there is a speciality SF bookstore in Ottawa called The House of SF, neither it nor its owners should be mistaken for *Yarrow*'s Peter Baird and his bookstore. By the same token, Cat Midhir's writing habits, inspirations, and the course of her career do not parallel either my own or that of any other writer I know.

—Charles de Lint
Ottawa, Spring 1986

Fantasy from Ace
fanciful and fantastic!